a little harmless lie

A HARMLESS WORLD NOVEL

THE ORIGINAL HARMLESS FIVE
BOOK FOUR

MELISSA SCHROEDER

EDITED BY
HEIDI SHOHAM

COVER ART BY
SCOTT CARPENTER

HARMLESS PUBLISHING

contents

also by melissa schroeder

THE HARMLESS WORLD

The Original Harmless Five

- A Little Harmless Sex
- A Little Harmless Pleasure
- A Little Harmless Obsession
- A Little Harmless Lie
- A Little Harmless Addiction

Rough 'n Ready

- Rough Submission
- Rough Fascination
- Rough Fantasy
- Rough Ride

Harmless Trouble

- Harmless Secrets
- Harmless Revenge
- Harmless Scandals

The Wulf Family

- Faith

- Taboo
- Trust

A Little Harmless Military Romance

- Infatuation
- Possession
- Surrender

Task Force Hawaii

- Seductive Reasoning
- Hostile Desires
- Constant Craving
- Tangled Passions
- Wicked Temptations
- Twisted Emotions-coming 2025

THE CAMOS AND CUPCAKES WORLD

Camos and Cupcakes

- Delicious
- Luscious
- Scrumptious

The Fillmore Siblings

- Hate to Love You
- Love to Hate You

Juniper Springs

- Wild Love
- Crazy Love
- Last Love
- Imperfect Love

THE SANTINI WORLD

The Santinis

- Leonardo
- Marco
- Gianni
- Vicente
- A Santini Christmas
- A Santini in Love
- Falling for a Santini
- One Night with a Santini
- A Santini Takes the Fall
- A Santini's Heart
- Loving a Santini

Semper Fi Marines

- Tease Me
- Tempt Me
- Touch Me

The Fitzpatricks

- Chances Are

THE MELISSA SCHROEDER INSTALOVE COLLECTION

Dominion Rockstar Romance

- Undeniable
- Unpredictable
- Unexpected
- Tempted

Mafia Sisters

- Stealing Destiny
- Guarding Fable

Faking It

- Faking it with my Billionaire Boss
- Faking it with my Brother's Best Friend
- Faking it with my Frenemy

The Fighting Sullivans

- Falling for the General's Daughter
- Falling for the Girl Next Door
- Falling for my Best Friend
- Falling for my Baby Mama

Also Included

- Kiss my Tinsel
- Dad Bod Rockstar

Texas Temptations

- Conquering India
- Delilah's Downfall

Hawaiian Holidays

- Mele Kalikimaka, Baby
- Sex on the Beach
- Getting Lei'd

Once Upon an Accident

- The Accidental Countess
- Lessons in Seduction
- The Spy Who Loved Her

The Cursed Clan

- Callum
- Angus
- Logan
- Fletcher
- Anice

The Sweet Shoppe

- Tempting Prudence
- Cowboy Up
- Her Wicked Warrior

By Blood

- Desire by Blood
- Seduction by Blood

Hands On

- The Hired Hand
- Hands on Training

Telepathic Cravings

- Voices Carry
- Lost in Emotion
- Hard Habit to Break

Bounty Hunters, Inc

- For Love or Honor
- Sinner's Delight

Saints and Sinners

- Seducing the Saint
- Hunting Mila

Lonestar Wolf Pack

- Primal Instincts

Texas Heat

- Scorched

Spies, Lies, and Alibis

- The Boss

Single Titles

- A Calculated Seduction
- Chasing Luck
- Going for Eight
- Grace Under Pressure
- Operation Love
- Saving Thea
- Snowbound Seduction
- Sweet Patience
- The Last Detail
- The Seduction of Widow McEwan

hawaiian terms

Aloha - Hello, goodbye, love

Bra-Bro

Bruddah- brother, term of endearment

Haole-Newcomer to the islands

Howzit - How is it going?

Kamaʻāina-Local to the islands

Mahalo-Thank you

Malasadas- A Portuguese donut without a hole which started out as a tradition for Shrove (Fat) Tuesday. They are deep fried, dipped in sugar or cinnamon and sugar. In other words, it is a decadent treat every person must try when they go to Hawaii. If you do not try it, you fail. Do yourself a favor. Go to Leonard's and buy one. You are welcome.

Pupule - crazy

Slippahs - slippers, AKA sandals

dear reader

When this book was published, it was a surprise. I shouldn't say that. It wasn't a surprise it was published, but it had not been planned. A Little Harmless Addiction had already been signed by Samhain Publishing. But once readers met Micah in A Little Harmless Obsession, there was no going back. I just had to write him.

There are a few little differences in this book including an entire new chapter. I hope you enjoy the story of Dee and Micah as they are a favorite couple with my readers.

Mel

To my sister, Sharon.
Thanks for allowing your obnoxious little sister to follow you and your friends around, for sitting backwards in the car in the backseat of that Nova as Dad drove us through Europe (not to mention trying to devise a way to get him arrested by the East German guards), for being the best aunt my girls could ever have and for always remembering just how many steps there are up to that stupid reservoir. You are the only other person who truly understands how much our lives would resemble an episode of Everybody Loves Raymond if I moved in across the street. Melissa (the aforementioned obnoxious sister)

10 years earlier

"If you'd find something to do, you wouldn't be so antsy, Marjorie," Agent Michelson said. "Read a book."

Marjorie tossed a nasty look in the female FBI agent's direction and kept pacing. In forty-eight hours she had to testify against the one man she knew wanted to kill her. Even thinking about it had her head pounding, her pulse racing. She felt as if she'd drunk three gallons of coffee.

"I've read everything you have here. I don't think I can handle reading another *Field and Stream*, thanks. I'm not allowed to pick anything to watch," she said, glancing pointedly at the other FBI agent, John Brown. He'd deemed himself king of the remote the moment they'd gotten there.

Michelson smiled. Marjorie had actually liked the FBI agent. She was the first woman agent she'd dealt with after going into hiding. Just over forty, Michelson had grown up in the Bronx from the sound of her accent. It was about the only thing they had in common. Michelson wore her hair super short, was in desperate need of an eyebrow plucking, and wore some ugly-ass clothes—not to mention the fugly shoes. But she'd been nice since she arrived, even if she wasn't Conner Dillon, the man who had been in charge until two days ago. He'd headed up the investigation, been her main confidant and protector, and then he had left without a word. No explanation. She'd woken up and there was a new agent to take his place, and new orders. At least John Brown had stayed.

With a gusty sigh, Marjorie plopped down on the ratty recliner. There was no reason to be bitchy. Okay, she did have a good reason, and a lot of it started with the flea trap in which she was presently residing. For a girl who had grown up in luxury most people could only imagine, it was definitely a shock.

But that was her life before. Before she knew about the murder and before someone had tried to kill her.

"Have you been able to find my brother?"

There was a beat of silence and she glanced at the agents. They shared the same look they always did when she asked them about Mark. Conner and John had done the same thing. She knew there was something they weren't telling her.

"No. We haven't been able to locate your brother," Michelson said.

Marjorie looked in John's direction, but he ignored her. Purposively. They were hiding something. She knew the chances that it was something good, like they'd found her brother and had him hidden, were very slim. There was a higher chance that he was dead.

She blinked back the tears that threaten to spill over. What the fuck had happened to her life? She wanted to go back to what she'd had before. She wanted to be a regular seventeen-year-old with no worries other than getting her car keys back.

She turned away, stood and wandered to the window to stare out at the barren landscape. Not wanting to see it, to know just how horrible her life was now, she closed her eyes. But she couldn't escape the fear for herself, for her twin brother who was apparently missing, and she couldn't escape the fact she came from a family of jackals.

Michelson drew her attention by clearing her throat. She smiled and said, "Hey, Brown, why don't you let Marjorie pick something to watch?"

Brown grunted. "SportsCenter's on."

Marjorie couldn't keep from smiling. He was so laidback, so wonderful, she didn't mind his grumpiness. He was in his late thirties, crazy in love with his wife, and had the sad job of being a Texas Rangers fan. Of course, she was for the Yankees, so they argued about baseball all the time. But he had been kind, understanding and dependable. Unlike Conner who had abandoned her.

"SportsCenter is always on. How many times can you watch the same footage over and over?" Marjorie asked.

"Why, is Oprah having something special today?"

She ignored his sneer because he tossed the remote in her direction. Catching it, she smiled. He winked at her. He was gruff and he was a pain in the ass, but he had been her savior. And for the first time in a long time, he was a man she could trust.

"Fucking teenagers," he said with little heat.

She found the channel she wanted and settled in for watching her show. It was crap, she knew that. There was something about some man cheating or something like that, and she lost herself in the stupidity of it all. It had been a long time since she'd watched something that didn't have to do with sports.

She barely noticed the time slipping by, until she realized her room had grown dark. Rising, she walked to the floor lamp to turn it on. The moment she did, the house exploded in a rain of bullets. Marjorie dropped to the floor as glass showered over her. She crawled across the carpet, her heart pounding as the TV exploded. She couldn't stop the cry of fear that escaped. She pressed her back against the wall that separated the hall and the living room and drew in big gulps of air, trying to calm herself.

Closing her eyes, she remembered the instructions John had given her the day they picked her up.

Get to safety. Calm yourself. Assess the situation.

She did just that and the first thing she noticed was there was no returning fire. All of the shots were coming in the windows.

"Marjorie." Brown's voice was hoarse with pain.

She peeked around the corner into the foyer. She gasped at the sight. He lay against the opposite wall, and even in the dim light she could see the blood. It was everywhere, his shirt saturated with it.

Her stomach roiled as she moved to him. Tears burned the back of her eyes as she huddled next to him. She pulled the scarf she used to hold her rebellious dark curls back, and pressed it to his stomach. It was soaked within seconds.

"Forget it."

She looked up and saw the resignation in his eyes, the knowledge that he was dying. The bullets rained around them, glass continued to shatter but they were apparently in a safe zone in the hall.

"Take these." He handed her a set of car keys. "Just go. Go away, hide, don't look back."

"I can't leave you. I'll get Michelson—"

"Useless to us." And that meant the female agent was dead. "Go. You know where the car is. You know where to go until they leave. Go out the back, down the alley. Don't talk to anyone, no one."

She nodded, but it wasn't enough. He wrapped his fingers around her hand. With the level eye she had relied on since she'd been in his protection, he caught her gaze. "No one. I mean no one. No girlfriends, boyfriends, family...or the authorities."

Her heart stuttered to a stop then swung into a rapid rhythm. "W-what?"

"Someone knew where we were, Margie." He drew in a long, thready breath. Each word sounded as if it was ripped from somewhere deep and painful. "Someone told them. No one should have known about this. Disappear. Don't ever come back."

Her brain couldn't seem to assimilate what he was telling her. All the weeks of protection, of trusting the FBI, holding on to them like a lifeline, and now...

He drew in a shuddering breath and winced. "God dammit, fucking go, now."

It pulled her out of her thoughts, got her mind working in the right direction. She leaned forward and kissed his cheek. "Thank you, John."

"Go."

She nodded, then turned away. She slipped down the hall and into the closet beneath the stairs. Once she closed the outer door, she pushed on the panel that opened to another set of stairs. She grabbed the flashlight and headed down. It was dark and dank in the basement, but out of boredom she had found it the first day they had arrived. Only Conner and John knew about it, and as far as she knew they hadn't told a soul.

She knew there were bugs, knew there were probably big hairy rats, but she found the darkest corner and waited. She heard the pounding of feet, the shouts, the activity. She waited. The excitement seemed to fade, the knowledge that she wasn't there was setting in from the arguing she could hear. It didn't take them long, but it felt like a lifetime. The quiet house, the almost deathly stillness of it seeped through the floor above her head. And still, she waited.

Knowing she had to get out of there before the authorities arrived, she crept out of her corner. She reached behind the water heater and grabbed the bag of clothes. In it she knew there were documents for a new identity and money to get her where she needed to go. She slung it over her shoulder and headed to the stairs. Each step was agonizing as fear coiled in her gut. When she reached the top, she placed her ear against the door.

Nothing. Not a sound.

Drawing in a deep breath, she eased the outer panel of the wall open, then turned the knob and pulled the door ajar. She peeked out. She could see the front door was closed. With more courage than she felt, she slipped out of her hiding place. Glass cracked under her boots as she walked with her back against the wall down the hall. She looked around the corner and saw John Brown. Now she couldn't hold back the tears. He lay, blood pooled around him, his eyes open, his chest no longer moving.

Even considering her father and all he had done, this was the first time she had dealt with the death of someone she cared for. He had lost his life for her. John had been hard on her at times, but he had done everything to protect her. As tears slid down her cheeks, she inched closer, and even though she knew he would have griped at her for wasting the time and putting herself in danger, she slipped her fingers over his eyes and closed the lids.

"Thank you," she whispered.

She would not let him die for nothing. She held the keys in her hands and ducked into the kitchen. There was no sign of Michelson, but since John had said she was dead, Marjorie decided to just get out. She'd had enough up-close-and-personal dealings with death for the day.

She turned to go to her bedroom for more clothes, but then stopped. No. John said leave now. Go.

Instead of going to the garage, she slipped out the back, over the fence and then down the alley just as John had told her. She found the car three streets over, sitting in an abandoned lot. Five minutes later, she was driving down highway 395. She had one destination...Canada. She glanced at herself in the mirror, saw her trademark curls and knew they would have to go. And she would have to change her hair color. She needed to become someone else. Like John said, disappear.

Tonight, Marjorie Rizzoli would do just that.

one

"You're going to bore a hole in her back if you keep staring at her like that."

Micah Ross tossed his best friend and business partner, Evan Chambers, a nasty look. "What the fuck are you talking about?"

"Dee Sumner. You have an obsession with that one."

Micah snorted. "Not likely."

But even as he said it, his gaze traveled back to the monitor where his head bartender served drinks. He couldn't seem to keep his attention on anything else. He had a club to run, a profitable one that turned people away on the weekends. It was getting downright embarrassing. He'd been drawn to her from the moment she'd come to work for him, and it was getting worse.

She wasn't even his type. He usually went for curvy, soft women with a little height. Dee was short in stature with a tough little athletic body. He could see the sculpted muscles beneath her uniform. He would give a million bucks to see that tight ass of hers. Lord knew he'd spent enough time watching it the last few months. When he had first hired her, her hair had been short and curly. Now it was long, sleek and a lighter blonde. He preferred dark curls on a woman. But on her...it worked. It showed off her high cheekbones and that full mouth of hers. Her eyes were really what captured him. Blue, almost luminous...mermaid eyes. They took up most of her face and sparkled when she smiled. Like she was now, a full grin with those cute little dimples he'd come to love.

But he had rules, so he kept his hands to himself. He sat in his office above the main floor of his club, watching the monitors. Stalking her. She had a way about her. It was one of the reasons he had hired her. Each move was fluid, as if part of some dance routine.

"Micah."

He tore his attention away from the monitor and inwardly grimaced when he saw the smile on Evan's face. His fascination with Dee was something he wanted to keep under wraps. He would never be able to act on it, and while he was frustrated, he could deal with it. Maybe. Truthfully, he didn't know how he felt about the situation. It was probably the reason he couldn't seem to settle down the last few months.

"What?"

"Why not ask her out?"

He shifted in his chair. "She works for me."

Evan rolled his eyes. "Big fucking deal. I know you don't like to fuck the help, but that has never been a rule here."

He hesitated. It had been one of his personal rules, true. Running a BDSM club came with some complications. A relationship of any sort could quickly escalate into a sexual-harassment suit. And of course, there was the real reason he couldn't break the rules.

"She doesn't play."

Evan grunted. "Really? I find that hard to believe."

"What do you mean?"

"Just a vibe I get off her."

Micah knew what Evan was talking about. The woman might not admit she was a sub, but everything about her screamed it. He could see the way her eyes would flare with recognition and heat when he ordered her to do something. She was a woman who was made for submission.

Not that she was a wilting flower. She was one tough woman, as some patrons had found out when they'd tried to mess with her. The last guy sported a broken nose for his efforts.

There were times when they were together that he felt it. Felt her need to be conquered, to be controlled. Still, she denied it constantly. All of his employees had a free membership in the club. Since it was several thousand dollars, he knew it was a highly prized benefit. Dee never used hers.

"She's been working here for two years, there has to be some reason."

Micah glanced at Evan. "She says the tips here are better than other places. Plus, she says, other than the occasional jack-ass, our patrons are better behaved."

Including the one she gave the broken nose to. Even now he wanted to hunt the son of a bitch down and break his nose again for even thinking he had the right to touch Dee.

"So are we done here?"

Evan's question jolted him out of his revenge fantasy and he frowned. "Got somewhere to be?"

"May's closing up right about now." The smile Evan was sporting irritated as much as it satisfied him. Micah could take some credit for getting them together.

"Not bored yet?" He said it as a joke, and Evan took it that way.

"Yeah, sure. Would you ever get bored with May Aiona?"

A swift jolt of envy twined through Micah. May was a sub, an almost perfect sub. He would have loved to be the one who initiated her, but that had been for Evan. She had always been for Evan.

"We're done. Since you're whipped, you can leave."

Evan laughed again. "Man, you're nasty. You need to hook up before you start a fight with someone."

The problem with having a friend like Evan was he knew too much. All their years together, living on the street, then building Rough 'n Ready, the premier BDSM club on the islands, they had learned each other quirks.

"Not happening, bra. I have more work to do tonight and someone has to close up."

Evan shook his head as he headed for the door. "You're going to work yourself to death if you aren't careful. You need to take some time off."

"And who would run the club?"

Evan paused. "We have a manager and several assistants who are very well trained. You can take a vacation whenever you want. If you don't do it on your own, I'll arrange it."

"Are you talking kidnapping?"

Evan shrugged. "You need a break, Micah. I don't want you working yourself into an early grave."

He shook his head and flipped his hand at him. "Go to May."

"Oh, did you get that ad set approved for next month?"

Micah nodded.

"How does it look?"

Micah rolled his eyes. "It looks great. You approved it, you should know. May's waiting."

Evan didn't leave at first, but he sighed and then slipped through the door. Micah tried to concentrate, but his attention kept straying to the woman downstairs. He gave up and went to the window that looked out onto the floor. They had built the club from the ground up. With Evan's skills and Micah's vision, they'd designed something that was unique to the islands. The office overlooked the floor where their patrons mixed and mingled. Five bars were scattered throughout the area, although two of them were shut down since it was Monday, their slowest night of the week.

Still, the dance floor was crowded, as was the lounge area where chairs and sofas were grouped together in conversation pits. He glanced up at the few rooms that were on the same level as the office. Five luxury suites built for the ultimate enjoyment. Two were being used. He knew the rooms on the floors below the main floor were full. Not bad for a Monday night.

He should go find someone. There were more than a few willing subs out there, but as he looked them over, his gaze was drawn to the woman who had been driving him crazy for two years. She didn't look like much, that was for sure. Five-four, petite, with silky blonde hair, she resembled a fairy. She had luminous blue eyes, a cute little nose that was sprinkled with freckles. She wore the uniform of his staff, dark black pants, and tailored shirt. It was almost boring in a way. But on Dee... He sighed. The woman had a body. For being short, sleek and petite, she didn't lack feminine attributes. High breasts, slightly rounded hips...and her ass. Jesus the woman had an ass on her. He'd seen her a couple of times in jeans that molded to her rear end and almost passed out from blood loss to his brain.

She laughed at something a customer said to her, patted his hand and moved on. The man, who had a death wish, watched her walk away, his attention on her ass. Jealousy, swift and hard, pounded through Micah. He turned to head downstairs ready to tear the man's head from his shoulders before he caught himself.

He paused at the door and noticed the man was already moving on somewhere else, to someone else. Dee wasn't even paying attention to the loser. She was helping Keisha, one of his wait staff, fill an order. Before he knew what he was doing, he was walking down the stairs to the first level. To her. The moment he reached the bottom step, he frowned. Damn. Now that he was here, and some of his customers had seen him, he couldn't turn around and walk back up. He would look like an idiot. So, with practiced ease, he walked through the crowd, smiling, stopping to talk and shaking hands. All the while, one part of his brain was focused on the woman behind the main bar.

He was watching her again.

Dee mixed a Colorado Bulldog as she rolled her shoulders, but it didn't get rid of the feeling that Micah Ross was watching her. He'd been doing it most of the night and it was making her damned self-conscious.

"Is there something wrong?"

She looked up at Keisha and smiled. The tall black woman

had become one of her few friends since moving to the islands two years earlier. "Nope. Just a feeling."

"Oh, you mean the boss?"

She glanced up sharply and Keisha's smile widened. "It's kind of funny how he watches you all the time."

"Well, I don't like it. Makes me think he doesn't trust me." And while she did lie about some things, she had always been trustworthy in her job.

"Uh, honey, that's not why he watches you."

She turned to pull a beer. "Yeah, why else would he do it?"

Keisha said nothing and Dee looked up. Her friend rolled her eyes. "Are you that stupid?"

No, she wasn't. Most men were easy to read. They wanted one thing, and one thing only from her. Well, two things. First, their booze, then they wanted sex. She had avoided the second problem while making a good living off the first. Either way, she didn't like deep men. Those men were dangerous. They could hide things from you. Things that could end up getting you killed.

Micah Ross was deeper than any man she had met.

"There's a pool going," Keisha said.

That caused Dee to come to a dead stop. "A pool?"

"Yeah, we want to know how long it will be before Ross can't control himself. I have dibs on two weeks from Tuesday and I really want to go back to the mainland to see my mom."

"It's that high?"

Keisha laughed as she hoisted her tray up. "Honey, it's been building the last six months."

With that, she turned and sashayed through the crowd. Dammit, Dee hated that. She didn't need people speculating what was going on between her and Ross. She didn't like gossip.

It made her too interesting. That would cause her too many problems to count.

She rubbed her forehead and tried to get her mind back on work. It was bad enough she'd dreamt of him more than once in the last few months. Who wouldn't, she thought with irritation. He was gorgeous. Not the usual pretty boy, he was tall, over six feet, with long straight hair, a proud Native American nose and Jesus, his body. She'd seen him just about naked since he'd paired up with subs for the crowd a few times when she first started working there. Saying the man was built just didn't do him justice. Sinewy muscles, golden skin, not to mention a world-class ass.

Lord, she had to stop thinking about that. No men. That was her rule. She didn't trust easily, but men especially. She couldn't be sure that one of them wouldn't offer her up on a silver platter for the price.

And if that made her feel sad, she would just have to ignore it. Stupid girls got themselves killed. Falling for a guy like Micah Ross was definitely stupid.

Business was starting to slow down, so she decided to start looking over the bar, starting cleaning up and doing inventory. Mondays weren't that busy, but she never left her bar for the next worker without a good supply. In her position as head bartender, she didn't have to stock the bar. She could make the next bartender on duty do it, but Dee held herself to higher standards than that.

She picked up a bottle of Patron and made a note that she needed another one. Once done, she turned to put it back.

"How's it going?"

Her heart jumped to her throat, every nerve going on alert and the bottle slipped from her grasp. The crash was barely

16

heard over the roar of the pulsing music, but it did draw the attention of a few people sitting at the bar. Micah was behind her in an instant. He grabbed her by her upper arms and spun her around.

"Are you okay?"

She looked up at him, held immobile by his nearness. She had never been this close to him ever. She could see the concern in his eyes, feel his breath feather over her face. Even with all the people in the area, she could scent him. Bayberry...and Micah. It made her head spin and left her feeling vaguely aroused.

"I-I'm fine, Micah. You can let me go."

He looked down at his hands on her arms as if he didn't realize he still held her. He wanted to argue, she could see it when his gaze pierced hers again. After a moment's hesitation, he released her.

There was no reason for her heart to be beating the way it was. Her entire body simmered with heat. Good Lord, it wasn't as if she hadn't been that close to a man before. She was acting like a teenager.

"Are you sure?" he asked, his low, seductive voice easy enough for her to hear. He had moved closer, his lips within inches of her ear.

She nodded and turned to grab the broom. Without saying anything she cleaned up the glass. He stayed there, watching her as if she were a child who needed supervision. By the time she was done, her nerves were jumping.

"Was there something you wanted?"

He didn't say anything. She glanced up at him. His body was rigid, his gaze fastened on her mouth. A tremor of need shifted through her blood. Dammit. She cleared her throat.

"Micah?"

The heat in his eyes sent a shaft of need spiraling through her as she took a step back from him. From temptation.

"No. Just wanted to make sure you were doing okay tonight."

She frowned. He watched her a lot but he rarely worried about her taking care of herself. "Everything's fine. You know how Monday nights go."

He kept watching her mouth as she spoke. It was a bit disconcerting. A lick of heat raced up her spine. His gray eyes darkened, his pupils dilating. Every bit of moisture in her mouth evaporated. Her nipples pebbled, ached. It took all her control to lick her lips. The need to squeeze her thighs together to relieve the unbearable tension between her legs almost overwhelmed her.

He took a step closer to her. The music, the people, everything faded to the background. Without a word, he dipped his head, but jerked back at the sound of Keisha's voice.

"Hey, I need another gin and tonic."

He shot Keisha a look of death before glancing back down at Dee. She couldn't say anything. Hell, she could barely think at the moment. In that one second, she had wanted him with a need that was burning her up inside. Her entire body was pulsing, yearning. But the moment was over as he glanced around at the customers. He said nothing as he turned on his heel and stomped out from behind the bar. Dee pressed a hand to her chest, trying to calm her heart and then leaned against the bar.

"Hey, Dee? Wake up, girl."

She looked up at Keisha and offered her a weary smile. "I'll get it. Give me a second. And definitely, I owe you a thank you."

She cocked her head to the side, her chocolate brown eyes

twinkling. "Why? Because the big bad bossman looked like he wanted to gobble you up?"

Dee closed her eyes and shivered. "Yeah."

"Ohh."

Dee's eyes shot open. "What?"

"Well, I didn't know you liked him that much."

Dee inwardly cursed. She had kept her attraction to him under wraps until that instant. "I don't like him."

"Honey, you may not like him, but I could hear it in your voice. You want him."

"Show me a heterosexual woman who wouldn't find him attractive, and I tell you the woman is an idiot."

Keisha laughed. "No. This is different. I have never seen that reaction to any man in the two years you've worked here."

Dee finished making the gin and tonic and placed it on Keisha's tray.

"You're loco."

Keisha laughed. "Oh, you do. This is going to be good. Just don't do anything until my day on the pool. I need that money."

Before Dee could say anything, Keisha turned and worked her way through the crowd again. Without looking, she knew Micah was there, knew he was pretending not to pay attention to her. The fairest whisper of his gaze would move over her from time to time. She could feel it as if his fingers moved over her flesh. Dammit, she didn't need this.

One way or another, she would have to ignore him and every enticement he represented. Keeping entanglements to a minimum made her a smart girl. Smart girls stayed alive.

She glanced over and noticed he was talking to one of the regular subs...one that used to be his favorite. Her heart dropped to her stomach and she turned around. So what if it hurt? It was the way it had to be.

She pushed aside her foolish yearnings and started to shut down for the night. She'd learned years ago not to regret what she'd lost. There was nothing to be gained from it.

two

Micah grumbled as he let himself into his office. Three days. Three days since he'd dealt with being in Dee's presence. He knew it had been a mistake to touch her. From the moment he'd hired her, he'd been attracted. That had never been a problem before. Even now, knowing she wasn't into the life, or at least claiming she wasn't, there would be no chance with her. She had been pretty emphatic about that. It didn't matter that he'd been lusting after her, or that it was getting worse by the day. He needed to control, needed to be the Dom. It wasn't something he merely desired in the bedroom, it was something he needed to be complete.

He turned on his coffee maker, thankful that Freddy was a good assistant and had gotten it ready for him. It was early for Micah, just past noon, but he had an idea of getting work done and taking the night off. Evan had been right. He needed some time away and he would start with tonight. The night Dee was scheduled to work.

With a sigh, he sat behind his desk and turned on his monitors without looking at them. He had some paperwork to get done and the schedule for the bouncers needed to be set up. Every section of his club, from the bartenders to the waitresses to the DJs had a supervisor. All of them except the bouncers. Charles was his head bouncer, but Micah couldn't let him do the scheduling. He had tried that once, and it had blown up in his face. Thinking of the infighting he'd dealt with and all the work-related issues had him chuckling. Most people thought his job would be exciting and titillating. It was, to an extent. Working up schedules, dealing with taxes, publicity and safety codes dimmed some of the glow of being a Dom in his very own BDSM club.

When he and Evan had decided to open the club five years earlier, Micah had been happy to take over the managing. Evan had a say in everything, but Micah ran the place for the most part. He had a mind for numbers and marketing, so it worked.

His coffee beeped and he went to retrieve a cup. When he sat back down, he noticed someone was in the gym they had built for their employees. Most people didn't show up until right before their shifts, and none of them were slated until seven that night. He zoomed in, but even before he saw her face, he knew who it was.

She was boxing. He'd never seen her do it, but he had heard from others that she did a lot of it in the gym. Just as when she worked behind the bar, she was fluid in her movements. She lifted her leg for a kick and then punched the bag. Her muscles contracted, eased, contracted again.

Damn, she was a thing of beauty. He'd fought in the ring and he knew he hadn't been as good. Hell, he wasn't sure with her moves that he could take her easily. He could tell from the way she pointed her toes that she had danced at one time. What woman trained to be a ballerina then turned to boxing and bartending?

The clothing she wore clung to her, curved over that tight ass. The top was little more than a sports bra. The flesh rose above the fabric. He licked his lips. She pivoted on her foot for a roundhouse kick and he felt the arousal that had been simmering shoot to boiling. He would have never thought to be turned on by a woman sparring with a bag, but then, he wasn't sure there was much the woman could do that wouldn't turn him on.

He didn't even think when he rose from his chair, not really. The only thing on his mind was going to see her, watch her...touch her.

Dee landed another right against the bag as she tried her damnedest to fight the images that kept coming to her from her dreams the night before. For two nights running, she had dreamt of Micah, what he could do to her in bed. She might be a virgin, but she knew what went on. *Can't work at a place like Rough 'n Ready and not know*, she thought with a chuckle.

Left, right, left.

But then last night...her sexy dream had morphed into horrific memories. She'd been thrown back into that safe house, glass shattering on top of her, bullets flying around her. This time, though, she didn't get away. She could still feel the piercing of her skin, the burn of the bullet.

She turned and did another roundhouse kick.

MELISSA SCHROEDER

"You're going to hurt yourself if you push too hard."

She started, her breath coming out in short, hard chops and looked at the doorway. Damn, the man had to be here today. He never showed up this early. It was one of the reasons she came early, worked out and went home. Plus, no one bothered her when she arrived first thing in the afternoon.

"You have no idea what I can handle."

One eyebrow rose as he walked into the gym. Shit, he wasn't going to go away. She wasn't up to a verbal sparring match. Not today. Not after those dreams she'd had about him. She could still feel his hands moving over her, teasing her, taking her up and over that edge.

She turned away and pulled off a glove to grab a bottle of water. She took a large swallow and faced him. "What are you doing here this early, Micah?"

"I thought to get some work done."

Which was odd because Micah didn't do work early in the day. It was one of things she envied about him. He had no problems living his hedonistic lifestyle. He intertwined it with being a very successful business man, but he seemed to revel in the fact that he slept until two in the afternoon every day.

"Well, I'm trying to get my workout done so I can go home to shower, so..."

He shoved his hands in his pockets and rocked back on his heels. "So, what?"

She knew he wasn't dense. He knew she wanted to be alone and he was taking pleasure in denying her wish.

"I have a feeling you have better things to do than watch me work out."

He chuckled and the sound had every hormone in her body jumping to attention. Wet heat slipped through her body, over her nerve endings. "I doubt that. How long did you train in ballet?"

"Jazz," she said, and then silently cursed herself for allowing that information to slip out.

"I knew you had some training in dance from the way you move behind the bar."

She frowned. "What do you mean?"

He paused. "Well, there's just something in the way you move that speaks of some kind of dance training."

Crap. She thought she kept that hidden away, had for years. "I didn't know you paid that much attention to your employees."

His smile widened. "I don't usually. But you intrigue me."

Just hearing him speak the words had her heart whacking against her ribs. She turned and grabbed her towel to wipe herself down. If he wasn't going to leave, she would at least clean herself up.

"So, you're stalking my every move."

"I wouldn't say that."

"It's that obvious that I used to dance?"

Her nerves were jumping and not just with arousal. Maybe she'd been here too long. She had grown comfortable in her surroundings and that was never a good thing. But she had fallen in love with Oahu, the people and her job.

"No, not really. But since I used to fight, I pick up on things like that."

"Oh, I forgot you used to do those ultimate fight things."

"Things? I guess you could call it that. It definitely shouldn't be considered anything but a means to an end."

"Did you get hurt?"

He shrugged. "It was worth it. Helped me open Rough 'n Ready."

She nodded. "Well, I'm on my way home."

But when she tried to step around him, he moved into her path. Every nerve in her body sizzled.

"Why are you rushing out? People say that your workouts last at least an hour."

"Ross, back off. That *does* sound like stalking."

"If I wanted to stalk you, you'd have no idea, that's for sure. After my stint in the ring, you know I was a bounty hunter?"

She did, but only after she had taken the job. Since she rarely saw bounty hunters in the bar, she figured she was safe. Considering the six-foot-plus mountain of gorgeous muscle looming in front of her, that might have been a mistake.

"Okay, so you can stalk me. Gotcha."

She turned to leave, but apparently Micah wasn't ready for that.

"I didn't say you could leave."

She stopped in her tracks. Not because he ordered her. Not really. It was the tone of his voice. It had changed. Subtly. There was an edge to it that wasn't there before. Worse was her reaction to it. The dark order sent a tsunami of need flowing through her. She didn't need this, didn't want it. Hunger surged, battered at her defenses.

"I didn't ask."

He drew in a deep breath, his nostrils flaring slightly. *Even that turns me on*, she thought. Her blood pounded through her, her heart turning over at the fierce look he gave her. God, she needed to get away from him, away from this crazy longing he pulled from her.

She moved to get around him, but he wrapped his hand

around her upper arm. She didn't feel threatened. If she told him to take his hands off her, Micah would do it. There was a deep core of goodness in him, the type of thing that made him dangerous to a woman like her. He was dangerous in a completely different area. She wanted him. More than she had ever wanted another man. It was something she had avoided by keeping her interactions with men very superficial. She dated men who did absolutely nothing for her, so she wouldn't be tempted. Unfortunately, this man would tempt the most pious of virgins.

She looked down at his hand then back up at him. The heat she saw flicker in his eyes flared deep in her belly, shot straight to her sex. Dammit, he barely touched her and she was quivering, waiting. *Wanting.*

"What?"

He turned her, slowly, until they faced each other, so close that her breasts rubbed against him each time she drew in a breath. Her nipples were hard, her mouth dry. Her body was one big hormone begging for relief.

"I don't know what the hell it is about you, but..." He groaned, and before she knew what he was doing, he dipped his head and moved his mouth over hers. She didn't respond at first. She tried her best to resist, pretending it didn't affect her. But he pulled her closer and her breasts pressed against him. His hands skimmed down her spine to her ass. She could feel his arousal through their layers of clothing and she couldn't stop herself, or the hunger he seemed to wrench from her.

His tongue slipped over the seam in her mouth and she opened, willingly, craving this connection. Longing welled up in her, surged through her blood. She slipped her hands up his shoulders, behind his neck, and then she plunged her fingers into his long silky strands.

He groaned again and deepened the kiss while he lifted her off the ground. Everything in her body screamed for relief, one that she knew only Micah could give her. She pressed closer, wrapping her legs around his waist. Liquid heat pooled between her thighs. All her nerve endings seemed to shimmer. Every thought dissolved at the feel of his tongue sliding against hers, the way his heart pounded against hers, and how much she burned to feel his flesh against hers.

The sound of a door slamming in the distance brought them both back to their senses. They pulled apart, their breathing choppy. He eased her down, grimacing when she slid against his erection. Both of them groaned.

"That should not have happened," she said between gasps.

"It was just a matter of time, Dee."

She shook her head. "You live a lifestyle I don't."

It wasn't exactly true. Secretly, she read BDSM and had a thing for big, bad Doms as the heroes, but she definitely would never admit it. Not to the big, bad Dom standing in front of her.

He eyed her with suspicion. "You don't know until you try it."

She shook her head. His face was flushed with arousal, his breathing still unsteady, and she was sure without letting her gaze dip, wonderfully aroused. She squeezed her thighs together to try and diminish the pulse of need between her legs. It just made it worse.

"I can't." She could hear the regret in her voice. For the first time in her life, she realized what she was missing out on with her personal agreement for no sex. "I need to go."

She grabbed her back pack, eased on her slippers, and walked to the door.

"Dee." She stopped but didn't look back. "You don't have to come in tonight."

She glanced back over her shoulder at him and swallowed. She could see desire for her in his expression, and it made her heart tremble, her body yearn. In all her twenty-seven years there had never been a man who tempted her as this one had.

"No. I can do my job. Unless you would rather I wouldn't?"

He shook his head and offered her a small smile. "You're the best. And you know how Thursday nights can be busy."

She hesitated, then nodded. She hurried out of the club, glad that she hadn't run into anyone. As quickly as possible, she slipped into her car and started on her way home. By the time she was on Pali highway, she drew in a deep breath, trying to calm her nerves. She knew she shouldn't have done that, shouldn't have touched, been touched, but she had been. Never before had a man gotten that close, mainly because she never let them, hadn't until today.

Damn, she didn't want to leave, but maybe she should start thinking about it. She had come to love Hawaii and the way of life there. The moment she stepped off the plane over two years earlier, she had felt some kind of connection as if she were coming home.

She smiled. Who would have thought a girl raised in New York City would think that? But she did. It stirred something in her blood every day she saw a rainbow, watched the sun rise, or smelled Plumeria and salt in the air.

And then there was the man. She wanted him, more than was good for her health. She couldn't, wouldn't put either of them at risk. There was still a price on her head, although she hadn't heard anything lately. It didn't matter. Not safe for either of them. She'd have to keep her hands to herself.

And for the first time in ten years she felt regret because she was sure Micah Ross would be a man who knew just how to handle her. Dee just couldn't take a chance. With another sigh, she hit the gas and let the Hawaiian wind fly through her hair. She was going to enjoy Hawaii as long as she could.

three

Dee smiled when she saw Kai Aiona step up to her bar.

"How's it going tonight, Dee?"

From the moment she'd met him several months earlier, she'd liked May's big brother. He was average height, but most people didn't notice it. He was big everywhere else, especially his muscles. The man worked on the docks and it showed in his sculpted arms as he leaned on the bar. He had a wealth of tattoos, mainly Hawaiian symbols. And she knew from the few times she'd seen him on the beach, he sported a nipple ring to match his earring. In fact, rumor was that he had more interesting piercings.

"Same as usual. Busy, but then it's a Saturday night. Surprised to see you here."

He rolled his eyes. "My soon-to-be brother-in-law has been after me to come in."

She laughed. "Somehow I don't see you hanging out some place like this."

He cocked his head to the side. "Now why would you say that?"

She leaned forward over the bar. "For one, you've never been in here before, even though I know Evan would've let you in for free, being family."

"And?"

He leaned forward, his face just inches from her, his gaze on her lips. Oh, crap. Men often took her genial manner with them as flirting. She'd always been more comfortable with them than with women. Truthfully, Kai was the sort of man she should be interested in. He was a caretaker. She could feel it to her bones. But even with him this close, with the scent of sea on his skin and his gorgeous body, he didn't interest her in the least.

She shrugged and moved away, as casually as possible. "I just think if you were really interested, you would've shown up before now."

He didn't say anything for a few moments, and she looked up from pulling a beer.

"Might be I don't like to be some place where I might see my sister naked."

A laugh bubbled up at the pained expression on his face. "Brothers are always squeamish about their sisters."

The moment she said it, she regretted it. His gaze caught hers and she saw the interest, the speculation. She had been so careful not to reveal any information about her family.

"Brothers?"

She nodded.

"How many?" She hesitated and he shook his head. "Never mind."

She sighed. "I just don't like talking about my family. I had a...disagreement with them years ago. We don't talk."

"It's odd for me to even imagine that with my crazy family."

Keisha came up and smiled at Kai. "Hey, Kai. What have you been up to, bra?"

Dee took Keisha's order and listened to the two of them chat. It was easy to forget just how well everyone knew each other on Oahu. It was like one big little town.

"Don't be a stranger," she said, as she hefted her tray and walked away. Kai watched, his gaze zeroing on her ass.

He must have felt Dee's attention because he glanced over at her and had the decency to flush.

"Talking me up and then watching another woman." She tsked. "I'd hate to see what May would make of this."

Kai smiled. "My sister knows I'm like that. If I thought I had a chance with you, I wouldn't look at another woman, but I don't think I do."

She said nothing, just crossed her arms beneath her breasts.

"And secondly, Keisha and I go way back."

She arched an eyebrow. "How far?"

He pursed his lips. "Eleventh grade, prom."

She leaned against her bar and watched his gaze go back to Keisha. The relationship her friend had been in had been...well, bad. The guy hadn't been too happy when she'd ended it, which had resulted in Dee having to threaten the asshole when he'd had the stupidity to show up at her place looking for Keisha. Those self-defense moves had come in handy, and he had left with a broken nose and talking in a higher octave.

Keisha needed an easy relationship with no complications. Kai was a good guy. He slept around a bit, but she didn't know a lot of men who didn't. A girl who had two brothers knew what men were about. But unlike a lot of other guys, Kai was decent. He never hurt a woman. In fact, he was still friendly with most of his exes from what she could tell. Knowing Keisha needed someone to make her happy, if even for one night, Dee made her decision.

"I'll let you in on a secret."

He tore his gaze from her friend. "What?"

"Her and that loser, Ruben, broke it off. She kicked him out."

Kai pursed his lips as his attention returned to Keisha. "Really? Well, maybe I should stick around."

She laughed. "Yeah, she might need someone to help her mend that broken heart."

Kai offered her a smile and a wink. "I'm just the man to do it."

She watched him as he eased his way through the crowd to follow Keisha. Kai was just the type of guy she should get involved with, if she was wanting to get involved with anyone. He was easygoing, so laidback he never let anything ruffle his demeanor. Not like a certain someone with long silky hair and a hard-on for ordering her around.

Jesus, when was she going to get that man out of her head? It had been two days since the kissing incident. She swore she could still taste him there, lingering on her lips. This wasn't like her at all. She did not get hung up on men. Sure, they were fun, but getting involved was complicated, especially with her life.

"Was Kai Aiona bothering you?"

She jumped when she heard Micah's voice behind her. Damn, he was sneaky. Granted, the music was loud, but she usually could sense a person coming up behind her. Micah's ability to sneak up on her was another worry.

She drew in a deep breath and turned to face him. He was behind the bar again, a place that he'd never ventured in the two years she'd been working for him. Not until this week.

"No. Kai is just hanging out. I have a feeling Keisha and him might be rekindling some of their high school romance."

His gaze didn't leave her as she pulled a beer for a customer and then took the man's money.

"I just wanted to be sure."

She drew in another breath. The man was dangerous to her psyche, to her body, to her very life. He made her want to be stupid, to just jump his body and take what he wanted to offer. A man like Micah Ross might not want attachments, but going to bed would be complicated. And damn, it would be good. Really good.

She pushed that thought aside as she wiped down the bar.

"Ross, I can take care of myself."

He shook his head and opened his mouth, but apparently thought better of it. "I need to talk to you after your shift tonight."

She frowned. It wasn't that odd, except she couldn't think of anything they needed to discuss. She nodded. He hesitated, then turned and walked away. People moved out his path without probably knowing what they were doing. He projected just what he was, top alpha in a club filled with them.

God, she wanted to know what he was like in bed. It was a hunger that had been simmering for months. Now that he seemed to be completely and absolutely focused on her, it was hard to keep it off her mind. It was consuming her daytime thoughts and still invading her dreams. Something had to give.

She shoved thoughts of Micah Ross to the back of her head as another waitress came up to the bar for an order.

What the fuck was he doing?

Micah asked himself that over and over as he watched Rex let the last of the workers leave. It was just the two of them and one more employee left. She was wiping down the bar, finishing up her work. He could tell she was taking her time. Hell, she had avoided him for the past two days and he could understand that. He felt like an ass for his behavior in the gym. Anyone could have walked in on them. Kissing her definitely would have caused a commotion in the club. Worse, it might have diminished her authority, and that was something he could not allow. Almost everyone who worked there looked up to her. Especially the bouncers.

Apparently finished with her work, she walked toward the stairs to his office. His palms were sweating, his heart thundering. Damn, he was acting like a fifteen-year-old.

He wasn't even going to touch her. Other than apologizing, he had no plans to do anything in that quarter. But then things never went as planned with Dee.

She knocked on the door twice before opening it.

"What did you need to talk to me about?"

She was straightforward as usual. He stayed seated behind his desk. Normally he would have risen as a show of respect, but he didn't really want to embarrass himself. He was already half-aroused. He motioned to the chair in front of his desk. She hesitated, her hand still on the door knob. Then she released her breath and stepped forward.

Once she was seated, she stared at him expectantly. What

the hell had he called her in here for? Damn, when she focused all that attention on him with her luminous eyes, he couldn't think. Before meeting her, he had never seen that shade of blue. They were so deep, dark, they were almost violet. The dark lashes that framed them were natural.

"Micah?"

He shook his head. "Sorry. Long night. First, I want to apologize for the other day."

She shrugged, acting as if it wasn't a big deal. And it shouldn't be. Hell, it was a tame kiss compared to what he was used to. But he could still remember the way she tasted, the way her breath caught just before he pressed his mouth against hers.

He shifted in his seat, trying to ease his pain. Unfortunately, the fabric of his pants rubbed over his erection, further frustrating him. Damn, he needed to start wearing underwear.

"Is that all?"

He shook his head. "No. I want to take a few days off and wondered if you would be okay with handling all the ordering for the bar while I'm gone."

"Sure. I do most of the ordering right now."

He looked at her. "I thought Eddy did it."

She rolled her eyes and crossed her ankle over her knee. "I come up with the list. Eddy tends to wait until the last minute. I like a well-stocked bar. Why wouldn't he be doing it if you're gone?"

"I'm asking him to take over while I'm gone."

Another eye roll.

"You don't agree."

She sighed. "I like Eddy. He's a great guy. But he's too much of a pushover when it comes to the women here."

"What do you mean?"

"He's great at keeping things hopping, taking care of the customers, don't get me wrong. But when one of the waitresses wants to go home and you aren't here, they go to Eddy, even if Sylvia is here. They know that she won't let them go home early if there is work to be done. They just have to bat their eyes at Eddy and he lets them do what they want."

"He's not screwing around with any of them is he?"

She laughed. "Lord, no. He loves that crazy woman he's married to. But he's a pushover when it comes to women. If you haven't talked to Eddy, I would put Sylvia in charge. She's the Domme out of the two of them."

He studied her for a long moment. "You talk like you know the life, when I know you don't practice."

She snorted. "I've been working here for two years. I'd have to be dead to not know the life."

He smiled. "You definitely aren't that."

Her smile faded and she looked away.

"Is that all you wanted?"

"No. But I can't have what I really want."

Just like that, the air in the room grew hot and his pulse doubled. He shouldn't have said it. Even now he wanted to kick his own ass for it, but he couldn't keep his mouth from saying it. No way. He'd wanted her for months, probably since the moment he'd hired her. He wasn't a man who was used to denying his needs. Damn, the woman didn't know just what she was doing to him. He hadn't had a woman in weeks. Hadn't wanted one. He wanted her, in his bed, submitting to him. He could imagine just how she would look strapped to his mattress—

"I thought we decided it would be best to ignore that."

"No, *you* decided."

"You know as well as I do, I'm not in the life. That's what you want."

"That's what I need." He corrected her. "Have you ever tried it?"

She shook her head but still didn't look at him. It was starting to piss him off. She was the type of person who met your gaze head-on, toe to toe. Refusing to meet his gaze was like she was dismissing him, as if he didn't matter.

"I have a feeling you would like it."

She looked at him then, her eyes wide with surprise. "Well, if I did, I would probably be a Domme, so what would that have to do with you?"

He didn't say anything for several seconds, letting the silence grow around them. She didn't look away this time, but she shifted in her seat. He hid a smile, but it was hard. Dee only fidgeted when she was nervous.

"Why do you think you would be a Domme?"

She did look away then, but it didn't bother him this time. He could see her pulse beating in her throat through her fair flesh.

"I like being in charge."

Again, he said nothing, allowing the silence to stretch out.

"That's not what makes someone the Dominant."

She glanced at him through her lashes and he bit back a groan. The look was so coquettish, so not like Dee, it sent a shaft of heat to his dick.

"I would think the need for control would suggest that you need to be the dominant in the relationship."

He shook his head. "You might have worked here for two years, but there is a difference between the need to control...and to be controlled. Many subs are people who have a large amount of control in their professional and personal lives. They need to relinquish it to feel complete."

"Hmm. Well, if that's all?"

She said it hopefully, but for some reason he couldn't let it go. He wanted her to understand that while she might not practice the life and actually avoided talking about it despite working at the club, she was a submissive. A bottom.

He rose, now not even trying to hide the fact he was aroused. He settled on the top of his desk in front of her.

"Dee."

She hesitated and he fought down a growl. He didn't have the right to expect her immediate compliance. But he wanted it. The need to be the one who gave her orders, who gave her pleasure, who saw her eyes go blurry with bliss, burned in his gut.

She raised her gaze to his. Her breathing was shallow, rapid.

"What do you like in the bedroom?"

"Micah, this isn't important."

But it was. It was more important that she understood she was a submissive, that she would do better by taking orders from her Dom. From him.

He pushed that thought aside.

"I don't like talking about it, okay. Especially with my boss —who I've seen naked."

He let one eyebrow raise as a blush stained her cheeks. Damn, she was cute when she did that. It didn't happen often, but when it did, he wanted to do nothing more than pull her into his arms and cuddle her. And he wasn't exactly the cuddling type.

"Okay, not completely, but you forget you used to perform a lot as Dom when I first started working here."

"Ah. And you liked that?"

She shifted again and this time he couldn't help the curving of his lips.

"What's not to like? You're a pretty man and you know it."

He laughed at that. "Pretty isn't something I've been called before."

"Then you haven't been paying attention to the women who have been talking about you."

She fairly bit out the words. Was she jealous? He cocked his head to one side studying her.

"Enough about me. The question was about you. What do you like in the bedroom?"

"Micah—"

"Tell me." He didn't raise his voice, but he heard the authority in his tone, and so did Dee. There was a flash of anger in her eyes, but something else. Something he had seen before when he ordered her to stay in the gym. Arousal. Then the look dissolved into calculation.

"I like a good time."

It didn't ring true. Normally, he would let it go. If she wasn't interested in the life, there was nothing he could do. Forcing someone to accept a D/s relationship wasn't very smart and in his opinion, downright criminal. But right now, in this moment, he knew she was lying to him. About what, he didn't know. He had tried not to think about her having sex with other men. Thinking back, there had been one or two comments made about her and who she was dating. There hadn't been many.

"Listen, I really need to go. I have to be up early, and it's already past four."

She rose.

"Sit."

She frowned at him. "I don't take orders outside of work from you. I think we discussed that a few days ago."

"You better sit your little ass in that chair before I pull you over my lap and smack it red."

He growled the words. He couldn't help it. The silence that followed told him that he had stunned her. Well, he had shocked the hell out of himself. It was a loss of control to say things like that, especially to an employee who wasn't a sub, didn't play in the life. It went over the line of sexual harassment. Something he'd never had a problem with. Until Dee.

"I told you what to do."

She slowly sat in the chair, her blue gaze never leaving his.

"I want an answer from you."

"I said I have no problems in bed, Micah. I don't know why it's your business, but I can assure you that there isn't anything to worry about."

There was something there, something she was trying to hide from him. In the sane part of his brain he knew she had a right to her privacy. But the warrior in him wanted her compliance. He wanted to know everything about her.

"So, you've never been spanked?"

Her breath caught, just the barest of sounds, but he heard it. She was aroused. By the discussion...and by the thought of being spanked. His appetite increased. Just knowing that she was turned on by it had his blood draining southward.

"No."

"Never been tied down...controlled."

Her breathing hitched again. He couldn't see her nipples through her vest, but he'd bet a million bucks they were hard.

"So, you don't know the pleasure of having someone take

the control from you, take possession, be the lucky man to give you pleasure."

She shook. Her tongue darted out over her fuller lower lip, wetting it. God, he needed another taste. The lure of her sweet mouth tempted him. But, he needed her answers more.

"I bet you would be a pleasure to initiate. You would definitely be fun to conquer."

"I-I need to go."

But she didn't get up, didn't move. He wanted to shout with excitement but he kept it under wraps. He'd wanted her to be a submissive so badly, he hadn't known if he had been imagining it the past few months. Now he knew. Keeping his hands off her was not going to be possible.

Not when he knew she wanted him. Her pulse was hammering. She shifted again.

"I think you would flourish with the right Dom. Tell me, have you ever had an orgasm?"

"I'm almost thirty, of course I have."

"A lot of women don't. Especially if they don't know what they need in bed."

"Well, I can assure you that I have. Can I go?"

Even as she asked it, he knew he had her. An hour ago, she would have told him to go to hell. Now though, she wanted to hear, was turned on by his questions.

"With a man?"

Everything in her stilled.

"Ah, so no man has ever given you one."

She swallowed. "It isn't that uncommon. You said so yourself."

"Do they just not understand what you need?"

She looked at him again. "I still think this is highly—"

"I didn't ask you what you thought." His words were a little harsher than he expected, but he didn't regret it. It shut her up. The woman had been driving him to distraction for months and all he wanted was one damn answer.

"So, tell me. What goes wrong in bed?"

He tried to soften the question, but even he heard the simmering desire in his voice. The idea that he could be the first man to give her an orgasm, to give her the pleasure she deserved, was almost too much to take. Definitely too big to ignore.

"I don't think—"

He took her chin in between his fingers. "Again, I told you I didn't want to know what you think. Answer me."

"Fine. You want to know? I've never been to bed with a man."

For a second, he couldn't compute what she had said to him. He dropped his hand from her chin. His brain just didn't seem to be able to figure out what the words meant. A look of irritation then embarrassment moved over her face.

"Fuck. I can't believe I just said that." She crossed her arms over her chest as if trying to protect herself. "Aren't you going to say anything? No smart-ass comment from you?"

He opened his mouth, but no sound came out. The whole idea that this delicious woman, one that fairly shimmered with sensuality, was a virgin had short-circuited his brain. He couldn't believe it.

She jumped out of the chair. "That's it. I'm done."

Again, he couldn't think of anything to say as she stomped out of the office and down the stairs. He shook his head, his brain finally seeming to start functioning enough for him to watch the outside monitors. Rex, their bouncer, walked her to her car.

Micah watched as her taillights faded into the dark Hawaiian night then plopped down in his chair.

She is a virgin.

How had that happened? The woman was twenty-seven years old. It wasn't as if she was a prude, and he didn't think she was saving herself for marriage. He closed his eyes, need crawling through his body, his heart hammering against his chest, his dick at full staff.

She apparently thought telling him she was a virgin would be a turn off, and usually it was. He didn't like to play with women who didn't know the score. Virgins also didn't understand BDSM, didn't understand the life. Dee was different though. The woman understood it, and from the flash of arousal and fear, understood it more than most. She had some kind of idea that she was sub and didn't like it...and definitely didn't want to admit it to him.

He should back off, and usually he would. But the need to conquer, to take her under his command, surged through him. He opened his eyes as he promised himself one thing.

That woman would learn just what she needed, and she would learn it from him.

four

"So, what's going on with you and big bad bossman?" Keisha asked Dee as they settled down to a pizza they'd brought back to Keisha's apartment. They had a rare night off together and they sat out on Keisha's balcony that overlooked Kalakaua Avenue. Later, they planned on watching Jakob Wulf's newest Romantic Comedy, 'Tis the Damned Season. It wasn't the holidays, but Dee didn't care. She had a thing for Jakob Wulf. Rumor was his brother was a member of Rough 'n Ready but Dee had yet to see him.

"Nothing's going on," Dee said around a bite a pizza.

"Girl, you're insane if you don't know the way he watches you."

She swallowed the pizza, enjoying the spicy sauce, the gooey cheese. "We talked about that before. Whether he does or doesn't really isn't the issue. And I think he might be avoiding me for the most part."

"I heard something was going on between you two in the gym."

Dee choked on her soda. "What do you mean?"

Keisha laughed. "Something did happen. I wasn't sure until I saw your reaction."

Dee took another big gulp and tried to keep her face from heating. She failed.

"Nothing really happened."

"Oh, no you don't. I always give you my dirty details."

"I will point out that I don't want to hear the details, you push them on me."

Keisha laughed. "Well, considering the jackass I just kicked out, I can understand that."

Concern wiped away all of her embarrassment. Keisha had been through a rough patch with her ex before she'd finally kicked him out the door. "Are you sure you're doing okay? I mean...I know you were ready to get rid of him, but how are you really doing?"

Keisha drew in a deep breath. "Okay. He's called a couple of times, but it really hasn't been that bad. If he cared enough he would have been beating down my door when he found his clothes on the street." She narrowed her eyes. "But don't think I'm letting you get away with distracting me. What went on with Micah?"

Dee shook her head. "It was really nothing. We had a little argument."

"About what? And it couldn't have been that little if you blush every time you talk about it."

She threw her pizza down on the plate in disgust. "Okay, fine. We argued about nothing big, but then he grabbed me and kissed me."

Keisha's eyes went wide then she fell back in her lounge chair giggling. "Oh. My. God. The guy has it for you bad."

"I have no idea what you're talking about. Micah isn't the kind of guy who keeps his sexual interests hidden."

"You sound like a prude when you use that tone—not to mention pissed."

Keisha was right. She didn't condemn anyone who came to Rough 'n Ready. Seriously, she thought everyone had a right to do what they wanted, but every time she thought about Micah taking another su—*shit*.

"You're jealous."

"I am not jealous." Dee closed her eyes in mortification. Even to her own ears, she did sound jealous. "Damn. It wasn't that much. Not really. Just a kiss."

"I have to ask for clarification here. Was there tongue?"

Dee's eyes popped open. "What difference does that make?"

"So, yeah, I'm going to say a lot of tongue, and probably more." She reached over and knocked Dee on her head. "What's your problem, woman?"

"He's into the life and I'm not. And while I might not think much of it for myself, I understand that it is something a person needs in the bedroom. I don't think I can give that to him. And I really don't want to get involved and have it blow up in my face. I like my job."

Granted, she was thinking of leaving, knew she would soon. But she would be damned if she would spend her last few months on Oahu watching Micah take other subs. It would break her heart.

"Ah, well, I hate to tell you, girlfriend, you reek of submissive."

Dee narrowed her eyes at her friend. "How the hell would you know?"

"Jeez, I've worked there a few years, I know. I'm not into it, although I tried a couple years ago. *So* not my thing. But Dee, don't think I don't know what books you read."

Dee frowned. "Even so, I wouldn't know what to do when I got there. When he started asking me about my experience—"

"Wait. Do-everything-by-the-book Micah Ross asked you about your sex life?"

Dee nodded.

"You do know you are fighting a losing battle?"

Sighing, Dee said, "I hope not. I definitely wouldn't know what to do with a man like Micah in my bed."

Keisha studied her. "Is this because you're a virgin?"

Surprise then embarrassment shifted through her. "How did you know?"

Keisha rolled her eyes. "I've watched you date a lot of men the last couple of years. They never spend the night at your place, and I've never seen you do the walk of shame."

Dee sighed. "Well, that makes three people who know. Jesus, I thought my sex life was personal."

"In a place like Rough 'n Ready? Please. Wait, did you say three people? You told Micah?"

Again, fire lit her face. "I couldn't help myself. He asked me to come talk to him last night. He kept insisting I was submissive and I just wanted out of his office, away from him. And he kept asking over and over what I liked in bed, if I had ever had an orgasm and I blurted it out. I couldn't help it."

Again, Keisha fell back in her chair giggling.

"Oh, great, I'm glad to have given you some joy."

"I'm so sorry, but I can't help but laugh. I mean, what did Micah do?"

"Nothing. He said nothing." And that was the humiliating part of it. She had yet to meet him face to face since the incident, so she had no idea if he was avoiding her or not. She was both thankful and pissed off.

"What do you mean he said nothing?"

"I blurted it out, then he got the strangest look on his face. He opened his mouth but said nothing. I was so embarrassed I bolted out of the office. I haven't talked to him since."

"Oh, woman, you are in some serious trouble."

Dee jerked her shoulder. "I have a feeling it got rid of any interest from him. Micah never fools around with the inexperienced."

"You're different."

"Yeah, I'm special." Sarcasm dripped from her tone.

"You are."

She stood, wanting to get away from her friend and the conversation. Keisha latched onto her arm. "He has done a lot of things he doesn't do with you around. He's pursued you, somewhat, while you worked for him. He kissed you, at work. Asking you about your sex life, that is so not like Micah. If you had gone to him for advice, that would be different. You didn't. He approached you, then you blurt that out. He might be figuring things out, but I have a feeling you're about to know what it's like to have a big bad alpha come after you. And darling, seeing the way you feel about him, I don't doubt that something is going to happen."

"I can't handle it. Him."

Shame crawled through her. One of her biggest faults was pride. She hated admitting it. She was a grown woman and wasn't able to handle going to bed with a man. Especially this man. Resisting them had always been easy, or somewhat easy. Micah wasn't a man who would sell her out, and that made it worse. She knew there was a good chance she could take what he offered, and definitely enjoy it, with no harm to her life. But she knew if she did it, there was a good chance she'd never be completely whole again once she walked away.

"You can. At least think about it. If you really like those books—and I've seen you download three in less than two days and devour them, so don't think to lie to me about that—maybe you can explore this with him. One thing about Micah is you can trust him."

"That's true."

She gave Dee a quick hard hug. "Just don't let the opportunity pass you by. That man wants you, and I can guarantee that he will make it worth your while."

Monday afternoon, Dee dragged her butt into work. She wasn't in the mood. Not today, probably not ever. For the first time in her adult life, she had thought about calling in sick. It was the coward's way, she knew that. But as she parked her car in the lot for the Rough 'n Ready employees, she truly hated her need to prove she wasn't a weakling.

It would be the death of her.

She shivered and looked around. The lot was deserted, which was normal this time of day. She'd come early to exercise as usual, although she wouldn't have time to run home to clean up. With a sigh, she grabbed her bag and walked to the club. Mondays were slow days with long boring nights, and she wasn't in the mood for that. She wanted the night to go by fast, but she knew it wouldn't.

She pulled out her keys as she approached the door. Once she stepped in and shut and locked the door, she knew she wasn't alone. The lights to Micah's office filtered over the open bar area. Shit. Well, she knew she couldn't escape, but she could hide for a little bit. She needed to work off steam and well, sexual tension.

She turned and headed for the gym. One of the best benefits of this job was the gym they had. It was private, just for the employees. It allowed her to train without worrying. It only took her a few minutes to store her gear and pick the music she wanted to hear. Eminem's voice filtered over the speakers and she slipped on the boxing gloves.

She had a lot of aggression to release.

"Damn."

Micah looked up at Evan and noticed his friend's gaze was on one of the screens. He looked at the monitor and felt everything in him tighten.

"She's freaking talented."

Micah nodded. He couldn't do anything but stare as she went through the same kind of routine he'd watched her do earlier that week.

"You said she had some kind of dancing in her background?"

"Yeah. Jazz, she said."

"I tell you, she might've trained as a dancer at one time, but that definitely is one lethal woman now."

As if to prove his point, she did a pirouette and connected with the bag. The strength behind the kick would definitely hurt. "Shit, she could fight professionally."

Micah snorted. "Like I would allow that."

Evan's head whipped around, his eyes wide. "What did you just say?"

"I didn't say anything." Micah pulled up another set of numbers. This one for new memberships. "I think we're okay with membership levels now, but we might have to have a cutoff next month. We are dangerously close to having too many members. If they all showed up one night, we would break some fire codes."

When Evan said nothing, didn't even make a joke about him being a pain in the ass for worrying too much, he looked up at him.

"You didn't just snort. You said something about allowing it."

Dammit. Did he say that out loud?

"I didn't."

Evan shook his head and laughed. "Oh, shit, this is going to be too much fun. And don't worry about memberships. If we get too many, we can look into getting another club, maybe on the other side of the island. Near the North Shore."

Which meant that Evan had been thinking about it too. "You see a property you like, let me know. Moving on—"

"I want to get back the lethal little prize fighter down there." He nodded toward the screen. Micah tried not to look, because he knew what would happen. He couldn't help but stare at her, especially when she was going through a routine.

"What about her?"

"She looks trained."

He didn't look at Evan when he spoke. "Yeah. I told you."

"No. Look at the way she handles herself."

Micah did, watch her muscles move, tense, release. She balanced herself perfectly on the balls of her feet. The dancer was there, but there was something beneath the surface that gave him pause.

"She knows how to defend herself." Micah couldn't believe he hadn't seen it himself.

"Yeah. Not that I see anything wrong with a woman learning self-defense, probably smart considering her job. But most women don't learn something to that extent without an experience."

Micah glanced at him and realized that Evan was serious.

"What are you getting at?"

"I'm saying she might have been in some trouble."

Micah shook his head. "Not likely. If there had been we would know by now. She's been here for two years, and has yet to have an issue. Hell, she's never called in sick."

But something was niggling at the back of his brain and Evan must have sensed it.

"I understand you're hung up on her. You don't want to think she did anything bad."

That made him laugh. "Please, son, I have no problem with a bad woman."

Evan chuckled as Micah had hoped. "You're such an ass. I'm just saying you might want to have Carino check her out. He'd probably be happy to run a background check on her. See if she has a nasty husband after her."

Micah smiled despite his irritation. "I'm pretty sure there's no husband in her background."

"Still," Evan started then looked at the screen. "That woman was trained to defend herself for some reason. And not the weekend kind of classes where suburbanites play at self-defense. You might want to know that before you get involved with her. That's all I'm saying. Are we done with this thing? I gotta get home and finish packing. May and I are flying to the Big Island for a couple of days."

"Eloping?"

Evan rolled his eyes. "If I could, I would, but I think her father and grandfather might kill me."

They talked about a few properties Evan had been keeping an eye on, ones that might work for a smaller club on the other side of the island. But they were soon done and Evan left Micah to watch Dee finish up her routine.

She rolled her shoulders, which thrust her breasts out. She wasn't full-chested, but damn, if they weren't gorgeous. Not that he had seen them without clothing, but he could tell they were nicely rounded and high. He could imagine just how her skin would taste. She liked a hard workout and he could imagine how she would be in bed. Hot and sweet, enough to keep up with his demands. He shuddered as his cock hardened. Damn.

Since she had confessed her lack of experience, Micah could barely think of anything else. It had always been a turnoff to him. Virgins were too much work, boring, and he would rather take an experienced woman any day.

This was different. *She* was different.

He'd never had this need, this desire, for a woman before. To take her through her initial submission, take her virginity. He closed his eyes and counted back from ten. He was probably going to have issues keeping his head straight until he got her in bed. It was dangerous to continue to operate without much blood flowing to his brain.

He knew he would have to be slow with her. There was no doubt in his head about that. He couldn't just seduce her. He had to entice her. She was wary, of him, of what was between them. Being that she was inexperienced just added to the complications, not to mention he had to be careful since she worked for him. He knew she would understand it wasn't sexual harassment, but he still wanted to be cautious. Micah sighed as he watched her leave the workout area and head back to the showers.

Tonight he would start his pursuit in earnest. He just hoped he didn't pass out from being lightheaded and fall at her feet. He had a feeling she wouldn't think it very romantic.

"Do you have a second to talk?"

Dee started at the sound of Micah's low, seductive voice. They hadn't opened up and her nerves were still vibrating. The workout she'd put herself through hadn't helped one bit. As she turned, her heart jumped, her whole body heated. It was the first time she had faced him since confessing her lack of experience the other night. Even now, she could feel her face heat.

"Did you need something?"

He said nothing for a moment or two, then, "I was wondering if you were busy tomorrow night."

She blinked. "Well, no. I took the night off because I worked four in a row. Do you need me to come in?"

"No. I was wondering if you would like to go out to dinner?"

For a second, her brain couldn't seem to understand what he was saying.

"Dee?"

She licked her lips. "Uh, are you asking me out on a date?"

"Yeah."

"But you don't date."

He frowned. "I haven't lately, but I do take my lovers out."

"First, even if I agreed to go out with you, that isn't going to happen."

The smile he shot her told her that he didn't believe it. Of course, why would he? She didn't really believe it herself.

"Secondly, it isn't from my observation, but most people around the club say you don't date. You engage—and definitely not with the help."

He glanced around the room and it was then she realized how quiet it had gotten. She followed his line of vision and was amazed at the sudden explosion of activity. The staff all apparently found something to do, at the same exact moment.

He waited for her to return her attention to him. "I date. It's true, I don't always bring them by the club, and I've never pursued something like this with someone who is working for me. You won't suffer anything if you say no to me."

She snorted and crossed her arms over her breasts. "You don't have to tell me that, Micah. You're the fairest boss I've ever had. And let's be honest, you don't need to force women to go out with you."

He cocked his head to one side and she couldn't help but watch as his waist-length hair slid over his shoulder or the way the light danced over it. She could still remember the way it felt as it slipped through her fingers.

"Thank you."

She shrugged, suddenly embarrassed by his intent stare.

"What I wonder is why you make me sound like a prize."

She laughed. "I didn't say that."

"But even more, why would you refuse to go out with me?"

Because I can't trust myself. She knew she couldn't say it out loud. It was too embarrassing. This was the one man that had tempted her like no other. Right now her body ached to lean into him and brush her mouth over his, run her fingers through the smooth strands of his jet black hair.

"It's a date, in public. Hands off, unless you ask me." As if to prove his point he held them up.

"I thought you were going to leave the island for a vacation."

"Changed my mind."

After she told him she was a virgin. Now he seemed to think of her as some kind of project. Just what she needed. She sighed. She should say no, and he would let her. It didn't mean he wouldn't ask again, but she knew that he would let it alone for a few days. Then she could gather some of her armor against the man.

But then if she went out with him, proved to him—and herself—that she could resist him, he might lose interest.

"Okay, you got it."

He smiled, the sight of it holding her completely transfixed. The man was gorgeous, and she had seen him offer many kinds of seductive smiles. This one didn't have the cynical edge all the others did. This one, dammit, reached his eyes and tugged at her heart.

"I'll pick you up about eight, okay? I thought maybe we could hit Dupree's."

She nodded, especially since it was one of her favorite spots. "Sure."

He just kept standing there, staring at her. She could feel her face flush again. She had done more blushing in the last week than she had in the last ten years.

"I gotta get back to work."

He stepped forward as if to kiss her. Panic had her stepping back and shaking her head. He looked around at the employees and sighed.

"Sorry. I forgot myself. Until tomorrow night."

He turned and walked away, and she couldn't help watch him as his hair swayed over his back. God, the man was built. Her gaze slipped to his ass and she almost moaned. She would give anything to see that ass bared, feel it flex beneath her hands.

"So, you got a date?"

She turned and gave Keisha a nasty look. "It's just a way to prove to him that he really isn't interested in me."

"Uh-huh. Sure. Of course, you are the first employee he has ever dated."

She frowned and moved down the bar to make sure everything was in order. They had about fifteen minutes before they would be hit by customers.

"I'm sure there's been someone. Just because we've never seen it doesn't mean anything."

"Well, what if I told you that Sylvia has never seen him ask one of his employees out?"

That gave Dee pause. Sylvia had worked for Micah and Evan since the beginning, starting out behind the bar.

"In fact, there was one woman, Tina I think. She pursued him hard. Definitely his usual type and someone who loved to play. But he refused to do anything with her."

Crap. "Well, either way, I'm making sure we don't get too involved. And seriously—" she leaned forward, "—it is a free meal."

Keisha laughed. "Girlfriend, you won't know what hit you."

As Keisha walked away, Dee started to wonder if her friend was right.

Former FBI agent Conner Dillon frowned as his sister, Maura, walked through the door. She had her long inky black curls up in ponytail, her green eyes bright behind her glasses. Something was up from the excitement he could read on her face.

"Sure, come in. Just trying to run a security agency here."

She frowned at him and dipped her wire-rimmed glasses down her nose to peer over them. "One of these days, I'm going to shoot you with your gun. Because of my superior intelligence, I'll be able to work out a way to make it look like it was Zeke. Then I'll be super rich because of all your hard work, Zeke will be in jail, and I will cry false tears at your funeral."

He laughed. "My partner wouldn't let you frame him."

"He's not that bright."

"What do you have?" he asked with a chuckle.

"I have something you've been looking for. Of course, it's because of my face recognition software, so you do owe me a trip to Alaska."

He shook his head. "Why anyone would want to go to Alaska is beyond me, especially when you live in Florida."

"It's hot here, there are bugs and well, you and Zeke. But I will settle for a weekend in New Orleans, during the winter."

"I knew my ears were burning for a reason," Zeke said as he

came through the opened door. The tall half-Jamaican/half-Irish man smiled as he said it, but Conner knew better. He was raring for a fight.

Conner saw the look in his sister's eyes and knew if he didn't cut this off at the knees, it would end up in another shouting match between his sister and his business partner.

"Listen, I love both of you, but I have a business to run."

With one fulminating look at his business partner, Maura turned to him. "I found her."

He didn't have to ask who. He knew from the way she said it.

Marjorie Rizzoli.

"Where?"

She slapped a piece of paper down in front of him. It was an ad for a BDSM club. "Hawaii."

He looked over the ad, searching for the face that had haunted him for ten years. He had let her down, left her open for an attack, and that is just what had happened. Worse, he had lost his best friend and partner because of it.

"She's a whore?" Zeke asked.

His sister sighed. "No, you jackass. It's a BDSM club. They don't pay people for sex there. People pay to be members to hook up. It's a safe environment for people to explore their desires."

"Well, I do believe our little Maura knows a little more about BDSM clubs than she should," Zeke said, irritation and something else Dillon didn't want to even think about humming in his tone.

"Would you two shut the fuck up?" He looked through the pictures. It was a full-page ad, four different pictures, all tasteful. But he didn't see her there.

"Where?"

His sister sighed, as she often did with him, and moved to behind his desk. "Right here, behind the bar. Looks like she's one of the bartenders from the way she is dressed."

He squinted and then grabbed his magnifier. Zeke stepped up on his other side and leaned over his shoulder. "How did you see her in that?"

"I used that new program I came up with. Remember, I came in and said that I used it?" She said it as if he were an idiot. "I can set it up to scan sites looking for pictures to fit."

"I knew there was a reason we kept you around here," Zeke said, but Conner barely heard him. He was zeroed in on the petite blonde behind the bar. Her hair was no longer curly or golden brown. Blonde straight locks dripped over her shoulders, giving her a more chic look. She was always a clever girl, smarter than her father or brother gave her credit for.

"Damn, it is her. Do you know her name?"

Maura shook her head. "I thought about calling, but my worry is that if we do, and it gets back to her..."

Conner nodded. "She'll run. And if she hears her father's trial is heating up, she'll definitely go underground."

"I thought I could go."

He glanced at his sister, surprised. "What?"

"I mean, she doesn't know me, right? I checked out the club, and they allow you to pay a one-night fee to explore. I could do that, find out what name she's using. She'll be easier to track that way."

Conner sat back in his chair as Zeke shook his head. "You can't let her do it."

"Why not?"

"Well, she's not trained."

She huffed out an irritated sigh. "First, I am trained. You guys use me all the time when you need someone to go in and check things out."

"That's here. Not at some BDSM club."

"Zeke's right. I want to make sure this is done right." He looked from one to the other. "You guys will go together."

"What?"

They both yelled it together.

"Zeke, you just finished up with the Markinson case. So why don't you just go along, make sure Maura stays out of trouble." He turned toward his sister. "You're the best observer I know. You can watch with Zeke there to make sure nothing goes wrong. Make the arrangements."

Neither of them said anything for a moment, but he knew they understood they had no choice. He couldn't go. Marjorie would freak out and run. This way they would get out of his hair and find out everything he needed. And they both knew when he had made a final decision.

"I'm flying first class," Maura tossed over her shoulder as she stomped out of the room. "And I am not sharing a room with him."

She slammed the door and Zeke sighed. "You're lucky you're my best friend. Or I might find a way to lose your sister over the Pacific."

He glanced up at his friend. "I trust you to protect her. I know Maura can be a pain, but you know she's good. You wouldn't have closed the Markinson's case without her. Just try to keep the beatings to a minimum."

Zeke sighed. "I'll try, but it won't be easy."

Once Zeke left him alone, Conner stood and walked to his windows. The buzz of the Miami rush hour was just getting started as he looked down at the stop-and-go traffic. He couldn't believe they'd found her.

Ten years. Because of his obsession, of his stupidity, he had lost her and his career. He knew she wasn't dead, had actually gotten a few leads on her, but the trail had died and the FBI had been happy to sweep the whole fuckup under the rug, along with his career. He probably could have salvaged it, if it had not been for his insistence that they look more closely from within the bureau. He knew it had been an inside job.

With a sigh, he turned back to his desk. No use thinking about what he should have done. He would fix his mistakes, give Marjorie back her life, and then get back to his.

He just hoped they were the only ones who noticed her in that ad. If not, there was a good chance her brother or father would kill her.

five

You never know what each day will bring. It was the only thing that came to mind when she stepped over the threshold of Dupree's on Micah's arm. She had learned it early enough in life that was for sure. It was one reason she never planned, never even thought about the future, other than the next name she needed to use. She noticed a few people look in their direction, but she knew it wasn't her they were looking at. It was the man now causing her whole body to simmer.

She didn't blame them. Micah was a man who commanded attention. Most women at least turned their heads to watch him walk by. Being so tall, with the waterfall of black hair down his back and his lean, sculpted body, it was easy to understand the female infatuation with him.

Someone other than May was working tonight, and she led them to the back table, one of the prized places to eat in Dupree's. Of course, since Micah was good friends with Chris, the owner, she knew it had all been arranged. Not that she was complaining. It had been so long since she'd been on a real date, she was happy just for the experience. He waited for her to slide into the round booth, then he followed, scooting close enough for her to feel his heat, but without touching her. She glanced at him and he gave her a knowing smile.

After the hostess took their drink orders, they were left alone.

"So, what's your favorite here?" he asked.

She stared at him for a moment longer. "I like the Kahlua Pig Pizza."

He smiled but didn't look up. As the silence stretched, she looked around the restaurant. It wasn't that busy tonight, but they always had customers at Dupree's. It was gaining a reputation as one of the best places to eat in Honolulu, for price and quality of food. As she returned her attention to the man in front of her, she frowned. He still had said nothing, and she was starting to feel uncomfortable.

"Is there something wrong?"

He glanced at her and then back down at the menu. "No. Just deciding what to eat."

More silence. It was definitely making her self-conscious. "It's just that you're acting like you don't care if I'm here with you."

He looked at her now, his gaze capturing hers and his nostrils flaring. This was not the nice guy who had picked her up.

"If I spend too much time looking at you in that outfit, I'm going to throw you on the nearest table and fuck you."

Every word was bit out as if he was barely controlling himself. The waiter arrived with their drink order as she tried to catch her breath. When he asked what they wanted, they both ordered the pizza. When they were finally alone, she glanced down at her clothes, then back up at Micah who was spending a lot of time on his iced tea.

"What do you mean dressed like that?"

He gave her a glance out of the side of his eyes. "You really don't know?"

She shook her head. She knew she looked good. In her life before, she'd had the ability to shop at the finest stores and had been taught at her mother's knee just what to wear and when. But she didn't think she looked particularly sexy.

He sighed and then faced her, sliding his arm behind her. "I'm used to you in your work outfit. This is different. Your uniform pants aren't as snug. And while most women would look boring in a pair of jeans and a black T-shirt, you make it... sexy."

She opened her mouth, but he shook his head.

"I should have never said anything and I wouldn't have if I had thought you knew what the hell you did to me."

She felt a bubble of laughter threaten to spill out. She cleared her throat. His eyes narrowed.

"Oh, you definitely deserve a spanking for that insubordination."

His words flashed out, and they should have irritated her. Instead, the slow steady beat of arousal thrummed through her blood. She licked her lips.

"Ah, I have a feeling you would like spanking." His voice was low, intimate, seductive.

Her nipples tightened as his tone deepened. His anticipation of something so naughty, so forbidden, had arousal flaring in her tummy. The idea that both of them were aroused turned her on even more.

"But it will have to wait. You aren't ready, and well, Chris would be pissed if I gave a public display in his restaurant."

He leaned back against the booth and, odd as it felt, she laughed. He smiled in reaction.

"Yeah, I have a feeling Chris might not like that."

"And I'm assuming since you didn't even look at the menu, that you come here often."

"Yeah. I like the variety of food. Plus, it is one of my favorite places for the pig pizza. You just can't find anything like that back where I'm from."

"Oh? I guess that's the mainland. I've been here so many years I forget that they don't have those things there. Until I have to go back for a visit."

"You have family back on the mainland?"

He shook his head. "No family. You?"

She sighed. "Nope. Well, I do, but we aren't speaking. Haven't for years."

He nodded and didn't push. She could feel he wanted to, and that should scare her. Anytime a guy tried to find out her background beyond what she wanted him to know, she broke it off. Men could easily be bought off.

With Micah, she wanted him to want to know more. She was pretty sure he did, but there was a part of her that thought he still thought of this as some kind of game. And just what the hell was she thinking? Wanting a man was simple. That she had dealt with. This was different. Especially when she yearned to tell him everything.

The rest of dinner went without incident, both of them being surprised by how much they had in common. Both had been on their own a very long time and both had a thing for Striker Force One, a computer game. As they strolled down the sidewalk at Waikiki, she breathed in the warm fresh night, and Micah.

"I would have never guessed that you liked to play games like that."

She shrugged and was brought aware of the fact they were holding hands. It was odd to be walking along the beach, like a normal person on a regular date. Especially knowing the things he wanted to do to her. The things she wanted him to do to her.

"What is going on in that quick mind of yours?"

She looked up, surprised at his description.

"What?" he asked.

"It's just odd. My family never thought I was that bright. Well, except my brother." Even thinking of Mark made her sad. The reports of his death came about two years after she'd started running.

"What happened to him?"

"How do you know something happened to him?"

He stopped and looked down at her. "You're estranged from your family, but I have a feeling this brother and you were closer? There was something in your voice."

She nodded, thinking of Mark. "We were twins. He died a couple of years after I left home."

"I'm sorry."

She glanced up at him and noticed for the first time ever someone was offering her real sympathy.

"Thank you."

"And your father has to be an idiot not to see how smart you are."

She smiled and started walking again, tugging him along. "Yeah, well, I'm dyslexic, but I didn't know it at the time. It took some work to finally understand why I didn't see words right."

"Still say he was stupid. You're pretty clever."

She smiled at him. "And now why would you say that?"

"One, you know how to manage well, and you know just when someone has had too much to drink."

"That's not smarts. That's just years of working in bars, most of them not near as nice as Rough 'n Ready."

"Two, you add things in your head."

Again, he'd surprised her. "How do you know that?"

"I watch my employees. I noticed right away that you could add up a large and complicated order without using the register."

She smiled. "Anything else?"

"Well, you have somehow convinced me to walk in public along the beach so that I can't touch you."

She shivered at the dark intent in his tone. It slid over her skin, sank into her blood.

"You're holding my hand." She lifted their joined hands. "Besides, I thought you wanted to do this."

He stopped and pulled her closer. There was no mistaking the erection pressed against her stomach. The simmering lust she had been fighting all night exploded, sending a rush of heat dancing through her blood.

"I think I established pretty early on what I wanted. But I can be patient."

She shook her head even as her body yearned for him. "Micah, I am not going to do this with you."

"Not tonight, but maybe we can have a little fun."

The way his voice moved over the word fun had her body

humming with need. "Why don't we head back to your place? If you don't want me touching you, you can kick me out."

She sighed. She wanted to tell him to go to hell and take his cocky attitude with him. But instead, she nodded and hoped to God she had the control to kick him out of her house when things went too far.

Micah smiled as he followed Dee into her house. The night had been part heaven and part hell for him. Being near her had his entire body yearning to strip her naked, take her, claim her. He could just imagine how it would feel to slip into that tight snug passage, feel her pussy pull on his cock.

He counted backwards from ten. He had been doing that a lot tonight. He wasn't sure he would even get to touch her, let alone be allowed the privilege of sinking between her thighs. From what he knew of her, could gauge from her reactions, he would not be in her bed tonight. He pushed aside the disappointment. It would happen soon.

It was a small house. She'd been living in Waikiki in an apartment, but he remembered she'd moved here a couple months ago. It wasn't huge, more like a cottage. He noted there were no family pictures, but there were lots of pictures of the ocean, taken by herself and professional. A picture of a Wyland whale filled the wall behind her couch. There were precious few things that would tell him much about her.

"I like your place."

She looked at him as she dropped her keys on the small dining table. "Yeah?"

He didn't miss the skepticism in her voice and he smiled.

"Yeah. It suits you. Clean lines, uncluttered, straight-up sexy without being tacky."

She arched an eyebrow at him. "Really. That's a mouthful of words for such a little space."

God, he loved that sassy mouth of hers. He couldn't wait until she used it on him. "As I said, it fits you."

She looked away then, but not before he saw the flash of hunger in her eyes. To keep from touching her, he shoved his hands into the pockets of his pants. He got the idea that while she had been dated, there hadn't been a man who tried to romance her. At least no one recently. Keisha had made it very clear that Dee rarely dated, and she had yet to get serious. Of course, he knew that, especially after what she'd blurted out the other night.

"Would you like something to drink? I don't keep alcohol, but I do have some sodas and homemade lemonade."

He chuckled and watched as she shivered at the sound. God, keeping his hands off, or at least keeping his needs at bay, would be hard. He wanted her so damn much, and if there was a woman in need of a good, long hard fucking it was Dee Sumner. But he knew she was skittish.

"A bartender who doesn't keep alcohol at home. I'll take a glass of water."

She looked back over her shoulder and made a face. "By the time I was twenty-one, I was working in bars. And some of them make dives look good. There were a few with chicken wire to protect the band. Drinking alcohol had lost its thrill by then."

She handed him his glass of water and then poured one for herself.

"I've got a nice lanai if you'd like to go sit outside."

What he'd liked to do was toss her over his shoulder and take her to her bedroom. But that wouldn't be possible, and the back porch was probably the safest place at the moment. He nodded and followed her out. As he stepped out, the simplicity of it matched the interior. She had a small table, enough for two people, cheery red cushions on the black wire chairs. He waited for her to shut the door and settle in a chair before taking his.

She took a deep breath. "God, I love nighttime here. The air is so sweet."

He licked his lips and then caught himself. He was starting to act like the wolf in *Little Red Riding Hood*. "You said you worked in bars by the time you were twenty-one. I take it you lied about your age."

She laughed and glanced at him. "Most of those places paid under the table."

He studied her for a second. "Yeah? How old were you when you started working at them?"

She rolled her shoulders and he hid his smile behind his glass. That was definitely one of her tells. When a customer was irritating her, Dee tended to do that with her shoulders. It was nice to know that he was getting to her.

"Eighteen."

She glanced at him again when he said nothing, just sipped his water.

"What, you have nothing to say against that?"

He shrugged. "What am I going to say about that?"

She relaxed against the chair. "People always seem to have an opinion about it, like I should have done something else."

"I can't talk. I was working the tables with a fake ID in Vegas when I was sixteen."

Her eyes widened at that. "Sixteen? I could have never gotten away with that. Especially in Vegas."

"Vegas isn't any different than anywhere else. Just have to know the right people."

She paused and then looked at him. "Yeah, I guess, but with my stature, most people questioned my age up until a couple years ago."

"That's not something that I had to worry about. Not at my height."

"You were this tall at sixteen?"

He nodded. "I was over six feet by fourteen."

Her eyes widened. "Wow."

"So, you worked dives. How did you end up here?"

It was her turn to shrug. "I just needed a change of place."

The vague answer irritated him. Granted, he had talked to the man she had worked for in Seattle and he had told Micah how much he'd hated to let her go. So apparently there hadn't been a problem with the work situation. He wanted to press, more than was good for him. The woman intrigued him on so many levels, but he had learned too many questions would have her closing up.

He let the silence stretch as they enjoyed the Hawaiian night. It was hard, because he wanted her. Her spicy scent mingled with the Hawaiian air. Every fiber of his being was telling him to take her, to pull her up out of that chair and lay her across the table, strip her naked—

"Micah?"

"What?" He bit out the word, his fantasy dissolving as he

looked at the woman who had been the featured star of every one of his fevered dreams for the past six months.

"Did you say something?"

He pulled in a deep breath and shoved his hand through his hair. "No."

She lapsed into silence. Great way to seduce her, Ross. It didn't escape his notice that he'd always been the one in control of the seduction, the way he liked it, and he was damned good at it. With Dee, he felt like a bumbling seventeen-year-old.

By the time she led him back into the house he could feel the evening slipping away…along with his chances. He knew he had to go slowly with her, had to awaken everything he saw beneath the surface. It had taken him almost two years and there was no way he wasn't at least easing her to step one tonight.

She set their glasses in the sink and before she could turn around, he approached her. He stopped directly behind her and placed his hands on each side of her on the counter. Leaning forward, he closed his eyes and drew in her scent.

"Micah, I said this wasn't going to happen."

Even as she tried to be strong, he heard the tremor in her voice. The sound of it tripped over his heart, dug deep into his soul. He knew he affected her, knew that she wanted him. But with her resistance, it never hurt to get a little reminder to boost his ego.

"I heard ya. I just thought we might do a little—" he drew in a deep breath and started to nibble on her ear, "—necking."

"Hmm." She shivered and moved her head to the side to give him better access.

Just as he expected, her skin was as sweet as the woman. He pressed closer, settling his jean-encased cock against her ass.

When she said nothing else, he slipped a hand up her torso to her breast. Through the layers of fabric, he could feel her hardened nipple. One little brush against it had her moaning his name. It was the sweetest sound he had ever heard. It took every bit of his control to drop his hand and step away.

She fell forward as he took another step. It took a few moments for her to gather herself and turn around. Her breathing was rapid, her eyes dilated.

"Just what was that about?"

"I..." He drew in another deep breath, calling on the patience he'd promised himself he would have for her. His inner warrior was screaming to be let loose. "I got a little carried away."

She studied him for a moment and then looked away. He slipped his finger under her chin and turned her to face him again.

"Look at me."

Slowly, she raised her gaze to his. Arousal was there, but there was a hint of fear. It was understandable. He also saw a flash of embarrassment.

"You shouldn't be ashamed of your feelings."

She sighed and looked away. "I'm not ashamed."

He knew then he couldn't push her any more tonight. He wanted to. His body was begging him to ignore her feelings, coax her into the bedroom and take her. She would do it. He knew he could convince her, but she would regret it afterwards...and maybe hate him. That was something he could not accept. Ever.

He cupped her face with his hand, rubbed his thumb over her bottom lip before leaning closer to kiss her again. The sassy, sweet taste of her lured him like no other woman. He pulled back a moment before he lost control.

"I think that's my cue to leave."

"Thank you for dinner."

He smiled. "How about lunch tomorrow?"

She hesitated. "Sure. Where do you want to meet?"

"I'll give you a call in the morning." He allowed the screen door to close before turning around. "I told you it wouldn't be that bad."

"I didn't say it would be bad. I was afraid that if you asked for more, I wouldn't be able to say no."

With that, she closed the door on his face. He was frustrated as hell and his body was ready to revolt against him. But he couldn't help whistling on his way back to his car.

six

Dee leaned her head back and closed her eyes. The midday Hawaiian sun warmed her face as the sound of fellow patrons of the ocean-side café faded into the distance. It didn't take her long to feel the weight of Micah's gaze. Ignoring it wasn't easy, but she did for a moment or two. She pulled her head back up and opened her eyes.

"What?"

"It just struck me that we've never really spent time together during the day."

She cocked her head to the side and said nothing as she studied him. She couldn't. Because as soon as he'd said it she'd realized he was right. They had spent a lot of time together or at least in the vicinity of each other, in the last couple of years. They had never spent time outside together in the sun.

While he was a man who was dangerous in the moonlight, he was vivid and beautiful during the day. He would probably scoff at the idea, but he was. The golden undertone to his skin, along with the hint of copper from his Native America heritage, added a depth to his image that she hadn't seen before. She had never observed him dressed so casually, if she didn't count the times she'd seen him dressed in...well, almost nothing at the club. The sunlight allowed her to see the blue-black tone to his hair. She looked out over Waikiki Beach and sighed.

"You're right. But both of us are usually sleeping, until probably noon, right?"

He laughed. "That's true. Still, there's something to be said for spending the day at the beach. Especially in Hawaii. I just find it odd that you love the sun so much but you work at night."

She shrugged. "Not really. This way I can spend time enjoying it during the day. If I had some kind of daytime job, I'd only have my two days off. And after several years in the Seattle area, I needed the sun."

"That was your last town, right?"

She nodded. He knew that much because she'd had to apply for the job. "I had to get out of there. Nine months and I couldn't shake the feeling I was sick all the time. I ached some days."

"Ah, so you have that disease where you can't take the gloomy days."

"Yeah. Doc suggested California, but I figured if I was going to be at a beach, I couldn't go wrong here."

He laughed. "That's true."

"How did you end up here?"

He took a sip of water. "I'd come over to find a fugitive, then I talked Evan into coming over for a vacation. We knew then that we wanted to live here. Neither of us had any family, so it was easy. I know Chris has a hard time with his family back on the mainland."

"Yeah, not having the ties makes things easy."

"But then, I have ties here now."

She looked at him as he studied the beach.

"Ties?"

He glanced at her. "Chris and Evan, their soon-to-be wives. The club. It has become sort of a family atmosphere."

"Yeah, but we never do anything like this during the day. Maybe we should."

"Like a picnic for Rough 'n Ready?" he asked with a chuckle. "It might work. Hell, I know that we could close down on Monday and not really hurt. I'll talk to Evan about it."

She nodded and looked over as a kid went running by, squealing as his older sister ran after him.

"Are you going to keep me at arm's length now?"

She smiled. "I have no idea what you're talking about."

"I didn't count you for a coward."

A sigh of irritation escaped before she could stop it. "I'm sorry, but I told you that there would be nothing else."

"You can say it all you want. It doesn't mean that you don't want it. Don't need it like every sub."

She looked away from him again, out to the crystal blue of the ocean, wondering just how she could explain it to him. How did she get him to understand things about her without revealing too much?

"Dee."

She sighed again.

"Tell me."

It wasn't a question or a plea, it was an order.

"I grew up with a very rich and very domineering father. Ruthless. He picked my friends, my boyfriends, he controlled just about everything from the clothes I wore to well, just everything. He isn't a man who takes the word no that kindly. And I didn't like that feeling. I didn't want to be told what to do, even at seventeen."

"Especially at seventeen."

She smiled at him, then felt it fade. "My father would stop at nothing to control what went on in my life. People are easily influenced."

He studied her for a second, two. "You know it'd be different with us. You do have some control over what happens...a little."

She shook her head. "Giving you that power is something I'm not sure I can do. Jeez, I haven't even done it the normal way, let alone..." She gestured with her hands, mindful of the people around them.

"Power is given, not taken, so it would be up to you. I can promise that you would benefit greatly from it."

"How?"

"What?"

"How do you know that? I don't even know what I like. How could you?"

His lips tipped up arrogantly. "I think I have a little more experience at it than you do. Plus, we would take it slowly. Promise. But it isn't just about the power exchange. It is about trust. You have to trust your partner to allow them that control."

"And there you go. I don't trust men."

That was easy enough. There would never be a man she could trust enough, and that was the sad truth.

"Because of your father."

She shook her head. "Partly. He was a man who lived two lives. 'Do as I say, not at I do' was his motto."

"But there was someone else."

"Micah, I grew up with everything I wanted, every little toy, pretty shiny thing, it was mine. My father used those things to control me. He used them to control other people."

"Men."

"Men can be bought. Quite easily."

He nodded. "People can be shits. I've known enough of them in my life. But you need to wonder if you will allow them to rule your life, or if you will take life on despite them."

She knew he was talking of his own experiences. Micah wasn't a man who would allow anything to push him the way he didn't want to go. He made his own destiny, did his own thing.

"I'm not sure I'm brave enough for that."

He smiled. "You are."

Dee gave him a skeptical look. It was then it struck him that it had been a long time since he'd had this type of conversation with a woman. He'd had plenty of lovers, even female friends, but he hadn't sat and had a conversation outside of work. He wasn't sure what that said about him, but it did say something about his relationships. Building the club up had taken all his time. The relationships he'd had were shallow. He knew that. He hadn't had the time to pursue something more with anyone he had been dating. Or maybe, he hadn't met a woman to entice him enough to look further. Until Dee.

"You know about being powerless," she said, her words measured as if she chose each one carefully.

He nodded. "I guess you know I came from little. Truth is my mother abandoned me. Father was long gone."

He didn't see pity in her eyes. Women usually got upset, wanted to soothe. Instead, he saw...admiration.

"Then I was in juvie. When I got out I got a little money and started working. When Evan and I were a little younger, our mid-twenties, we had a club in Vegas. Did some good business there until we were forced out."

"Forced?"

"Yeah, ever heard of Peter Rizzoli?"

She cleared her throat. "Uh, yeah."

"Well, Mr. Rizzoli didn't like the idea that we were taking business away from his strip club down the street. I don't think we ever were. Our clientele wasn't looking for a little bump and grind. But Rizzoli and that idiot son of his decided that we were in their way. They did everything they could, nothing stuck. Until our club burned to the ground."

The stricken look on her face worried him.

She swallowed. "Did anyone get hurt?"

He shook his head. "It happened on a Tuesday night, the one night of the week we were closed. We had insurance, but not enough to help us rebuild. So we decided to find somewhere else. It would've been useless to try and build again."

She nodded. "Then you found Hawaii."

"Yeah. You know, that bastard had the nerve to call me to tell me how sorry he was that we'd had a fire. Smug son of a bitch. And I could've gone off the deep end. I could've gone after him. But I didn't. I knew I would lose, and I wanted more out of life than to end up dead at twenty-five."

"Why don't we head to the club?" she asked.

Her abrupt change of subject caught him off-guard, and he

studied her for a minute. He didn't know what was going on in that beautiful head of hers, but something was bothering her. He hesitated, not wanting to leave the solitude they'd created at the ocean-side café. But he realized it was getting late and he had to input data from the night before.

"Sure."

They had walked from the club earlier since she was on the roster to work that night. They paid their bill and then started walking down Paoa Avenue. She was trying to pull away from him. He could feel it, but he wouldn't allow it. After her explanation, he understood her issues with trust. He would just have to work to overcome those worries, those fears.

He slipped his arm over her shoulder and pulled her against him. It wasn't easy to walk down the street that way, but he refused to let her go. For the first time in his life, he wanted everyone to know she was his. Maybe it was the fact they hadn't had sex that made him feel he needed to mark his territory. She wasn't truly his. And the tenuous thread he felt he'd tied the other night seemed ready to break.

"Was there something I said?"

She shook her head but said nothing more.

He didn't like it. She hadn't looked him in the eye since he'd told his story. Dee didn't strike him as insensitive. But why would she behave this way? They walked past the Hale Koa and he spied an alleyway. With ease, he stepped off the main street and pulled her along with him.

"What are you doing?"

He said nothing but turned her toward him and backed her up against the building. Without any words, he slammed his mouth down on hers. For a moment or two, she resisted. He pulled back slightly. "Don't. Don't keep yourself from me."

His voice shook when he said it, his emotions too raw to control. She looked up at him, those blue mermaid eyes watching him. Then she shuddered, closed her eyes and leaned into him. He wanted to shout with triumph, but instead, he slanted his mouth over hers and swiftly slipped inside past her lips and teeth. Her tongue danced alongside his as she slid her hands up his chest and then over his shoulders. He leaned in closer, skimming his hands down her back to her ass. He pulled her tight against his groin. The moment he felt the contact, he groaned and deepened the kiss. Micah knew he would never get enough of this woman. She was innocent and sweet with a dash of temptress. It was enough to make a man go insane. The blood in his veins roared, heated. Arousal, need and torment twined together and clutched at his gut. He needed her, now. It was at that moment he was thinking of stripping off her pants and taking her. In an alley, in the middle of the day, in Waikiki.

He pulled back, his body protesting. They were both breathing heavily.

He raised his hand to scrub it over his face and realized it was shaking.

"Dee, I'm sorry."

She wasn't looking at him, her head bent down.

"Dee?"

She did look up at him then. The desire still holding him by the short hairs simmered in her eyes. Her lips were swollen, her face as red as a passion flower.

"I'm fine."

"Dee."

She held up a hand. "No. I'm fine. I just..." She shook her head.

"What?"

"You make me want to forget all the rules."

The words were a punch to the gut. Damn, if the woman was going to drive him crazy. Micah considered himself a man who could manage any kind of seduction. But handling a straight-forward virgin like Dee was a little too much to ask of him. Especially when he had been wanting her for months. She didn't even try to play games. Hearing what he did to her didn't help cool his libido. If anything, it made him want her to call in sick for the evening so he could take her back to his place.

He stepped forward and she shook her head. "No. I need a clear head to work tonight."

He wanted to push. His body was pleading for him to push her, take her, and she would go along. But this wasn't the time. Instead, he offered her his hand.

She looked at it, then up at him. With a small smile, she slipped her hand into his and walked with him to work.

Dee's head didn't clear that night. Or the next. Her need for Micah seemed to grow each day, becoming an itch under her skin. Of course, the only way to relieve it would be to let him take her to bed. She had lain awake for hours the night before, trying to remember just why she shouldn't.

She wiped down the bar as she went over the conversation she'd had with Micah the day before. Her father. Her father had ruined his business. It didn't seem like a big thing to him. It was to her. What if her father found out about her relationship with Micah? Knowing her sadistic father, he would use it to hurt her.

Of all the men in the world, she found herself intrigued with one her father had tried to destroy. What were the odds in that? She inwardly sighed. High, considering her father had ruined a lot of lives not only back home in New York but also in Vegas and who knew where else.

"Where are you, girlfriend?"

She looked up as Keisha walked toward her. She was still wearing her windbreaker and carrying her purse.

"Off in dreamland. Are you early?"

Keisha shook her head. "We open in forty-five minutes. Let's get back to those day dreams."

"What?"

"Are they about a certain bossman?"

Dee rolled her eyes. "No. And why are you so preoccupied with what I do with him?"

"I got money on it, honey."

"What about Kai. Isn't he keeping you busy enough?"

Keisha smiled. "Kai knows how to keep a girl happy. And damn, the boy has definitely learned a lot since our prom night."

"I can imagine," she said with a chuckle.

"But I'm not going to let it go." Then something caught Keisha's attention over Dee's shoulder. "Oh, I guess I will. Bye."

Dee didn't have to turn around to see what had made Keisha flee. Even without looking, she knew who was there. Her body seemed to be able to pick up on the vibes coming from him.

His hand slipped over her waist, then around her tummy. He bent his head and nibbled on her ear.

"Good evening, Dee."

The arousal she heard simmering in his voice had her heart tripping. "I thought you didn't like public displays at work."

He drew in a deep breath and she had an idea that he was sniffing at her. She should be irritated with him, but there was something so primal about it that spoke to her soul. She didn't have the heart to tell him to go away when she wanted him to touch her so badly.

"We aren't open yet. And I did leave you alone to stock the bar."

She had known he was there. His Vette had been parked out front in his space. And she had been a little disappointed that he hadn't shown up when she'd come in. Although she wouldn't admit it to him.

"That's true."

He shifted closer, his body melding to her, his front against her back. He didn't do much more than that, except lick her lobe. She closed her eyes as heat that had been simmering started to boil.

"I had to have a taste. You look so cute in your uniform."

She snorted. "Yeah, not as good as Sheila."

Sheila was one of the weekend workers, who had saved all her tips up to add a cup to her bra size.

He chuckled, his breath feathering over her neck. "Fishing for compliments?"

She shook her head.

"Sheila definitely has special attributes...but I find myself drawn to tight, little athletic bodies."

With each word, his voice deepened and her lust soared. He was barely touching her, barely trying to seduce her, but she could feel herself losing control. Every hormone in her body was begging her to turn around, grab him and kiss him until she couldn't think straight. A state she wasn't far from anyway.

He sighed and stepped away before she was ready for him to do it. She liked the feel of his body heat against hers, the clean fresh male scent of him.

"I need to let you get back to work."

She looked back over her shoulder at him. His dark eyes were watching her, lust easy to see simmering there. "Micah."

He raised his hand. "No. You and I both know it's going to happen." He stepped closer. "It's just difficult to wait."

A yearning she didn't know she had, something that almost overwhelmed her, rushed through her, pushed her up on her toes and had her brushing her mouth against his. Just that taste wasn't enough, would never be enough.

She sank back to her feet and looked up at him. A flush darkened his cheeks.

"Thank you for being so patient."

He nodded once, then turned and strode away. She'd known from the beginning he was a temptation that would be hard to resist. He was just what she loved to read about. A hard-headed Dom, an alpha with a nice gooey center. While he might expect and demand everything from her, he had enough respect to take his time.

God, she was in very big trouble.

Micah woke up, his body covered with sweat, his heart smacking against his ribs. His cock hard and insistent against his belly. It was the fourth time this week he'd woken up from a dream so vivid he almost came. Seriously, he would have taken a wet dream over waking up frustrated. But apparently his body wasn't going to give him the easy way out.

He sighed. Waiting on Dee was right, but it didn't make it any easier on him knowing that. Although, he figured if she wasn't ready soon, he might just go insane. He was patient. He was actually legendary for it. But with each passing day, he was being pushed closer to the edge.

He knew that she was pretty damned close to being ready. He hadn't done much more with her other than a little kissing and petting, once after another dinner, then another time when she'd shown up in that little outfit she liked to wear to work out in. It had been almost liberating to sneak her up to his office and neck.

It was almost as if they were courting. It was an old-fashioned term, but it fit, especially without sex. It was a totally new experience for him. He'd been living on the streets of Atlanta at such an early age that he didn't do the high school dating thing. He didn't have fond memories of backseat seductions or necking under the bleachers. His first woman had been a fellow juvie inhabitant, who did just about anything for five bucks. Crack addicts usually did. After, the women he'd been involved with had wanted him because he was a bit on the dangerous side, but they knew they could trust him on some other level. Then as he became known as a Dom, one who owned a club, ran a website and spoke to groups, women came to him to experience submission. And yes, there had been some sharing on the personal level, but nothing had felt this intimate before. Ever.

Was it because she was virgin? He didn't think so. He'd felt connected to her from the beginning, before he had even touched her. He must have sensed it on some level and that is why he'd avoided her for so long. But now he didn't have those barriers, and the full force of his attraction was getting the better of him.

He glanced down at his erection and sighed. Wrapping his hand over his cock, he stroked it. He closed his eyes and immediately a vision of Dee popped up. He couldn't even summon the image of another woman. No other woman had monopolized his time. He knew once he had her, it would only get worse. He had seen two of his friends go through the same thing, and he knew he was sunk. The important thing was that she didn't find out.

He picked up his speed, his body quickening for his upcoming release. He could imagine Dee as she kissed her way down his body, her mouth moving over his stomach, her tongue darting out over the head of his penis.

His balls drew up, his entire body locked up as he arched off the bed. He groaned her name as he came. Long moments later, he sighed and got out of bed. Something had to happen, and soon.

Skilled hands moved over Dee's flesh as she arched against them, her body shimmering with need. Wet heat wound through her veins.

"You know you want to submit to me."

She threw her head back and forth, denying him even here where he did actually control her. His mouth skimmed the inside of her thigh, his teeth scraping over the tender flesh. The pressure between her legs increased, but with his body there, she couldn't press them together to relieve the ache.

"One of these days, you will give in to me."

Again, she denied him. She hungered for it, needed it more than she needed to breath, but giving in would be giving too much. She could never protect herself against him, against the emotions that he pulled from her every time they were together.

His breath feathered out over her skin. She couldn't stop the shiver. Oh, God, she needed this, needed a release. Breath warmed her sex the moment before he set his mouth on her. His tongue swept in, slipping easily between her dripping lips. With practice and ease, he pushed her, built her up, the tip of his tongue brushing up against her clit. It felt as if she had been shocked with an electrical wire. Shots of current threaded through her blood as the pressure built, her body stealing her sanity as it raced to the orgasm she knew was shimmering there right out of reach.

The ringing of her phone brought Dee out of the fantastic dream. A thin layer of sweat layered her body, her heart beat against her chest and her breath came out in short, violent chops.

She didn't get to the phone in time. Her mind was still bleeding with images of Micah's hands, his mouth, his body.

Dee. Pick up.

She narrowed her eyes at the phone when she heard Micah's voice. Dammit.

If you don't pick up, I am going to assume that you are hurt, bleeding and need me to come there to take care of you.

With an aggravated sigh, she leaned over and grabbed the phone.

"I'm not hurt."

He chuckled, the rich sound wrapping around her heart. "I figured."

He was silent for a moment or two, and she wondered then where he was. It was early for both of them. It was just after ten and both of them had closed. She sat up and leaned against her headboard.

"Is there something you wanted in particular?"

"I think we established that a few nights ago."

She rolled her eyes. "If you want to be all cryptic and not tell me, fine. I'm going back to sleep." And hopefully without the dream she was just having. She didn't need any more temptation, real or imaginary.

"I was wondering if you were busy this evening?"

She pulled the receiver away from her ear, looked at it and then replaced it. "This is Micah Ross, right? I mean, it is Saturday night."

He chuckled again, and the sound sank under her skin.

"Yes. I noticed you weren't scheduled to work."

She pulled her bottom lip between her teeth. It was her first Saturday off in two months, and she had planned on working on plans for her move. The move she hadn't told a soul about, especially Micah.

"Dee?"

She cleared her throat.

"I..." No words came to mind. She knew he wanted her. He had made that pretty clear. "You want to go out again, as in on a date."

"Yeah. That's why I called you and asked what you were doing. It's not the first time for us." He said it as if she were three years old.

Yeah, they had, and each time they went out, each time he'd touched her over the last week, she had barely been able to keep her head straight. The last time they were together, she had almost begged him to take her. And that was a mistake. Although...she wondered now at her idiot decree. Granted, it had kept her safe over the years, but the way her body yearned to be touched...she was thinking she might have made a mistake in judgment.

"And you're still convinced you need to go against your personal decree of dating employees for me?" She couldn't keep the disbelief from her voice.

"Yes."

Just that one word, the tone, sent a rush of shivers racing over her body. He offered no more, but Micah wasn't used to explaining himself. And truthfully, what woman wouldn't go for it.

A smart girl.

Shut up, smart girl.

"So, are you busy?"

Of course, she wasn't. He knew that more than anyone other than Keisha. She had actually planned on working on her new identity.

The moment the thought popped into her head, guilt stole through her. God, she was sick of it, sick of being someone else, of pretending that her life was normal. For once she wanted it to be. She wanted to be the normal girl on a date with a sexy man, especially one that women yearned for. After just the few encounters, she knew she wanted more. More of him.

She would just have to keep her head screwed on straight.

"Okay."

He released a barely audible sigh. Had he thought she would say no? What woman would say no to him?

A smart one.

I told you to shut up.

"I'll pick you up at eight."

"Okay."

"Until then."

He said nothing else as he hung the phone up. Dee clicked hers off and held it against her chest. What the hell had she just done? She knew going out with him tonight would probably be a mistake. Ever since that first kiss, hell since she was first hired, she'd wanted him. With each passing day, she was drawn to him more. He was wooing her. She felt it deep in her bones. It struck her as odd for a man like him. Doms weren't always the most romantic, but apparently Micah was. That combination of romance and domination probably made most women fall for him hard.

She would enjoy the evening and pretend for once that she was normal. Tomorrow was soon enough to start working on her new life, away from here, away from Micah.

Micah pulled the door to Dupree's open and right into his face. With a few muttered curses, he stepped over the threshold, looking for his wayward business partner. He was at his wits end on why he kept walking into things, dropping things... Hell, he was worried about walking down the street at the moment. It was a wonder he made it to Dupree's without killing himself. Of course, he knew it had to do with a certain virgin who had been driving him crazy. And that would end. Tonight.

The door slammed shut behind him. May was manning the hostess stand.

"Hey, Micah. That looked like it hurt."

He could feel his face heating up. "What?"

She frowned at him. "You didn't hit your head hard enough for a concussion, did you? I mean, you remember hitting your head, right?"

He didn't miss the twinkle in her eye or the humor lacing her tone. He decided ignoring her was the best option.

"I wasn't watching where I was going. Is your lesser half around?"

"Yes. He's back with Chris."

He nodded and headed back.

"I can get you some ice for the bump if you need it."

He didn't growl at her, but it was a close call. The woman had a mouth on her. He didn't know how Evan put up with her. Of course, considering who he was hung up on, he had no room to talk.

By the time he made it back to the office, he had calmed himself down. Still, he felt...odd. It wasn't something he was used to, not anymore, not since he'd gained control over his life.

The door was open and he found his two friends laughing.

"Hey, Micah," Chris said, a welcoming smile on his face.

Evan turned with a look of surprise in his eyes. "What the hell are you doing here?"

"I thought I would chase you down and see if you'd be at the club tonight. I'm taking tonight off."

Evan frowned. "So. I told you, we have good managers."

"I know that, but it's Saturday night so I thought it would be good if you were there."

He cocked his head to the side. "Ah, so you broke down and asked her out again?"

"Who?" Chris asked.

"Dee."

Chris nodded. "They were here a few nights ago."

Evan looked at Micah with his eyebrows raised.

"What the fuck? Why is everyone so interested in my love life all the sudden."

"Because you haven't really had one in about six months," Chris said.

Evan settled back in his chair. "That's when he started stalking Dee Sumner."

"I'm not stalking her."

"Yeah, I know. I got some money in the pool." Chris glanced at him. "Could you hold off for another week?"

"Pool?"

Evan laughed. "Yeah, everyone at work has money on when you're going to bed the woman."

He frowned as he collapsed in the chair. "Why would they be interested, and just how did they know?" he asked Evan with a suspicious glare.

Evan held his hands up and laughed. "Don't look at me."

He narrowed his eyes on Chris. Although he hadn't been

around much, he still had a lot of friends at the club. "You have to know they've been watching you, watching her. You haven't been with a regular sub for at least six months. Granted, I'm sure you keep it away from the club—"

Evan made a choking sound. Chris looked at him. "What?"

His business partner's smile curved evilly as he leaned forward. "I would bet you a thousand bucks our friend here hasn't had a woman in that long."

Chris glanced at him, a smile curving his lips. "Really?"

Evan nodded. Micah's face heated as his temper soared.

"I have no idea why the fuck you two are interested, but I have seen a sub outside of work."

Evan glanced at him and then said, "She wasn't a student?"

Irritation now crunched down Micah's spine. So the woman had been a student, someone who wanted to be trained as a Domme. For someone to get the right to be a Dom/Domme at their club, they had to go through training as a sub. They had to understand the psyche.

"What does that matter?"

Chris started laughing. "Oh, God, he's worse than you. You were sleeping with everyone in sight. This one locks down, and lordy, he gets pissy when he doesn't get some on a regular basis."

"Fuck you."

"No, thanks," Chris said. "I have an idea Cynthia would disagree. Plus, you aren't my type, even if you haven't had any in six months."

"It hasn't been that long." *Five months and sixteen days.*

"Damn near close, bruddah," Evan said.

"I just want to know if you are going to check in tonight."

"Sure. I mean, it's dangerous to let you go without getting some."

He said nothing as his friend cackled. He knew he would be doing the same thing to them, and had given Evan a pretty hard time when he was going after May. But damn, neither of them had had to deal with a virgin.

"What did you just say?" Evan asked.

Shit. "Nothing."

"No, he grumbled something about a virgin," Chris said.

Dammit. What the hell was wrong with him?

Evan hooted with laughter. "You're telling me the woman is a virgin?"

"I didn't say anything and if you want to keep your balls intact, you better make sure that you keep your voice down."

"You don't scare me."

"I might not, but that little woman might. She's small, but she's tough. I have a feeling she wouldn't think twice about relieving you of your manhood. I'll talk to you tomorrow."

Not wanting to face their speculative study, he slipped out the door. He said nothing as he passed May at her stand. Without looking up, she said, "There's a door there, be careful."

"What the hell was that about?" Chris asked when they were alone.

Evan shrugged, realizing that Chris was just figuring out what he had understood for a while.

"He's been hooked on her for months. At first, they were fighting all the time about work. Then he simmered down to that stalking thing he does."

Chris shook his head, his brow furrowing as he frowned. "No, I mean, did you hear the way he talked about her?"

"Of course." He had been lusting after Dee for months and now it was finally going to happen. The idea that he was waiting, being patient and not moving on to another sub already in the life told Evan it was serious. "Yeah. He's stuck."

"Stuck?" Chris asked.

"That man doesn't have any idea what he's about to get into, but I have a feeling he's about to learn a thing or two."

"From a virgin?"

Evan nodded. "A virgin who never flirts with him or tries to get his attention."

Chris frowned. "He likes a challenge."

"But have you ever heard him say he went without sex?"

Chris's eyes widened. "Holy shit."

Even chuckled. "Exactly. Our friend is about to have some of his asinine theories about falling in love with a woman tested."

Chris practically rubbed his hands together. "This is definitely going to be fun."

SEVEN

Dee looked at herself in the mirror and frowned. The dress looked great. She'd bought it over a year ago but this was the first time she'd worn it. It made her feel...odd. She didn't wear dresses or skirts that often, but for some reason she wanted to dress up tonight. Sadly, this dress was her last choice. She loved it, but found it a little too snug for her liking. The blue soft fabric clung to her hips and it was a bit too low cut for her liking. She glanced at the small pile of clothes on her bed. She was out of options at the moment. This was the end of the line.

Micah would be here any minute and she was far from ready.

She turned and looked at the back of the dress...or the back of the halter that was missing. Maybe this was a really bad idea. Okay, the whole date thing was a bad idea. She'd blurted out that she was a virgin to the man, allowed him to talk her into several dates, and basically drive her crazy for the last week. Why he wanted another date, she had no idea. She couldn't seem to help herself. She wanted to be near him, with him. And for once, she found herself wanting to be a girl.

She wasn't a woman who could dress up that often. She worked, that was it. Every now and then, she would go out with Keisha, but that was just for girls' night out. Her dates had dwindled in the last six months or so, mainly because she was just so damn sick of explaining why she wasn't in the life, why she wasn't going to sleep with the guy on the first date. They all thought she was a woman with loose morals because she worked at the club.

Drawing in a deep breath, she grabbed her lip gloss. A quick brush or two and she replaced the cap just as the doorbell rang. Damn. Her heart slapped against her chest and the breath in her lungs stalled.

She ordered herself to calm down and went to the door. This was just a dinner, nothing big. They had done it before. It wasn't as if they were going to go to Rough 'n Ready and get it on.

Her nipples tightened against the fabric of her dress and her body heated. Crap, the thought of being taken publicly by him should not turn her on. But it did. More than any kiss she'd had in the last few years.

By the time she got to her door, she'd settled herself down. Or at least talked herself off the ledge. Opening the door, she lost her ability to think.

Micah was always a gorgeous man, and he was one who dressed for his job. Meaning, as the owner, he wore suits most of the time. But nothing compared to what he now wore.

Dark steel gray fabric fit over his large body as if it had been made for him. Of course, knowing the kind of money he made, there was a good chance it had been. Her father had worn the best of clothes, always tailored to fit. This definitely had the mark of a hand-tailored suit. His hair shimmered down his back. She could imagine it sliding over her skin, the silky strands slipping across her bare breasts, teasing her nipples.

She squeezed her thighs together as he turned. His gaze slipped down her body and then traveled up to meet her eyes. One side of his mouth curled up and her heart started smacking her chest again.

"Wow."

His voice deepened over the one little word. God, the man was making her melt and all he was doing was looking at her and saying wow.

"I have to get my purse, if you'd like to come in."

He nodded and followed her into her house, shutting the door behind him. He made her living room look miniature. He was a large man, larger than most of their patrons. Added to his solid six-foot-four-inch frame was a wealth of sinewy muscle. It was shame she had definitely sworn off sex, because she was sure Micah would know just what to do. She turned away from the temptation and grabbed her purse.

When she faced him again, she found him studying her living room. When he zeroed his gaze on hers, the air backed up in her lungs. His gray eyes always had that ability. They wiped whatever thought she had from her mind. How could this man do this to her? Before the mess her life had become, she had played with guys. Teased, and had gone as far as oral sex. But she had never had a problem turning down a man. Oh, there were times she wanted sex, had needed it. She might be a virgin, but she understood desire. Still, there was never a time when she'd felt an overpowering craving for just one man. It constantly took her by surprise.

"Well." She fidgeted. She never fidgeted. Humor lightened his eyes, informing her that he recognized her tell also.

"I take it you're ready to eat."

Dammit. With anyone else, that would sound like a normal question. But with him, nothing was simple—or normal.

She straightened her spine. There was no way in hell she was going to let that seductive smile work on her. Sure, she knew it promised long nights of loving, controlling, dominating, beyond anything in her dreams. That wasn't what she needed to be thinking about.

"Sure," she said, offering him a smile.

He chuckled but said nothing else as he followed her out of the house. She stopped on the step and he took the keys from her. She frowned as she watched him lock her door.

"You know, this is the twenty-first century. I can lock my own door."

He finished the task and gave her back her keys. "Of course you can. You can do a lot of things. I told you the other night, you're going to have to learn that some things are better left up to others."

She could feel her face heating. Hell, her whole body was sparking with enough electricity to light up Waikiki Beach.

Without another word, he offered her his arm. "Ready?"

Looking up at him, she felt her mouth dry up. Those gray eyes always captured her attention. They hid so many secrets, desires. She would give him this, allow him this little dominance. It wasn't that big of a thing. She slipped her hand onto his arm and she heard a barely audible sigh.

Had he been worried? There is no way he could have. Micah Ross crooked his finger and women came running. If he didn't get her into bed, bent to his will, he would move on to someone else.

As they walked to his black vette, she wondered why that thought gave her equal parts arousal and pain.

Micah tried not to hum. It was hard not to since his whole body was humming. Having her beside him, giving in to that little bit of dominance he had shown her, shouldn't have thrilled him. He had gotten women to do more with little effort. This woman was going to make sure to fight him all the way. He was too self-aware to not understand that was part of her appeal.

"Do you mind telling me where we are going?"

He smiled. It had taken her about five minutes of talking about the weather before she'd finally given in and asked.

"My place."

He didn't look at her as he punched the gas to pass a slow-moving sedan, but he could feel her gaze settle on him.

"Your place. I didn't agree to that."

He wanted to laugh at her suspicious tone, but he instead he smiled. He couldn't remember the last time he'd enjoyed a woman's company this much before he got her to bed.

"You said you would have dinner."

She didn't respond for a few seconds. He could almost hear her thoughts turning over in her head. "You said this is only dinner?"

He shrugged. "Up to you. You want more, you get more. Just like the other night."

She sighed and crossed her arms beneath her breasts. Even from the corner of his eyes, he could see her succulent flesh move above the neckline of her dress. Micah was still amazed he could function. From the moment she had opened the door, most of the blood in his brain had headed south. In the two years she'd worked for him, he had never seen her dressed like this. The fabric clung to her curves, leaving little to the imagination. He knew without a doubt that she wasn't wearing a bra or panties. There were absolutely no lines beneath the fabric.

Arousal thrummed through his blood. His control was legendary. Micah never had a problem drawing out the pleasure or waiting until a woman was ready to take that final step. With his bastard of a birth father, a rapist who liked to beat his wife on a regular basis, Micah had never wanted to be like him. Never wanted to cross that line. It was one of the reasons he had been drawn to BDSM. He had been afraid too much of the bastard's blood was in him, and Micah did have a temper.

"So, just dinner."

He could tell she was trying to get some kind of promise from him. "And dessert."

"Micah." Her voice held a lethal warning. He knew he had to be careful around her. One little slip up and she would be out. It would take him months to get back to the position he was in now.

"I got a cheesecake."

There was a beat of silence. "Cheesecake."

When he saw the expression on Dee's face, Micah wanted to kiss Keisha. When he'd peppered the waitress for answers about Dee's likes and dislikes, she had let him know about Dee's love of New York Cheesecake. In fact, her friend said it was her one big weakness.

"Yeah, New York style." She said nothing so he glanced over and shrugged. "You don't have to eat any."

She shook her head. "No I l—" she licked her lips, "—I like cheesecake."

He laughed. "Well, then we do have one thing in common."

"I have a feeling we have a lot in common."

That gave him pause as he slowed down for a stop sign. "How so? I mean, I don't think I would be wrong in thinking that you don't want to be involved with me. Or I should say, you don't think you should be."

She ignored his last comment. "What I mean is that we both have control issues."

"That's true, but I don't think you understand yours."

"Oh believe me, I understand mine."

The sadness he heard in her voice pulled at him. For the first time in a long time, he really wanted to get to know a woman. His lovers in the last few years had been players, there for the challenge of being his sub. He hadn't really known them beyond the bedroom. He didn't work out their issues, know of their families, their habits. Hell, he already knew more about Dee than he did most of his previous lovers and he had yet to get her into his bed.

"Understanding them and dealing with them are two different things."

He took the exit to his neighborhood.

She sighed. "I know. I just don't have the ability to figure those things out. And sometimes things are out of our hands, don't you agree?"

He thought it over, thought about his temper, his father's proclivities. "I do to a point. But how can you live a satisfied life if you don't deal with it?"

"Sometimes surviving is all you can hope for."

Loneliness threaded her tone, tugged at his heart. He knew

there were things in her past she let no one know. Not even Keisha knew exactly where she had grown up. She never had anyone visit her and she rarely left the island. He didn't either, but he had no idea where his family was, and he was pretty sure they could care less about him. He wanted to know what caused her to run at the age of seventeen. Was it abuse? He knew there was more to it than just a controlling father.

But that could wait. It would drive him insane, but he would try for patience. He had yet to initiate a reluctant woman. This was a first. And wasn't that just a bitch. Micah knew he'd been spoiled the last few years. Being the main Dom at a BDSM club offered him a lot of benefits, one being that women regularly threw themselves at him. He didn't have to try. With Dee, he'd had to pursue her.

He pulled onto his street and then made the right into his drive. Dee had no idea just what a big deal this was for him. He kept an apartment in town, had his own private bedroom at the club. He rarely brought anyone back to his house. It was his sanctuary, where he could be himself. He also never wanted to share this part of himself with women he barely knew. It wasn't until he'd been planning their date tonight that he realized what he had been doing all these years. He parked in the driveway, then got out and rounded the hood to let Dee out of the car. By the time he reached her, she already had one leg out of the car. He grabbed the door and offered her a hand. She looked down at his hand, then back up at his face. Those luminous eyes danced with humor.

"I can get myself out of the car."

"Like I said, some things are better left to others."

She blushed but took his hand. He led her to the front porch, his heart pounding harder with each step. After unlocking the door, he stepped aside to let her enter. He followed her in, closing the door and leaning against it.

Until this moment, he hadn't realized just how much he wanted—needed—her here. He loved his house, had spent a fortune building it. Now, for some reason, for the first time it seemed like a home.

He brushed the thoughts aside as he led her toward the kitchen. He watched her as she studied the Corinthian counter-tops, the ceramic-tiled floor and the Viking appliances.

"Wow. You could fit about five of my kitchens in here."

She didn't sound upset by that fact. He didn't want to win her over with his money. Although, he had to admit, there was a part of him that did. He wanted to impress her with the money he'd earned, and just how far he'd come in life.

"I take it you like to cook?" she asked.

She hadn't stepped into the kitchen and he smiled. He had a feeling that Dee wasn't much of a chef. He took her hand and led her in.

"I love to cook." He pulled out a chair at the breakfast bar. "I know you know a little bit about me."

She nodded. "Of course people talk. It's natural since you're the boss. They don't know as much as I know now. As you said, you came from nothing."

He chuckled as he pulled out the ingredients for dinner. "I came from less than nothing."

He put the container of sea scallops on the counter and pulled a pot off the rack to fill with water for the pasta. Setting it on the burner, he turned the gas on and looked at her. Again, a sense of rightness stole over him. In his kitchen, at this moment, with this woman.

He leaned over and brushed his mouth against hers. A small

taste and his body was yearning for more. He had to use a large amount of control to push it aside.

"What was that for?" she asked.

"For a while," he teased.

He smiled when she frowned at him. Turnabout was fair play in his humble opinion. The woman was already driving him beyond sanity. He pulled out the pasta and he felt the weight of her gaze again. It was one thing he had learned these past few weeks. Dee was a cautious woman, one that weighed every option before coming to a decision. He set the box on the counter and glanced over at her.

"Do you need some help?" she asked.

"Sure. Why don't you start on the salad?"

Dee took one more bite of the seared scallops and closed her eyes in appreciation. Damn if the man didn't know how to cook. Granted, it wasn't anything hard to do. A few scallops with garlic, pasta and roasted asparagus, but it had been so long since someone had cooked for her. The simple delight of having another person take time for her, make her a meal, it was a little too wonderful to ignore.

She opened her eyes as she swallowed.

"I take it you liked the scallops?"

She offered him a smile. "Considering I'm trying to control myself enough not to lick the plate, I would say that is a yes."

He smiled as he sipped his water. She'd had one small glass of wine, but switched to water like Micah. She knew from experience that he didn't drink much. She had never seen him get drunk, never heard of him losing control like that. Of course, he always seemed to be able to master his emotions. There was no way he would allow himself to drink too much. It should comfort her since her oldest brother had been well on his way to being a drunk when she'd run—and a mean drunk at that. But there was a tiny part of her that was afraid of a man like Micah. A man with that much self-restraint should make any woman scared.

She smiled. "Odd that you seem to know some of my favorite foods."

He said nothing.

"So, been spying on me?"

He laughed as he stood and took both their plates. "No. Your friend Keisha was happy to help in my date plans."

She could feel a flush of heat fill her face. "Trying to win the pool."

"What?"

"Nothing." She watched him as he cut a generous portion of the cheesecake. He returned to the table and slid into the chair beside her with one plate and a seductive smile. She didn't know which tempted her more, the man or the cake.

"You're not going to have any?" she asked.

He nodded. "We'll share." He cut off a piece.

And then his gaze followed the fork as he moved it to her lips. He didn't mean to feed her, did he?

"Open up."

Well, crap. Fear and arousal twisted through her. She didn't want this. It was almost too...intimate. This was all about proving she wasn't for him, but no matter what, he kept slinking past her defenses.

She shook her head.

"You want some, you better open up."

She frowned as butterflies fluttered in her tummy.

"I told you, some things are better when someone does them for you."

The way his voice rolled over those words, she knew the meaning behind them. She would have to be an idiot not to understand. She wanted to refuse. Being fed by a man was...a little bit too much for her to take. He slid the fork along her bottom lip. The scent of the graham cracker crust and the sweetness of the cake filled her head. She raised her gaze to his. His attention was on her mouth.

"Open up, baby. You won't regret it."

Yearning for the cake, for the man in front of her, had her head spinning. Never in all her twenty-seven years had she wanted someone so much. He hadn't really tried to seduce her, and she was ready to jump up on the table and offer her body to him. But she kept all this inside, locked away, because it was better that he never know what was going on in her head. A man like Micah Ross might be good, but he definitely would use it against her to get her into bed.

"Dee."

Her name snapped out. Not loudly, not enough to scare her. But enough to let her know that he was not happy with her. She should take exception to his tone, the way it bit out from between his teeth. Instead, she found herself wanting to please him as her nipples hardened. She opened her mouth and he slipped the dreamy dessert between her lips. The sweetness exploded over her tongue. God, it had been a long time since she'd had good cheesecake. She could pay for the good stuff. She had the money to spend on air-shipped cheesecake.

But she knew she would eat the whole damn cake by herself. She opened her eyes to find Micah watching her, his face flush, his gaze intent on her mouth. The air between them thickened. Everything in her tightened, her hormones dancing.

She swallowed the bite. Before she could say anything, he had another bite for her. He held it in front of her mouth.

"Aren't you going to have any?"

He shook his head, said nothing. She got the feeling he was holding on to an invisible thread of control. From watching her eat cheesecake?

She wanted to refuse him, wanted to tell him one bite was enough. But...she couldn't. As she opened her mouth, she gave in to the delightful treat. Damn, the airiness was just like New York, just the right amount of sugar, the crust substantial, but not overwhelming the cake itself.

She had barely swallowed the second bite when he had another at her mouth. She took it this time without hesitation, closing her eyes and humming. The fork clattered on the plate. It was the only warning she got. She opened her eyes to find Micah reaching for her, pulling her out of her chair and onto his lap.

He crashed his mouth down onto hers, his tongue sweeping in and taking immediate possession. Like every time he kissed her, it set off an explosion within her. She didn't resist, couldn't. As her head spun, she slipped her hands through the silky strands of his hair, and tried to move closer. Her breasts ached, her nipples painfully hard. She turned in his lap to press her chest against his, trying her best to gain some relief.

He groaned and tightened his hold. The sound of it came from deep within him as if he were in pain. It touched something in her, had her heart beating so hard she was amazed she didn't pass out.

She slipped her tongue against his and his hands convulsed on her waist. Damn this felt good, right. Nothing had ever felt this right before. In all her times with men, before and after the incident, she had held herself back, made sure she didn't lose her head. But this time, this one time, she didn't want to stop. She wanted it to keep going—needed to feel his body on hers, in hers. She shifted in his lap and felt his erection. It should be a sign to run, to not get in deep with this man. But she wanted him. Wanted everything he could offer her, take from her. Nothing in her life had ever been so important. She wanted him. Now.

He apparently knew what she was thinking and pulled back. Without a word, he lifted her in his arms as if she weighed nothing and carried her through his house. Her body was still humming with need, still begging for relief. She knew where he was going, and she should stop him. But the need he had built up wouldn't allow her. She needed this more, seriously more than she'd wanted anything else in her life. That should scare her. It did a bit. As he turned down the hall that led to the back of the house, to his bedroom, her mind started doing somersaults.

He paused at the doorway. She peeked up at him. He drew in a long, and what sounded painful, breath. Then he turned his head and his dark gaze clashed with hers.

"Dee?"

She knew what the question meant, what he asking. It was on the tip of her tongue to say no. It would be better if she just walked—ran—out of the house. But she saw the flush of arousal on his cheeks, recognized the lust in his eyes. For a man not used to denying himself, he was asking permission. And she knew what it meant if she said yes. He would be in control, the one calling the shots in bed.

His jaw flexed. Just that little movement told her how much power she had over him. She had a feeling if she had been another woman, he could have easily seduced her into bed. But with her, a woman who had never really been with a man, he waited...gave her the choice.

It wasn't something big, nothing that would normally make another woman's heart melt, but the fact that he would wait, that he would give her that choice and not try and roll over her, tightened her chest. Her life had been a myriad of choices made for her, situations that she couldn't control, and although he planned on controlling their love making, he let her know with that one word, just her name, that it was her choice.

She wanted to say so much, wanted to tell him just what it meant to her. She was sure he had no idea, but instead, she held the words inside her and allowed her lips to curve.

"Yes."

eight

Micah wanted to shout with triumph, but he thought that might be pushing it. Dee was still skittish, even if she had agreed. He wanted to do nothing to upset her and lose his chance. Just getting her into his house tonight had been a major victory. Now having her in his bedroom...well, that was the gold medal and Nobel Peace Prize wrapped up into one big trophy.

Even though he felt like running to the bed, he forced himself to walk, slowly. He could feel her nerves. They were easy to see. He knew she wanted this as much as he did. Damn, no, wait, it was probably worse on his side. He had initiated a lot of subs, but he had never in all his thirty-five years had a virgin. He'd never had the pleasure of introducing a woman to the ecstasy she could have, she would remember every time she took another man to bed.

A growl threatened to erupt from his chest at the thought of another man touching her. He didn't want that, couldn't even think of that. It had never been an issue with him before, but he couldn't deny the possessive feelings now surging through him. He wanted to be the only man to touch her. Ever.

He brushed that feeling aside, and laid her on his bed. Again, he had this sense of rightness, a feeling that this was exactly where she belonged. Forever.

He moved away from that thought. For the first time ever, he saw her looking nervous. She always put on such a brave face, and he hated to see it. Mainly because she would hate it. The fact that he wanted more than anything to please her, to make her happy, wasn't a new feeling for him. Women were to be treasured, loved. But the bone-deep need to make her happy, that her happiness was somehow entwined with his, was a little too scary to contemplate.

She glanced around, looking surprised.

"Where's the dungeon?" she asked, her voice threaded with nerves and a bit of amusement.

He chuckled. "I have a secret room for that."

He pulled open the nightstand drawer and pulled out the red blindfold he'd bought earlier that day. She watched him, her big blue eyes solemn, more serious than he had ever seen her.

"I bought this for you today. The moment I saw it, I knew it was for you." He slid the silky fabric through his fingertips. "Like I said, sensual, no-frills sexuality."

"I'm not sure that's something I would like."

He heard the fear there, understood it. It was a little thing, the only thing he would ask of her tonight. He would have stopped if he hadn't heard the arousal threaded in her tone. She wanted to give over to the power, wanted to let him be the one in charge. Knowing that, having his suspicions confirmed, sent a jolt of lust spinning so fast through his blood he almost groaned. The fabric of his pants was rough against his erection and every move he made heightened the friction.

He slipped onto the bed next to her and couldn't fight the

smile when he heard her breath catch. After so many months thinking she wasn't aware of him, it was balm to his battered ego to know that she was in fact very aware of him.

"You understand why I would do this to you? Put the blindfold on?"

"To be in control."

This was going to be harder than he thought it would be. He could all but see her closing off to him. He knew it shamed her that she wanted him in control. She craved it. Her responses to him had proven that. But a tough woman like her might see it as a weakness to be ashamed of.

"No. Well, partially. But another aspect of it is allowing you to feel, taste, touch...all the senses but your sight. It will heighten your pleasure."

She didn't look completely convinced. In fact, with the wary look she was offering him, she was probably just seconds from crossing her arms over that very delectable chest of hers.

"There is always a way to call a stop to it. You need to come up with a safe word, one that tells me that I've gone too far."

She threaded her fuller bottom lip between her teeth. He wanted nothing more than to lean forward and kiss her into submission. With another woman, especially a sub who knew what was going on, he would do it. But he knew this was important. She had to make this decision without his interference. Of course, if she decided against it, he might change his mind.

"Dee?"

She looked at the slip of fabric and nodded.

"First though, you need a safe word."

She drew in a deep breath. "Hawaii." The word was said with such reverence it made him smile.

He leaned forward. "Remember, if at any time you feel like it's too much, that you are being pushed over an edge that scares you, use that word. It is very important that you understand that."

She nodded.

He slipped the fabric over her head, tying it in back. He brushed his mouth over hers. "Good girl."

He moved from the bed, pulled off his jacket and his shirt. He knew that she could hear his movements, hear the fabric being removed. Her breath sped up, and when he turned around to face her, he noticed her pulse was throbbing in her neck. As in most Hawaiian houses, he had removed his shoes when he'd entered, so all he wore now was a pair of pants. He wanted nothing more than to pull them off, but he knew better. He needed some kind of barrier to keep from jumping her.

He approached her, reminding himself to take it slowly. It wasn't something he usually had a problem with. It was one of the things he was proud of. But thinking about her for the last six months, wanting her, dreaming of her, had shredded a lot of his control.

Normally, he would make a sub strip. It was one of his favorite ways to exert power over the situation. But right now, he knew this was all she could take. Hell, she wasn't just a virgin sub, but a virgin, with all the nerves that went along with it. He didn't think she was scared, but even knowing about sex, knowing what went on, didn't really let her know how it felt to connect to another human being in such a way.

"I'm going to remove your dress."

She opened her mouth, but he pressed his index finger against her lips.

"Unless you are going to say Hawaii, don't say anything. I don't want a peep out of you unless you're moaning my name."

She shivered, her breasts swaying with the action. As he reached behind her, his fingers skimmed her soft flesh and he sighed. Just that simple contact had his libido in overdrive. He wanted nothing more than to shred her clothes and devour her.

His fingers were shaking by the time he undid the knot behind her neck. The halter fell away, baring her breasts to his view. God, she was gorgeous. Pale skin with just the smallest hint of a tan line. Her breasts weren't huge, but just the right size. He couldn't stop his hand from sliding down to tease first one, then the other nipple. She sucked in a breath and he felt it as if she had touched him.

"You can show your pleasure, as I said before. That I have no problem with. If you have a question, you need to ask permission, but I prefer to be addressed as Sir."

She frowned at that, and he chuckled. She would not go easily. It would take a while, he knew that, but he also knew she would fight him all the way. He actually preferred a spunky sub. He wanted a woman who could stand up for herself. Not someone weak-willed.

When she said nothing, he leaned forward and pressed the flat of his tongue over her nipple. She moaned then, the sound long, drawn out and filled with such need he almost lost his control. Over a tiny moan.

He grazed his teeth over her nipple then pulled away. He took a little time as he slipped the dress off her body and placed it on a chair beside the bed. When he turned around, his breath stopped short in his lungs. Seeing her here, against his red sheets, filtered through his blood, warming it to boiling. She was gorgeous. He knew that. Her body was trim and muscled, but not too tough. She had nicely curved hips, shapely legs. The nest of dark curls between her legs drew him. The urge to bury his face there, to take in her scent, taste her cream, almost had him scrambling on top of the bed.

Instead, for her, he counted backwards from ten. Twice.

"Lay back, Dee."

She did as he asked and he smiled. She might think she was independent, but the woman was made for being a sub, at least in bed. He sat beside her and again noticed his hand shaking when he placed his palm on her stomach. He smiled when the muscles beneath his fingers jumped.

"Your pleasure will be heightened by losing your sight. Of course, all your pleasure is for me to give. You do not take."

He skimmed his hand down to her pussy and laid it there. The heat of her sex warmed his hand. Her curls were damp, dripping with her arousal. He could imagine just how she would feel against his cock as he slid in.

"Do you understand?" he asked.

"Yes."

"Yes, Sir," he insisted.

She hesitated and he raised his hand and smacked her pussy. Her gasp was filled with arousal and irritation. She swallowed.

"Yes, Sir."

He rewarded her compliance with a caress, slipping his finger along her slit.

"I don't ask for much tonight. I understand that this isn't just your first submission. But I do expect some respect. And if you want to come, you will obey me."

She bit her lower lip as he continued to slip his finger up and down her slit. Since she said nothing, did not defy him, he allowed the tip of his index finger to slide against her clit.

Fuck, it was already hard.

He lay down beside her, slipped his hands to her arms and pulled them above her head. "I do not want to use restraints tonight."

That was a big fat lie, but he wanted to ease her worries. He couldn't wait to tie her up as he fucked her senseless, but he knew that would be a bit too hardcore for their first time.

"But I do want you to hold on to the rungs in my headboard."

He watched as she complied, her agile fingers slipping over the wood. She had dainty hands, slim fingers. He didn't know why he'd never noticed it before. Before he could stop it, the image of her hands slipping down his stomach and wrapping around his cock solidified in his mind.

"Ah," he said as he allowed his gaze to slip down her body. "I like that. You should see your breasts. That position offers them up to me so nicely."

He bent his head and took a nipple into his mouth as he plucked and teased the other. They were perfect. Her flesh was sweet, as were the little moans she tried to keep at the back of her throat. The idea that she was still trying to control her reactions made him think he needed to take it up a notch. The woman would not give an inch.

He kissed his way down her stomach, dipping his tongue into her belly button as he continued down to her pussy. He came up to his knees between her legs. She spread them enough to allow him room, but that wasn't enough for him. Placing a hand on each thigh, he urged them apart farther, until he could see her pussy.

"Damn, that's pretty." And it was. Her clit was hard, her

pink lips glistening with her arousal. He slipped a finger along her slit and she shuddered.

"We will be shaving this." She stiffened. "Not tonight, but we will. It's my right."

He knew she wasn't happy about it, but he didn't give a fuck. Really, at the moment, he had to use every bit of his control not to rip his pants off and fuck her until they both forgot their own names. Dee needed to understand just where they stood and who would be in charge.

Needing a taste, wanting it more than his next breath, he leaned down and set his mouth on her wet sex. He delved inside, the delectable taste of her crashing through him, over his taste buds.

Her legs moved restlessly against the sheets. Even tasting her wasn't enough. He wanted her with such a force it bordered on primitive. As he slipped his tongue to her clit and pulled the tiny bundle of nerves into his mouth, he fought with that inner warrior. He was screaming to take her, to slip inside her, to make her come over and over. But he knew if he didn't establish their D/s relationship from the start, it would confuse her. He continued to suck on her clit as he added a finger. Her inner muscles clamped down hard on his digit and he shuddered himself. Damn, she was tight.

It didn't take him long to push her up to the edge. He could sense that her orgasm was just out of reach, but he wasn't ready to let her fall. She needed to know that any pleasure she had she would get from him. He forced himself to pull his mouth from her as he continued moving his finger.

She moaned in frustration and he chuckled. It was about time she knew what he had been feeling for the last six months.

"You do not come unless I give you the right."

Her brow furrowed, showing her displeasure, but she didn't say anything. She had learned something at least. He rewarded her by pressing his thumb against her clit before pulling away completely.

He slipped off the bed, unbuttoned and unzipped his pants. She turned her head toward him and it was the one time he hated that she had that mask on. He knew that in today's world, even a virgin had an opportunity to see men naked. He was pretty sure she had seen a lot of men at Rough 'n Ready in various states of undress. There was a little part of him that wanted her gaze on him. It was a turn-on to see her excitement in her eyes, the way her pulse beat in her neck. It would have to wait.

Her tongue came out over her plump pink lips. Micah had always loved oral sex, giving and getting. But he knew tonight he could not ask for that, at least not this time. He pushed his slacks away and stepped out of them. Her tongue moved over her bottom lip again. He could only imagine how it would feel to drive his shaft between those lips, into the wet recesses of her mouth.

He shoved that thought aside, mostly, and joined her back on the bed. He touched his hands to her feet and then skimmed them up her legs. She was petite, athletic and he loved her body. Loved watching the muscles tense and relax. All that hard muscle encased beneath the softest skin.

He skimmed his hand over her pussy, happy to see her jerk at the touch. He wanted her off-center. He continued moving his hand up her body, lightly skimming over her breasts. She sighed, a dose of arousal and frustration in the sound. He smiled and slid his hand to her sex again. This time, he pressed against the clit with his thumb and slipped two fingers into her pussy as he slid down between her legs. Her body quickened, he could feel the way her muscles contracted on his fingers. He added his tongue, licking and sucking as he continued to move his hand. It didn't take long before he felt her orgasm take her.

"Come for me, Dee. Now."

He pulled back, keeping his hand on her, but watching as the pleasure consumed her. She bowed off the bed, her body shivering, convulsing as she came. Her fingers were still wrapped around the slats on his headboard.

"Micah." She didn't yell his name, didn't shout. Instead, she sighed it as she was coming down from her orgasm. It was such a sweet sound that squeezed his heart. He moved then, needed to continue the connection, knowing that he could take her up and over again.

He grabbed a condom off his nightstand, ripped it open and rolled it on in record time. He pulled her hips up as he rose to his knees. She drew her bottom lip between her teeth. Apprehension and arousal filled her expression, but without seeing her eyes, he wasn't sure just exactly what she was feeling. He took his cock in one hand and slowly started easing into her.

She was tight, very tight, and by the time he'd reached her maidenhead and pushed all the way inside of her, he was sweating. He paused for only a moment. Then with one quick thrust, he broke through. She drew in a quick, short breath and then released it.

He kissed her. "Are you okay?"

She nodded, and it was the only consent he needed. He began moving again, thrusting quick, short pumps, until he worked his way into her. Damn if he wasn't about to come. He could feel his orgasm there, shimmering, ready to take him over, but he didn't want to give in to it just yet. He did have some control left. Not much, but a little bit.

He moved in a slow rhythm. With each thrust in, he pushed himself closer, but he wanted her there with him. He moved his hand to her clit as he thrust into her. It only took a few flicks before she came again, her body pulling him in, her muscles grabbing hold of his cock. That one act had him losing control. He pulled her legs up around his hips and started to thrust into her, hard, fast, until he came. He couldn't stop the moan of satisfaction as he pumped himself into her. Nothing had ever felt so good, so wonderful.

He released her legs, pulled out of her and collapsed on the bed next to her. She had let go of the rungs on his headboard, but she still had the blindfold on. He used what little strength he had left to slowly raise it. Her eyes were closed, a smile curved her lips. He leaned closer and brushed his mouth over hers. Slowly, she opened her eyes. The luminous blue was deeper. Satisfaction filled him at the sight of it.

"Thank you," he said, as he brushed his mouth over hers.

"For what?"

She had no idea what she did to him. He hadn't been that fast in bed with a woman in years. He'd always been able to hold on to his control, but with her he couldn't seem to hold back. And he knew it was more than lust.

"For letting me be part of that."

She said nothing for a moment or two. She opened her mouth but not a sound came out. She swallowed.

"Get some rest," he ordered, his voice rough with emotion.

He pulled her into his arms and she came without protest. He gave a satisfied grunt as he settled back against the pillows and dozed.

nine

Dee woke to soft sunlight dancing over her face. For a moment she was confused. She kept her room darker than a dungeon, so the fact the sun was shining in confused her. Then she remembered.

Micah.

She opened her eyes and sat up, wincing when she felt the pull of muscles. It wasn't painful. Any more than losing her virginity had been. But it was uncomfortable.

It was morning. From the sunlight, she would say it was at least midmorning. She looked around the massive room and of course didn't find Micah. For a moment she sat there, bare-ass naked and smiled. She should feel bad, really bad. He had gotten in a position that she hadn't allowed any man. Closing her eyes, the memories from the night before flitted through her brain. She had made a lot of mistakes in her life, but this was definitely not one of them. She couldn't regret it. He had made sure it was wonderful. Most men would have rushed through it, as long as she had made him wait. Maybe that was why she felt so safe with him. She knew he would take care of her.

Whoa.

Panic rose out of nowhere, almost closing her throat and tightening her belly. No way. She didn't depend on any man. Her first thought was to run, get out, away from a man that was making her think stupid things.

"Stop worrying."

She looked up and found him watching her from the doorway.

God, he was beautiful. He always took her breath away, but now that she knew just how kind he was, he was completely irresistible. He wasn't wearing a shirt, and she was struck again by the sleek muscles of his chest and arms. Her gaze traveled down farther, taking in the jeans hanging low on his lean hips. If she were to make a man, she would start with Micah as the basis. Hell, he would be the man she wanted.

Stop it.

She cleared her throat, raised her eyes to his and blushed when she saw his knowing smile. Without a world, he went to a massive cherry dresser and pulled open the top drawer. He grabbed a T-shirt and walked over to the bed. He sat beside her, laying the shirt on his lap.

"Good morning."

Then he leaned in and kissed her. It wasn't seductive, wasn't something that should scare her. Sweet, gentle, almost chaste. Her heart melted.

When he pulled back, she sighed. "Good morning."

"As I said, don't worry."

"What are you talking about?"

"I could see you were having a little freak-out moment. Here's a shirt, take your time in the bathroom. I'm going to make some breakfast. Do you like French toast?"

She nodded. "But you don't have to wait on me."

He raised her hand to his mouth and his breath feathered out over her fingers before he kissed them.

"But I do."

Then he was gone.

She couldn't seem to make herself get up out of the bed. The odd feeling of having someone take care of her was starting to bother her. It had been years since she'd had people looking out for her. Ten to be exact.

Micah was a caregiver. She would have never guessed it, and that was the sad thing. She knew some of the prejudice came from her ideas about D/s. But he was a man who was very careful. He rarely made a stupid move.

With a sigh, she slipped from the bed and to the bathroom. Again, it was gorgeous. The man who came from nothing surrounded himself with luxury she had taken for granted for so many years. The large bathroom sported two sinks at the vanity, a deep garden tub and a separate shower. A peek into the tub told her that it had jets.

Oh, she would kill for a hot bath.

"Go ahead."

She jumped at the sound of his voice. Whirling around, she frowned at him.

"Quit sneaking up on me."

He chuckled. "Take a bath. It might make you feel better."

She opened her mouth to tell him she felt fine, when she realized what he was talking about. She might be a modern woman, but she still felt heat crawl into her cheeks.

"I thought you were making breakfast."

"I was about to, but I realized I should let you take a shower or bath."

He moved away from the doorway and took her hand, leading her to the tub. He sat down on the ledge as he started the water.

"Let me guess, you like the water cool."

She shook her head. "Boiling hot."

He smiled, one of those rare ones that reached his eyes. It made her entire body light up. She yearned to get him to smile like that more often.

"Then we could share a bath."

She swallowed, and he looked away.

"If you're comfortable with it."

She hesitated. This seemed to be a weekend of changes, of firsts, and while it probably wasn't smart, she nodded. The moment she did, he smiled again, and she felt her heart turn over. That smile was going to be the death of her.

He tugged off her shirt and helped her into the tub. He pulled off his pants and then joined her. He sat opposite her and sighed as he dipped into the water.

"I didn't truly appreciate a good hot bath until I built this house."

She smiled as he added bubble bath to the running water. "I take it that Evan did the work?"

He nodded. "He's my best friend, but I wouldn't have hired him if he wasn't the best. And in my opinion, he is."

"How did you meet?"

He cocked his head to one side, more of his hair dipping into the steaming water. "I've never had a woman ask me that before."

"Really, how odd."

"Why would you call that odd?"

"I just think, two such well-known Doms, there would be a

lot of speculation about where you met, how you came about opening the club."

"I told you about how we ended up here."

She nodded, trying to ignore the niggle of guilt for not telling him who she was. She didn't have to be truthful about her past. She lived in the present.

"We met in juvie. Evan was getting his ass kicked because of that mouth of his."

She laughed. "He is a smart ass."

"And he was skinny then."

Thinking of the contractor and all his bulging muscles, she shook her head. "That's hard to imagine."

"He'd been living on the street. Not fun for him. His life, well, it was much worse than what I went through. He was near starved when he came to juvie. Of course, that didn't stop him. I'd never seen so much bravado out of such a runt."

She smiled at the brotherly love she heard in his voice. "What happened?"

"He'd gotten in an argument about cigarettes. See, they're gold in a place like that, currency if you don't want to deal with drugs. Evan has a real distaste for drugs, so he was dealing cigs."

"You don't have a distaste for drugs?"

"Not like Evan. I've never really gone for them because there is that loss of power. That feeling that something else controls your destiny. I don't like that. Evan's mom was an addict, so he detests them. So he was dealing cigs and someone short-changed him. Evan decided to fight him."

"I would think that was normal in a place like that."

He laughed. "Yeah, pretty common. Except Evan barely weighed one hundred and forty pounds, and his opponent was well over two hundred and fifty. When I arrived on the scene, he was barely conscious. I don't mind a good fight, but it didn't seem that fair."

"So you saved him."

"And got my first broken rib thanks to him. It seems I tend to get hurt when Evan's around."

The memory of hearing about his wreck a few months earlier came rushing back. "That's how you ended up in the hospital."

"Oh, yeah. But that had more to do with May than it had to do with Evan. And that crazy bitch Lee."

"I'm glad you never hired her. She was bad news from the time she arrived at the club."

He reached for her then and turned her around. "How about I scrub your back?"

She smiled at the innocent question. The tone beneath it told her it had taken him a lot of his control not to have his hands on her before now. He used a bar of soap that smelled like him, sandalwood and musk, and moved it over her back. As he did, he used his fingers to release the tension.

"Tense? Why would you be tense?"

"I'm sitting in a tub, naked, with Micah Ross."

He chuckled. "Why would that make you tense?"

She laughed. "Yeah, it's normal every-day happenings for the former virgin."

He rinsed off the soap by splashing water over her skin and then he pulled her back against him. "I would think being a former virgin you would be a lot less tense. And this can be normal, is normal."

He said it as if it would be something they did all the time. She wanted to tell him right there and then that this couldn't last. Of course, he would ignore her, unless she told him the

A LITTLE HARMLESS LIE

truth. And nothing in the world would have her do that. Not now. Not when she was about to leave. Telling him would only put him in danger. If her father knew she'd been with Micah Ross, a man he had tried to destroy financially one time, he would do everything in his power to hurt Micah, possibly kill him.

"Relax," he said, as he kissed her ear, his hands coming around to cup her breasts. The steam off the water rose around them as he teased her nipples. And just like that, heat wound through her, a consuming hunger rising. She thought herself too sore to want to do anything today, but she wanted him. It was as if all he had to do was touch her and her body sprang to life.

He kept caressing one breast as he slid his hand down to her sex. He teased her clit, skimming over it, lightly, barely touching it. Her body responded and she moaned.

"You are so damned responsive." His voice had deepened. "But I have to remind you, do not come unless I give you permission."

She said nothing and he removed his hands.

"Dee, you understand?"

She nodded, anything to get him to touch her again.

He resumed, slipping one finger into her pussy. She was still sore, but not as much as she had expected. Easily, he worked another finger inside of her, sending little shocks of heat over her nerve endings. Tension gathered in her tummy, her body completely under his control. She wanted to come, needed it, but he hadn't given her permission.

He teased and tempted her, pressing a thumb against her clit over and over as his mouth tortured her neck. She couldn't stop the rush of energy that exploded through her. She came as she screamed his name, her body shivering with her release. It took her a few moments to recover.

"You're a naughty girl, Dee. I think you need to learn who is in charge here."

Before she could recover from her mind-blowing orgasm, Micah stood, pulled her out of the tub and into his arms. He set her on her feet. He grabbed a towel and quickly dried her and then himself. Her body was still steaming, her hormones still simmering. Watching Micah slowly dry himself, the towel rubbing over his flesh...she shivered.

He glanced up at her, an evilly seductive smile on his lips. It was then that she realized he knew what he was doing to her.

He tossed the towel behind him and came for her. The determined look on his face had her nerves jumping back to life, a laugh bubbling out of her. With a squeal, she turned and ran out of the bathroom, but she didn't make it far. One large arm wrapped around her midsection and hauled her up against Micah. He was warm, pleasantly, and he smelled of the oil he had poured into the bath. The combination was as intoxicating as champagne.

He easily turned her and hefted her over his shoulder. She laughed and he smacked her rear end. It stung, just a bit, but it definitely didn't hurt. If anything, it sent another trail of heat racing through her veins. He settled his hand against her ass and caressed it. The calluses on his hand sent an extra tingle of arousal through her.

He reached the bed and dropped her there. She squeaked as she bounced off the mattress.

Micah took hold of her waist and turned her over onto her stomach.

"You need to learn how to follow orders, woman."

She couldn't help but smile. His voice had deepened and it skimmed over the word woman. Shivers of anticipation showered over her flesh as she waited. He moved his hand to the small of her back, holding her still. She wanted to move, needed to. And the little imp in her couldn't fight it. She wiggled her hips against the bed. The brush of the sheets against her sex heightened her arousal. But nothing could have prepared her for the smack to her ass.

His hand connected, the palm of it hitting her right cheek. She squeaked again, then groaned as vibrations spilled through her body and straight to her clit. She was already swollen from her last release.

Smack.

Another wave of heat spread over her flesh.

Smack.

Her nipples tightened, throbbed. Damn. She needed to relieve the pressure, so she moved her hands up under her. Apparently, Micah had suspected she would do it.

"Don't. I did not give you permission."

The total control in his voice heightened her arousal. The discipline was there, but unleashed need vibrated in the background. Knowing he was turned on, that he wanted her as much as she wanted him, had another gush of liquid filling her sex. She would be embarrassed, but at the moment, the only thing she worried about was her release.

She didn't immediately comply and he slapped her ass again, harder.

"You don't obey me and I will make you pay, Dee. It'll be much longer before I allow you to come."

That threat had her moving her hands away from her clit. She might not know the total power of Micah personally, but she'd seen him work with subs at the club, and the man was insanely patient. Enough to do just what he threatened.

"Good girl."

She frowned at the term and stiffened her back, which pulled a chuckle from Micah.

"Oh, you are too much fun."

With one last hard smack, the hardest of all of them, he pulled her off the bed, sat down and then laid her over his legs. His erection was against her side, his hands skimming over her ass. Her flesh was still stinging from his spanking and the caress caused it to tingle even more.

"I've wondered just how fine an ass you had. I knew it was fine, but damn, woman, you have the purest skin.

He slipped his finger between her cheeks and she stiffened again.

"I want to take your ass. I know you would enjoy it."

She said nothing as he continued down to her sex, dipping a finger into her wet core. Her muscles tightened on him, and her swollen walls shivered around his digit. God, she wanted him again. She wanted to feel his cock deep inside her, stretching her again. Even thinking about it, remembering the way it felt to have him deep within her, had a rush of arousal shimmering through her.

He wet his finger and then pulled it back up to her anus. "I am going to try a plug on you. Not today, but soon. I cannot wait to be fucking that sweet little pussy of yours with your ass plugged up."

She should have been appalled. Naughty talk of any kind had never really turned her on. But then she had never been this far with a man. Maybe being with Micah, losing her virginity, allowed her to appreciate it.

He slipped his finger between her cheeks, teased her puckered hole and she tensed. She couldn't help it. His other fingers threaded through her hair as he leaned down.

"Relax, baby." The soft words, the way they rolled over the word baby had her melting. He slid his finger into her ass, and it was definitely a different feeling, but she wasn't sure she liked it.

He didn't push her though. Instead, he drew his delicious fingers away and smacked her ass. The already red skin burned anew, heat pushing through her. She squirmed on his lap and he groaned.

"You are so damned dangerous." He smacked her again and then pulled her up to his lap so that she was facing him. His eyes were deceptively sleepy, barely open. Not closing them, he leaned closer, took her bottom lip into his mouth and sucked on it.

"There is so much I want to do, want to experience with you, it is hard not to go faster."

She smiled at him. "You are the most patient man I know."

He chuckled. "You have no idea."

Feeling quite brazen, she rolled her hips, pressing her sex against his cock. "Why don't you show me?"

He leaned his head back and groaned. When he brought his head back up, his nostrils flared. He took her mouth in a devouring kiss, one that overwhelmed her physically and emotionally. His tongue invaded her mouth immediately and she lost any and all rational thought. It dissolved under the assault.

He pulled away before she was ready and then slid her off his lap.

"Kneel."

She was quivering with need, with an emotion that might

not have been exactly human in origin. It almost felt as if some kind of primal force was winding its way through her system. She couldn't think enough to defy him, and what's more, she didn't want to. She wanted to obey, to find pleasure in his control.

Kneeling between his legs, she watched as Micah wrapped a hand around his cock. He stroked it, slow, long. She knew he was watching her reaction. She wanted to take him in her mouth, wanted this more than anything before. It wasn't the first time she had done oral sex, but it had been over ten years. And she knew she wanted this, now. She licked her lips.

"Scoot up."

She did as ordered as he slipped his free hand around to the back of her neck to pull her down to his cock. He brought the head of his penis to her lips. He tapped it against her mouth.

"Open up and suck, baby."

The order given in such a crooning voice caused a race of tremors to move over her, through her. She opened her mouth willingly. She swiped her tongue over the head, collecting the wetness there, enjoying the sweet taste before pulling her mouth over the entire tip.

She loved hearing his groan as she slid down, taking more of him in her mouth. She added her hand, pumping him with each stroke, sliding her tongue over his penis to add to the torment. He was flexing his hips, pushing in farther, bumping the back of her throat with the head of his cock. He was close, she knew that.

"Dee, stop."

She didn't immediately stop. She was too much into the activity. But after a few more strokes, he pulled her back and tossed her onto the bed. He put on a condom, pulled her up to her knees and entered her from behind in one strong stroke.

She shivered at the intrusion. She was still sore from their first encounter, but she didn't care.

He leaned over her and kissed her shoulder. "I'm sorry. Are you okay?"

She turned her head to look at him. His hair spilled over her shoulders and onto the bed. "I'm fine."

He kissed her and then pulled away. He held her hips as he started to move. Soon her body accommodated him, and the friction of his movements had her arousal soaring to new heights. He held on to her with one hand, as he slapped her ass with his other, and then slipped his finger into her ass again. The feeling of having both holes penetrated increased her arousal. She was inching closer, spiraling higher. He reached around her and touched her clit.

"Come, now, Dee."

Panic welled up inside her at the command. She couldn't. Emotions swamped her, building a wall that kept her from falling into glorious oblivion.

"Dee, now."

He shouted the last word, the last of his restraint seemingly stripped away. He slammed into her hard, pressing against her clit, pushing her into the pleasure. She let go, allowing herself to feel. Thousands of bursts of pleasure scattered through her as she convulsed with her release. Micah shouted behind her, even as she continued to shiver.

They collapsed a short time later together on the bed. He pulled her up to the pillows and then into his arms. Her back was against his chest, his hair slipping over her body, and she started falling back to sleep.

He chuckled and kissed her temple. "No, you can't go back to sleep. Come on, baby. Let's eat."

He stood and walked into the bathroom for his clothes. It afforded her a great view of his ass.

He turned around, saw where her attention was and chuckled.

"See anything you like there, Sumner."

She smiled at him. "I see lots. But I really don't want to get out of bed."

Which wasn't like her. She wasn't someone who spent all day in bed. But...she wanted to with Micah. Not just for sex. But to cuddle, to touch, to experience being in his company.

"We need food. It's late and we're both working tonight."

She frowned at him. "Spoilsport."

He came back to the bed and placed a hand on each side of her head. "Tell you what, I'll start breakfast, then come get you."

She brushed her mouth against his. "You're the best."

"That's what I've been telling you."

He left then and she snuggled under the covers. He was the best. There was no doubt about it. What man would allow her the things he had, been so patient? Especially a Dom like Micah. The man was used to being in charge. Instead of coercion, he had used just enough seduction to get her into bed, but not too much to overwhelm her. And she knew he was doing his best to go slowly, not pushing her too much.

She sighed. She was dangerously close to falling in love with him.

ten

Micah leaned back in his chair in the office while Evan complained about something he could care less about. He hadn't heard a word for at least five minutes.

"Are you listening to me?"

Micah shook his head. "You said wedding and I tuned you out."

"I'm going to tell May you said that. I've been holding her off, but I warn you, she wants to talk to you. You're the best man and you have duties."

Micah shrugged and looked over at the screen. He thought having Dee in his bed would diffuse his infatuation. If anything, he craved her even more. Part of him thought it was the fact that she hadn't truly submitted to him. He wasn't sure when that would happen, if that would happen. He still sensed there was part of her that she wasn't showing him.

"Micah."

He glanced over at Evan with a smile. "What?"

Evan shook his head. "I'd be pissed you're ignoring me, but truthfully I am glad you finally did it."

"What?"

"I never thought you'd get her into bed."

Micah's felt his smile fade and he rolled his shoulders. He'd never had a problem talking about the women he was dating. Granted, he didn't go into details because that was just wrong. But he never had a problem with people knowing who he was sleeping with. Something about his relationship with Dee was different. It was like he wanted to keep it secret, away from prying eyes.

"I'd rather not talk about it."

Evan studied him for a second and started laughing.

"What?" Micah asked, not able to keep the irritation out of his voice.

"I love being right. God, I *love* being right."

"Right about what?"

He shook his head. "I told Chris you were stuck on her. I was right. Did you ever find out where she learned to defend herself?"

Micah looked at the screen. "Didn't really ask."

"I would if I were you, so you can be prepared if it shows up on your doorstep."

Micah nodded and said nothing. He knew better than to tell Evan he wouldn't be asking Dee. Their relationship was too fragile. With any D/s relationship, the Dom had to be careful not to order too much, want too much. Especially when this felt like the real thing.

A knot formed in his throat and he swallowed. He couldn't deal with that right now because he would just go crazy. He couldn't demand her compliance as his sub, it was wrong. He knew some did it, but it was a line he refused to cross. Especially since he felt as if this time he was playing for keeps.

"So, what do you think of the property."

"What?"

Evan sighed, got up and walked around the desk to his computer. After punching a URL into the browser, he motioned toward the screen.

"That."

Micah looked at it. It was near Sunset Beach, a little rundown, but had a lot of parking and he recognized the area. They would get a lot of touristy business. "That might do. What are they asking?"

Evan named the price and Micah frowned. "A little high for that area, doncha think?"

"Yeah, and especially for the state of the building. It's been sitting open for about three years. So, I'll talk them down if you're interested."

"How about we take a drive out there tomorrow, look it over?"

"Sounds good." Something caught Evan's attention. "I don't think I've seen that guy in here before."

Micah turned around and saw a man built like a prize fighter leaning over the bar and flirting with Dee. He watched as she smiled, took his order and set it in front of him.

"Not that I know some of the newer members."

Micah barely bit back a growl as the man settled his hand on top of Dee's.

"Whoa, son, you need to settle down."

His head whipped around as he narrowed his eyes at Evan. "Mind your own fucking business."

"You can't go down there and make a scene. Dee won't like it, and it won't be good for business."

"Let me ask you something, Evan. If there was a man touching May like that, flirting, what would you do?"

The look on Evan's face was enough. Micah stood and strode around the desk.

"Just remember to be diplomatic."

He ignored his friend, who followed him down the stairs and onto the main floor of activity. As he approached the bar, he saw the man lean over and watch Dee walk down the bar, his attention roving down her body.

"I'm going to kill him."

"No, you aren't. You're going to have to learn to suppress the need to hurt other men if we plan on staying open."

He pushed away from his friend, determined to find out just what the fuck was going on.

Dee knew the moment that Micah had entered the main floor area. It was like they were even more connected now than before. She smiled at the Irishman who was flirting with her as she tried to ignore the low hum of arousal filtering through her blood because Micah was in the vicinity. The Irishman was gorgeous, with skin the color of cocoa, dreadlocks down to his shoulders, and the most unusual green-blue eyes.

"I assume you're new to Rough 'n Ready?"

He smiled. "Yes. Here on holiday with the Mrs. She bought one of the nightly passes as an anniversary present."

Nightly passes allowed people to check it out, but not at full membership. They couldn't play in any of the rooms and the blue armband told other full-fledged members they were on a night pass.

"Lucky you." She noticed him looking around. "First time in a club like this."

He laughed. "Is it that obvious?"

"Naw. I've been working here for two years, so I pick up on the cues."

Just then, a woman—better yet, an Amazon—walked up beside him with a smile. She was almost as tall as her husband, with long wavy black hair and green eyes. She wasn't just pretty, she was almost model gorgeous.

"I'll take a shot of whiskey, straight up." She was American, probably from somewhere in the south from the accent.

Dee went to get her drink and turned right into a massive wall of muscle. She looked up, but Micah wasn't looking at her. He was giving the stare of death to the new patrons.

"Micah."

"What?" He growled the question. Of course, he was still looking at their customers.

She rose to her tiptoes so that her mouth was near his ear. "Stop looking like that. They're here for the night, for their anniversary. Having you stalk me behind the bar makes it hard to do my job."

His frown turned darker as he shifted his focus to her.

"He touched you."

"Oh, get over yourself. Just a little flirting. If I had to mention every time a woman flirted with you, we would never get anywhere. And from the look on his face, he's crazy in love with the Amazon he's with."

He glanced over, took in the situation, and his entire body

seemed to relax. She followed his line of vision, and found the husband almost devouring the wife at the bar.

"I would have never thought you would be the jealous type."

He sighed. "I'm not. Or I wasn't." When he looked at her the apology was easy to see.

"Listen, even if he has a sexy Irish accent, I can resist him. I survived almost twenty-eight years with my virginity intact. I mean you were good, but you definitely didn't turn me into a nympho."

He said nothing for a second and then chuckled. "I failed at my objective."

"Go away. I need to work."

He kissed her nose and then turned and joined Evan, who had been waiting for him at the end of the bar. The other owner winked at her and then followed Micah through the crowd.

She sighed as she went back to work. This was getting more and more complicated by the minute. The man was dangerous, to her head, to her heart.

"He's a big man to handle."

She looked up at the Amazon and smiled. "Yeah, and he knows it. Where'd hubby go?"

She rolled her eyes. "To the bathroom and then we're leaving. He's a bit too conservative sometimes."

As if on cue, her husband appeared by her side. "Ready to go, love?"

She rolled her eyes again. "Sure."

She watched the couple leave with another sigh. She could never have that, and for the first time in her life she regretted it. Micah was making her want things that could never be. And that was more dangerous than anything he could ever ask of her.

eleven

Three days later, Dee climbed the stairs to Micah's office, her back aching, her body so exhausted she wasn't sure she could make the drive home. It had been a hard few days. Two of her bartenders had caught the stomach flu, so there was a good chance it would blow through the club workers. It was going to be a long few weeks.

She knocked once, and then entered to find Micah working on his computer. The man was like the machine. He never seemed to need time off, never seemed to get tired, and she knew he was older than she was.

"How old are you?"

He hit a few keys and then looked up at her smiling. "You aren't supposed to ask that, right?"

"Nope, just can't ask women," she said, collapsing into the chair in front of his desk.

"Seems like a double standard."

"Yeah, well, when we make dollar for dollar in pay, you can keep an age a secret."

He laughed. "Thirty-five."

She frowned. "Not fair."

"What?"

"You have all this energy. I am ready to pass out."

"You stood on your feet all night. I didn't. I was up here working, and believe me, I know working behind the desk isn't as physically exhausting as working behind a bar. Plus, I knew I'd get you alone since we are both off tomorrow."

She frowned at him. "I'm not sure. With Stan and Vivi sick, we might have a few calls tomorrow."

He sighed as he rose to walk around the desk. Without a word, he plucked her out of the chair and into his arms. He turned and walked toward the back of his office. She expected him to drop back down in the chair. Instead, he hit a button beneath his desk and the wall slid open to reveal a bedroom. And not just any bedroom. It was luxury at its finest. Thick beige carpet padded his footsteps as he walked into the room. There wasn't much there. A dresser sat against the opposite wall next to the doorway to the bathroom. Dominating the room was a massive California-king bed with an ivory comforter and matching canopy. It was almost like a fairy tale.

"Wow. I had no idea you had this back here."

He walked through the doorway. "Push that button." He nodded in the direction of the white press button next to the door. She did as he asked and he walked farther into the room. "I had this put in when we built it because I knew I would spend most of my days here that first year."

"So, this was never used for...uh...other things."

His lips quirked. "No. In fact, other than letting Cynthia or May use the bathroom, you're the first woman I've had in here."

She looked at him then, saw the seriousness in his expression. The fact that his two best friends' soon-to-be wives were the only women who had been in the room did not escape her notice, or that he put her on the same level as them.

He waited, patient as always. She realized he was waiting for her to tell him differently, to contradict what he'd just said. He was waiting for her to deny him. She should. It would be the responsible thing to do. Leading him on, not letting him know that she would soon be gone, had to be gone, it wasn't the right thing to do. But she didn't want to give him up. This thing they had, the connection that grew stronger day by day, it was intoxicating.

"So you have this massive California-king bed back here and never let me know?"

He smiled at her, walked to it and dropped her. She squealed like she always did. He seemed to love tossing her on the bed, taking delight in her reaction. He was a Dom, very demanding in bed, but there was such a playful side to his nature that it always made her melt when she thought about it.

"I'll be right back."

He left her there and went back out into the office. Dee heard him talking to someone on the phone and she realized that he was telling the rest of the bouncers to leave. When he returned, he was no longer the smiling, playful lover. The intent she saw in his eyes had her heart turning over.

"I think you're ready for another step, Dee."

His voice was harder, a little distant, and dammit, it made her whole body shiver with anticipation.

She opened her mouth as he turned his back and said, "No talking unless asked or using your safe word."

She frowned, but said nothing. She'd known he would want this, want to take another step, but she wasn't sure she was ready. Although even now the anticipation had her nipples hardening.

He pulled a few things out of the drawer but left them lying there, just out of her view. He turned around, leaned against the dresser and crossed his arms.

"Stand up." She did as he ordered. "Strip."

For a moment, she couldn't comprehend what he'd just told her to do. When she finally worked it out in her brain, she gaped at him.

"I gave you an order. Do it."

His voice didn't rise. If anything, it lowered, sliding seductively over her nerve endings. He stared at her, waiting. Again. She remembered the first night he had said something about making her strip, and now apparently he thought she was ready.

In that next instant, she realized she was. The idea of having him watch her embarrassed and excited her on a whole new level. Without breaking eye contact, she unbuttoned her vest. His gaze dipped down to her fingers. She had a feeling that with every button released, she pushed him a little further. She slipped her gaze down his body and it wasn't hard to find him gloriously aroused.

She pulled off the vest and placed it on the chair beside the bed. She did the same with her shirt, and her pants followed. Soon she was standing in front of him in nothing but matching black lace panties and bra. Thong panties to be precise. Wanting to push him a little, knowing that she would like the punishment, she turned to give him a view. She thought she heard him groan, but when she looked over her shoulder at him, he was still in the same position, watching. She reached behind her, undid the bra and tossed it on the chair with her clothes. Now she slipped her fingers beneath the lace of her panties, then slowly slid them down her legs, bending over to give him an excellent view of her ass.

This time she was sure she heard a groan.

When she turned around his gaze zeroed in on her sex.

"Spread your legs."

She did as ordered once again. He approached her then, every step measured.

"You were trying to tease me," he said as he stepped beside her. He kissed her shoulder. "You will pay for that."

His dark promise had heat bursting through her blood. He slipped his fingers between her pussy lips.

"Ah, so it does turn you on being bad. I had a feeling you were going to be the most disobedient sub I've ever trained."

He moved his fingers over her clit, brushing the tiny bundle of nerves enough to tease. He slipped his hand over her breast, skimming her nipple, and then slid his hand around her neck and turned her head toward him. He kissed her then. His tongue dove into her mouth immediately, taking possession. Of her mind, her body, her soul. He pulled away, leaving her waiting, wanting.

He walked back to the dresser and grabbed a few items.

"Seeing how you like to be spanked, I think we need to try something new."

When she saw the butt plug in his hand, apprehension, fear and God help her, arousal twisted through her.

"You don't like it, you have a safe word."

She looked up at him. She didn't like the way he knew her thoughts, the way he could figure out just exactly what she was thinking. It made her feel too vulnerable.

"Get on the bed, on your stomach."

She didn't do it fast enough to make him happy.

"Now."

She obeyed, her body quivering. Fear and need had her heart beating against her chest.

He joined her, kneeling beside her. She heard the cap of something open, and a moment later she felt the cool gel of lubricant as he slipped his finger into her anus.

"Take a deep breath and relax."

He worked his finger all the way in and then started to move in and out of her puckered hole. Just like before, it sent a tidal wave of shivers ping ponging through her body. She liked the experience, had a feeling of what was coming later on. The anticipation had another coat of her juices wetting her sex.

Soon he moved his finger out and replaced it with the plug. It was a little bigger, but again, he went slowly, allowing her body to accustom itself.

Once it was in all the way, he said, "So, now you need to be punished."

His voice was controlled, but there was a thread of lust shimmering there. Dee wiggled and he slapped her ass. The hard hit stung, sending spikes of pain and arousal through her. It vibrated against the plug in her ass, then feathered out.

"You like to tease too much. Way too much."

He smacked her harder on her other cheek. The sting made her clench her cheeks together. With the plug in, it intensified her reaction.

He smacked her twice more. Her clit throbbed and her pussy wept with her arousal. She wanted to squirm, needed to rub against something to relieve the tension. But she knew that he would add to the torment.

He moved from the bed. She knew from the sounds that he

was removing his clothes. Soon his hands slipped over her hips and turned her onto her back.

He smiled down at her. "You're learning your place."

She wanted to say something. He laughed as he bent down and gave her a hard, quick kiss. "You're a joy."

The whispered words melted her irritation and made her sigh. They zeroed in on her heart, warmed her soul. He slipped down her body, settling between her legs. He set his mouth against her sex as he twisted the plug in her ass. The twin movements had her body humming. When his tongue thrust into her slit, she almost came there and then. He tasted her, groaning against her pussy. It sent a rush of vibrations over her slit, her body.

He wasted no time before moving up her body, donning a condom and then thrusting into her. She winced at the feeling of fullness, and he bent down.

"I'm sorry, love. I didn't even think."

With the plug in, he felt even larger. He started to move then, his movements slow, easy, frustrating. She wanted to come. She wanted to come right then. But she couldn't until he allowed it. He picked up speed and their bodies slapped together. She skimmed her hands up his arms, threaded her fingers into his hair and pulled him down for a hot, wet kiss.

As she did, she raised her legs around his waist. He groaned against her mouth and his speed increased. Satisfaction filled her as she felt his tension build. She was close, her body ready to release, and with one hard thrust, he pushed her over the edge. She pulled away from him and screamed his name.

He rose to his knees, pulling her up as he changed the direction of his thrusts. She wasn't even recovered from her first orgasm and he had her hurdling over into another one. This time, he joined her, groaning her name as he came.

He collapsed on her and she grunted from the hit.

"Damn, Micah, you weigh a ton."

He laughed. "I think I might be dead."

He turned his head to look at her. The warm look in his eyes had her body shivering. At the same time, her heart wept. She never wanted to leave. She wanted to see that sleepy smile every day of her life. Dammit, this was one of the reasons she should have never started this. Loving him could get them both killed. Without warning, tears sprung to her eyes.

He frowned. "Are you okay?"

She nodded. "It's just been kind of a long day."

He said nothing as he rolled her over and removed the plug. He rose from the bed and walked into the bathroom. She couldn't help but admire the way his backside flexed with each step. A moment later, she heard the water running and then turn off. He was smiling when he came back to her, that same warm look in his eyes. Slipping in next to her, he pulled her into his arms.

Gently, he brushed his mouth over hers. "Sleep. Don't worry."

Loose with her release, relaxed beyond belief, she allowed sleep to tug her into dreams.

twelve

Micah.

Micah groaned the moment he heard Harry's voice over the intercom. He cracked an eyelid up, noticed it wasn't even noon and closed his eye. He didn't want to move. He wanted to bury himself in the warmth of the bed, feel Dee's body next to his. He had never felt this attached to a lover, never overwhelmed each time he had her in bed with him. Only with Dee.

"You better answer him. He won't go away." Dee's voice was filled with sleepy warmth.

"You just want to go to sleep without interruption."

She smiled. "There is that."

He rolled her over and rose above her, pinning her arms beneath his. "I should spank you for that."

She smiled. "If I'm lucky."

And just like that, he wanted her, needed her like she was some kind of fucking drug his system craved. What was it about this woman? Yearning for a connection, he leaned down and kissed her.

Micah.

Harry's voice had risen an octave. Micah sighed against her lips. "Don't move." He jumped out of bed, grabbed his jeans and pulled them on. "I'll see what he wants and I'll be right back."

"Don't worry." She settled back against the pillows. "I'll take advantage of the break and take a cat nap."

She rolled back over onto her stomach and burrowed into the pillows, sighing with pleasure. And just like that, his heart dropped to his knees. He stood there, watching her slip into sleep, his shirt dangling from his hands, and his head barely able to comprehend what he'd just figured out.

Dammit, he was definitely up to his eyeballs in love with the woman.

He wanted to tell her, tell her right this moment, but he knew he didn't have the time. Instead, he put on his shirt and walked to the bed. Leaning down, he brushed his mouth over her cheek.

"Be right back, fighter."

She smiled and then it faded as she drifted into deeper sleep.

As he slipped out the door to his outer office, he pulled his mind back from the woman in the bed and the ramifications of his feelings. He'd take care of the problem, then he would do everything in his power to let the woman know how he felt. If he was stuck with the feelings, there was no reason she shouldn't have to suffer also.

By the time he made it to the lobby of the club, Harry was on the intercom once more. He had a feeling he'd probably woken up Dee again, but then Dee would figure out a way to pay Harry back later.

Next to Harry stood a tall blond man. He was dressed in a suit, which meant he wasn't from the area. Hawaiians weren't into dressing up with long sleeves, and this guy looked a little too intense.

"I'm here, Harry."

Harry whipped around, his eyes wide with a mixture of fear and irritation.

"Ah, Micah, this is Conner Dillon and he had some questions to ask you. I said I could answer them, but he said he only wanted you. I tried to tell him you were, uh, busy, but he wouldn't let it go."

"It's okay, Harry. You can go." Harry tossed a nasty look at the man, which was pretty impressive considering that Harry was three inches shorter and there was no way he was as lethal as the man who stood before Micah. This one had the look of a man who knew how to defend himself.

"Do you want to tell me what this is regarding?"

He shook his head. "I would rather talk in private. The things I need to say do not need to be overheard."

Micah sighed, thinking of the woman up in bed, and the fact this looked like it would take longer than he wanted it to.

"Come on."

He wouldn't be nice. He didn't want to. He wanted to be back in bed with the woman who had turned his world upside down. Micah said nothing as they walked up the stairs to his office.

He closed the door behind Dillon and motioned toward the chairs. He didn't offer him a drink.

"I guess you're going to tell me what you want."

"Is there a reason for the animosity?"

"You smell like a cop." Micah shrugged. "I don't like cops."

"Fair enough, but I'm a former FBI agent, not a cop. Now I run a security firm."

He pulled out his wallet and offered Micah a business card. Micah took it and read the name, his eyebrows rising.

"Not just a security firm, but one of the top security firms in the country."

Dillon shrugged.

"So, what do you want with me. I have no need of your services."

Dillon glanced at the monitors that filled the room. "Yeah, I can see that. What I have to talk to you about is personal."

"Look, if you want a membership you don't have to talk to me."

Conner laughed and pulled up the briefcase he had been carrying. "No. This goes back to my FBI days." He unlocked the case and pulled out some pictures. "I wanted to know if you know a woman named Marjorie Rizzoli?"

Micah shook his head.

"I know you know Dee Sumner."

He felt his heart constrict, but he made sure he showed none of his reactions on his face.

"Yes."

He saw no reason to deny it, because if Dillon knew, then he would paint him a liar.

He set a picture on his desk. Micah hesitated and then picked it up. God, it was Dee. Not the Dee he knew today, this was a teenager with big curly brown hair and a smile that told you she could take on the world. There was no way mistaking those eyes. Big, blue, luminous. Damn.

"What's this?"

"That's Marjorie Rizzoli, who has been missing the last ten years."

For a moment, his head couldn't comprehend what the man was saying.

"You show me a picture of Dee Sumner from her high school days and try to convince me she's someone else. I don't really give a damn."

He slid the picture back to Dillon, although he didn't want to. He wanted to hold it for a little while longer. It was a glimpse into a history she didn't let him see.

"No. That's Marjorie." He offered up the other piece of paper he was holding. It was a copy of a news clipping, Dee looking bewildered, surrounded by agents, being hurried along a street. Under the picture was the caption *Rizzoli's Daughter Turns Snitch.*

Shit. He remembered it now. The Italian princess whose father put a contract out on her. The FBI couldn't protect her and she was killed in a raid. It had been something he'd heard about Rizzoli after the fire that had destroyed his club. He remembered Evan saying that if Rizzoli had no problem killing his own flesh and blood, he wouldn't think twice about two nobodies like them.

Micah raised his head. "She's supposed to be dead."

Dillon grimaced. "That was my doing. It took a lot to convince the FBI to do that, to make sure that everyone did think she was dead."

"Why the fuck did you do that?"

"It was the least I could do. Jesus, thanks to a leak within the department, she was almost killed."

"That isn't how I remember it. I remember they said she had called a friend, exposing where they were."

Dillon shook his head. "Even if she had access to a phone, she wouldn't have done it. She was seriously scared of what would happen to her." He hesitated. "She saw what they did to that man. They didn't know she was there, but she watched them torture him. Or at least, heard what they did to him."

Just the thought of that seventeen-year-old in the picture hearing what they did to the man, the way he had been tortured, made Micah's blood run cold.

"So what does this have to do with me?"

"She works for you."

"Worked."

Dillon sighed, irritation thrumming in the sound.

"Dammit. She's always one step ahead of me."

"Maybe that's where she should stay. Really, Dillon, why is this your problem?"

He hesitated. "I was pulled off the case. I feel that if I had been there, they would have never got to her. And she definitely wouldn't be on her own."

Something in his voice told Micah that there was more to it than that. But he knew better than to push. It would show he had too much interest.

"Sorry. She lit out of here about two days ago. She said something about family issues and quit without notice. Odd for her, because she had always been so dependable and claimed to be at odds with her family."

Dillon nodded and reached for his card. He wrote something on the back. "Here's my personal cell. If you hear anything, anything at all, please call."

"Sure, but I doubt she would contact me. If what you say is true, she probably won't be back."

"True, but she did stay here longer than anywhere else. I thought she might have some contacts, some friends in the area. Her house didn't seem like she had left."

Micah shrugged. "I thought she had left the island, but I might be wrong."

"It would definitely be her pattern." Frustration seeped from every word Dillon muttered. Micah said nothing else as he saw Dillon to the door of the club. He wanted to make sure that Dillon didn't question anyone else. He would eventually, that much Micah knew. But Micah wanted enough time to get Dee out of here and to safety.

Before stepping out the door, Dillon turned. "Don't be heroic. The woman needs to be protected. Her father's on trial again, for the same murder, and a few other things. The DA dropped the case before because of the lack of evidence. This time they got one of the participants to turn on Rizzoli. There's a feeling that Rizzoli will do anything to avoid another trial, including finding any loose strings and cutting them."

Micah nodded. He watched until the former agent got into his rental and drove away. Then he hurried back to his office. Taking the stairs two at a time, he wanted to get to Dee, to make sure she was all right, that nothing had happened to her. His heart slammed against his chest as he pushed the door open and found the bedroom empty. The sheets were still tangled, her scent still in the air. But he realized now that she had gone out the back way.

Goddammit. Shit. Fuck.

"Micah."

He turned to find Harry watching him.

"What?"

"That guy is sitting down at the end of the street in a car."

Double fuck.

"Thanks for letting me know."

"Is everything all right?"

Micah shook his head. "No. But I am going to make damn sure I fix it."

Harry left him alone and Micah sunk down onto the bed. She had run. Not trusting him, she had run. It was bad enough that she had lied to him. Dammit, he was pissed and he had every right to be pissed. The woman he loved had been lying to him all along.

But fear was easily bleeding into his fury. She was out there, and he couldn't get to her. He wasn't sure he could shake Dillon. Granted, there was a good chance he could, but he wasn't sure. He didn't trust the man. He was a cool one, but to have tracked her for ten years...that was a little obsessive. What was it that Dee had said?

People could be bought.

There was every chance the man had been bought by her father. Conner might have been by the house, but if Micah went there now, he would probably follow. If Micah led them to her, he would never forgive himself.

He scrubbed his hand over his face, trying to cool the raging anger coursing through his blood. He needed to make sure she was okay. He needed to touch her. He needed to spank her ass red for lying to him. A lie by omission was still a lie.

Micah reached for the phone and called the one person he knew he could trust. He answered on the third ring.

"Evan. I need your help."

Dee turned in to her driveway, almost running over her mailbox. She gave it no thought as she scrambled out of the car. She should have run weeks ago, but she hadn't had the nerve. Couldn't. She dropped her keys on the porch, twice, then finally got her door open. She rushed inside and slammed it behind her. She listened, waiting for any creak, any evidence that someone was here. Dammit, she had been stupid. Now and then. She'd rushed into a house without first checking it out. After what she had heard in the office, she should be on alert.

But she couldn't stop the fear bubbling in her chest. It wasn't only her safety, but the fear that Micah would hate her. He hated liars, he had told her that. And that is what she was. A liar, a cheat, a dumb girl who still couldn't take care of herself.

She felt another tear trickle down her cheek. Shit. She was crying again. The man, the situation...she hadn't cried much in the last ten years. She hadn't had the time. But now she didn't seem to do much else.

She would have to leave. She had known that for weeks, had felt it was time to move on. But that would have meant giving up the time she'd had with Micah, and she hadn't wanted to do that. Even now, there was an ache in her chest that was worse than the fear pumping through her blood. She had no choice. She couldn't trust Dillon. He'd been the one she'd turned to time and again, until he'd left. And then they were attacked. She had figured out there had to have been a leak. John had been right. Someone had told her father's men where she was.

With a sigh, she walked quickly through her house gathering her things. She always kept a case ready to go, cash handy and a whole identity waiting to be used. She walked into her bedroom, pulled the case out and opened it. She reached for her book, knowing she would need something to help her ignore the way her heart was hurting. But as she reached out, a large hand wrapped around her wrist and another slipped over her mouth.

"About time you got home, sis."

thirteen

Micah grimaced when he walked through Dee's house. Nothing much looked out of place, except the bedroom. A suitcase sat on her bed, her clothes still in her opened drawers.

Evan walked up behind him. "She ran."

Micah shook his head even as the fear he felt choked him. "Look."

Evan stepped in the room and whistled. "She left without a pack. That doesn't look good."

They both knew how she had been living. They had never been hiding from a murderous brother and father. But they had always tried to stay one step ahead of trouble when they had been living on the streets in Atlanta.

Micah forced himself to walk around the room, his footsteps almost silent. He was careful not to mess with anything. He wanted everything left just like this, so he could figure out where she was and who had her.

"I take it you're going after her?"

"She's been abducted, Evan. Of course I am."

Evan sighed. "You would be going after her even if she'd run."

Micah raised his gaze. "I love her."

"Yeah, that much is easy to see. Well, you track her down. If anyone can do it, you can. I'll take care of things here, and maybe we can do something more to that Dillon guy."

Micah smiled a bit at the memory. They'd pulled the old banana in the tailpipe to get out of the club. Dillon would probably not be happy.

He looked over the room and then opened her closet. His blood ran cold. There in the corner was a wrapper, potato chips. Salt and vinegar. He remembered the face she made, saying her brother had loved them. Shit. The bastard had been lying in wait to grab her.

He would kill him.

"Let's go to the airport."

Evan looked over at him. "Why?"

"If they left the island they would have taken a plane."

Two hours later, he had the information he needed.

"Not very bright using a private jet," Evan said.

"Never said that family was very bright. She ran right into the arms of the family she was trying to avoid." Micah bit out every word, trying to keep his irritation and fear at bay.

"Not like she did it on purpose."

"She should have known."

Evan glanced at the security line. "Listen, don't be too hard on her. She doesn't know anything else."

Micah frowned. "Don't even try and get me on her good side. Once I get her, I am definitely going to make sure that she understands who is in charge. I still can't believe she ran."

If anything happened to her...a lump rose in his throat. God, he couldn't think about it. If he did, he would go crazy.

"I know how you feel. I went through all that with May."

Micah looked at him.

"Just go easy."

"You want me to be soft?"

Evan sighed and shook his head. "I just keep remembering something May said about her. She mentioned that Dee always looked like she was on the outside of every group, looking in. She wanted to be there, wanted to be one of the group, but she held herself back."

Another twist of pain filled his chest. That was exactly how she'd always looked. Micah wanted to kick his own ass. He knew now he'd been worried about asking too much, worried that she would leave him. The fear had kept him from finding just what darkness lurked in her life. Why hadn't she told him?

"She probably didn't have a choice," Micah said.

Evan nodded. "But as Dillon said, she stayed here longer than any other place. There has to be a reason."

"She liked her job."

"I'm sure that's what it was." Evan rolled his eyes. "You might not have been the reason she stayed here to begin with, but I can almost guarantee that you are the reason she has stayed for the last few months. She might have made a mistake, panicked and put herself at risk. While you make sure that she understands what she did was wrong, just make sure she understands how you feel."

Micah wanted to scoff at it, but he couldn't. Anger and fear tightened his gut. His emotions were raw, scorched. He couldn't come up with the words, didn't want to embarrass himself. He wanted to pour out every worry he had, but it would do him no good. Instead, he gave Evan a hug and stepped up to the security line.

He had one thing on his mind by the time he made it through.

Micah would kill the man who dared touch her.

With bone-deep weariness, Micah walked down the hall of Caesar's Hotel. Jesus, they were in a villa. He couldn't believe that after two days of not sleeping, following every lead, making sure no one was following him, he had arrived in Vegas to find out his woman was hanging out in luxury.

He was going to beat her ass red.

Of course, that was after he broke a few major appendages on her brother.

He followed the bellhop he'd paid down the hallway. Damn, he got angrier with each step. He wanted to think she had been having fun. But knowing her family, he was worried what he would find inside. As he'd been searching for her, Evan had done some research, and what he had found had chilled Micah to the core. He was amazed that such a sweet, loving woman had survived the pit of vipers she'd grown up with.

"D-do you want me to knock?"

Micah looked at the man and nodded. He hesitated and then did it.

"Yes?" a male voice said from behind the door.

The bellhop cleared his throat. "I have a package for you."

There was a pause. "Give me a sec."

The door opened slightly a second later. Micah shoved the bellhop aside, pushed through the small opening in the door and came face to face with Dee's brother. Dark hair, blue eyes, built like a fucking linebacker. Rage that had been building for two days rose up and took over. Before Micah knew what he was doing, before checking the room for more danger, or even looking for Dee, he wrapped his hands around the man's neck.

He struggled against Micah's grasp, his hands clawing at Micah's fingers. He swung his legs trying to kick Micah. Her brother missed, but both of them went sprawling onto the marbled floor with a thud, a hard whoosh of air escaping from the younger man. Micah held him down with one hand and smashed his face with his fist. The nauseating sound of bone cracking when Micah made contact fueled his anger. He heard a shout from the bellhop but he ignored him.

"Micah."

Someone was tugging on his arm. He ignored it for a few more seconds, as he hit her brother a few more times.

He turned to snarl when he realized it was Dee. All the hours of panic and anger welled up inside him. But he pushed it aside.

She was safe. She was alive.

He dropped her brother with a thump and rose to his feet. He grabbed her, pulled her against him and slammed his mouth down onto hers. Everything in him shifted. His heart warmed and the terror he had been riding for two days now drained. When he pulled back, he saw the tears in her eyes.

"Ah, baby, don't cry." He pulled her close and breathed in her scent. "I'm sorry. I didn't kill him, just hurt him a little."

"You broke my fucking nose."

He gave her a squeeze and then shoved her behind his back. He faced off with her brother. Blood dripped from his nose and stained his T-shirt. It gave Micah a sick satisfaction to see it, to know that he made the man suffer.

"You're lucky you're breathing, Petey."

His eyes widened at the name. "I'm not Petey."

"You're her brother."

He nodded and opened his mouth to answer, but Dee stopped him. Slipping in front of Micah, she looked up at him, her eyes filled with tears and happiness. "It's Mark. He's alive."

Dee couldn't stop touching Micah. Since she'd woken up over the Pacific, she'd been so worried about what he was thinking. Worse, she had been worried that her father could have found her and then found Micah. After Mark explained the situation, that her father was busy killing off anyone who could have knowledge of what had happened, she knew she couldn't go back. With each mile east, her heart had broken a little more.

Once Mark had paid off the bellhop to forget everything he'd seen, they had settled in the living room of the villa.

"Could you quit petting him?" Mark asked, disgust and embarrassment dripped from each word.

"I like it," Micah said with an evil smile. "Now, pick up where you tell me just why the hell you thought it was a good idea to abduct your sister."

Mark sighed. No, Dee thought. His name was Devon now. She had to remember that. Dee and Devon. The names still tickled her.

"I thought it would be best. I've been watching Dillon for a while now. I knew he was looking for her. When his sister and business partner took a trip to Hawaii, that was no big deal, but when Dillon booked the flight, I knew something was up."

"Dillon will be pissed when he finds out you were keeping tabs on him, and he didn't know it," Dee said.

Devon nodded. "But then I have the money and brains to do it."

"Did I tell you? He is the inventor of Striker Force One, the reality game?"

Micah gave her an understanding smile and patted her hand. "Yes, you did, love. But your brother abducting you and taking you on a private jet wasn't smart. Of course, holing up in Caesar's at one of the villas is definitely worse."

His voice was lethally soft, and she could tell from his expression he was barely holding on to his temper. Mark/Devon shrugged. "Not like anyone knows who I am. They think I'm Devon Striker. That's it. Not like we're going down to gamble every night. And I know for a fact my father still thinks I'm dead."

"So you fly to Hawaii, scoop up your sister, then neither of you thinks to contact me, tell me what is going on? You didn't think I would worry?"

"I wanted to, but M-Devon told me that it would put you in danger."

"And I don't like you."

She sent her brother a narrowed look. "I was leaving that out."

"That's okay, Striker. I don't like you either."

Devon looked away, out the window. "I don't know what the fuck Dillon was looking for, why he wants to find you so badly."

"I wondered about him for years, but really? I mean, they think I'm dead. And from what Micah said, Dillon is the one who convinced the FBI to pretend that I was dead."

Micah shook his head. "No, I got the same feeling."

Devon looked over at him. "There's something there. Something he doesn't tell anyone. But there was a reason he was pulled off the case."

She frowned and crossed her arms over her chest. "He was the one who gave me all the running options. He and John, but mostly him. He trained me to fight. Well, started it at least."

Micah shrugged. "While it pains me, I have to agree with your idiot brother. We can't trust anyone. And I mean no one."

He yawned and she noticed the dark smudges under his eyes, the fact that his entire body seemed to be shutting down.

"Hey, why don't you take a shower?"

He shook his head. "We need to discuss our options."

"I agree. But you can barely keep your eyes open. You haven't had sleep in forty-eight hours. Take a shower, clear your head and then we can talk some more. We need to get some food in ya too."

He smiled, cupped her face and kissed her. It wasn't the ravenous kiss he had offered earlier, but one of tenderness, sweetness...and love. She could taste it there, hoped she wasn't fooling herself. When he pulled back, he smiled at her. "I'll be right back."

She watched him walk to her room.

"He's not who I would pick for you."

She turned around to face her brother. "I didn't ask."

He laughed. "You haven't changed."

She felt her smile fade along with the lightness of the moment. So many questions had not been answered. They'd been tiptoeing around the past as if it didn't exist, or if one of them mentioned it, the other wouldn't be able to handle it. "But I have. You can't go through that without changing."

Regret shifted over his face. "I'm so sorry. I should have never left you there."

She waved her hands at him. "What? You were supposed to give up the opportunity to go to school early, get out of the house that drove you crazy?"

"I knew Dad was ruthless, I had no idea."

She snorted. "Neither of us did. I think Petey was the only one who knew. Probably because he is as sick as our father."

There was a beat of silence. "Was he there?"

Dee stood and walked away from the table, away from the feelings she still hadn't dealt with. She stared out over the strip as the last rays of sun disappeared over the brightly lit casinos.

"Yeah."

"Dee?"

She glanced over her shoulder at him, at the pleading in his eyes.

"What happened?"

She closed her eyes, that day rushing back to the front of her mind. "I was pissed at Dad. He had taken away my car keys because I'd been late on curfew again." She opened her eyes and smiled. "That's when I was dating Ken Totaro."

"You dated him? God, Dee, you had horrible taste in men."

She laughed. "He had a fast car. And he did whatever I wanted."

"Probably because he wanted in your pants."

She nodded. "So I snuck into Dad's Brooklyn office. I knew he wouldn't keep the keys at the house. I would find them there. I was searching his desk when I heard them coming up the back stairs."

She could see it as if it were yesterday. Hear the grunts, the cursing as they dragged that poor man up the stairs.

"I heard Dad's voice, and I knew he would punish me for being in his office. So I hid in the closet. I thought they would be gone in a few seconds." Tears welled up in her eyes as the man's screams filled her head. "It took over an hour, still not sure exactly how long."

She felt strong arms surround her, knew it was her brother. Not the man she needed, the one who knew just how to soothe her soul. But that would come later. "You know who it was, right? It was that sweet man who did the bookkeeping, Sam. He and his wife had just had a baby. They were just starting out in life."

"Marjorie," her old name slipped from his lips and she knew it pained him to hear, to know what she'd gone through. If he had been there, not away in England at school, would she have gone to him? She wasn't too sure. Not because she didn't trust him. But she wouldn't have wanted him dragged into it.

"They were accusing him of stealing from Daddy. And you know how he was about things like that." She leaned her head on his offered shoulder. "God, he was horrible. I saw the first fingernail they pulled and then...I closed my eyes. But no matter how much I covered my ears, I could hear him screaming. He begged for his life, begged without any kind of shame. Then... toward the end...he begged for them to kill him."

She felt his lips touch her temple. "I am so sorry. I can't..." His words trailed off as he swallowed. "After it happened, after all the news, I came home."

She nodded, knowing. She pulled away, grabbed a tissue and looked at him. Remorse and pain filled his expression. "I tried to find out just what was going on. I couldn't. Dad and Petey stonewalled me. I couldn't get to anyone. And then when you disappeared, the first time when you were in custody, that agent Dillon showed up. He told me that I should be watching my back. I sent him away, but the next day, the brakes went out on my car."

"You weren't hurt?"

"I wasn't in it. Rosalie was."

"Oh, no." His first love, his high school sweetheart, the woman he had planned on marrying. She squeezed him tighter. "I'm sorry."

He nodded. "After I got the report about the brake lines being cut, I faked my death and disappeared. I tried to keep tabs on you, but I couldn't seem to find you. Even after they said you were dead, I had a feeling you were still alive."

She nodded, feeling much older than twenty-seven. She didn't want this. She wanted to go back in time, to three days ago, snuggled up to Micah in his bed, feeling his body next to hers, his heart beating beneath her hand.

"Why don't you get some more rest? We can't do anything right now."

She nodded and leaned back to look at him. "How did we

not turn into something sick like those two? Why are we so different?"

He shook his head. "I think because once he had his first born, he didn't give a rat's ass about us. All he cared about was Petey."

"Well, thank God for that."

He laughed. "Yeah."

With a smile, he rubbed his hand through her hair. "Still can't get used to this."

"I changed a lot."

He nodded. "But you're still a pain in the ass. Go take care of your bodyguard in there."

"You really don't like him?"

He sighed. "A guy doesn't want to think about his sister and the guy she's with. In the case of you and Ross, it's worse because of what he does for a living."

"It's not like he performs anymore."

Devon closed his eyes then opened them. "Listen, I don't care about that, much. But knowing who he is, that he has a large business based on his sexual needs, I know what he likes in the bedroom. And you're the one in there with him."

She chuckled as she walked toward her room. "I'll keep that in mind."

"Tell Ross I'm going to take first watch."

She paused and looked at her brother. He was the same in so many ways. He was good, honest, smarter than he should be, and dependable. But there were edges there. Ones she understood, ones she felt in her own life now. Their lives hadn't afforded them many good things in life. But despite that, what he had suffered, the way he had to live now, he was still a good man.

"I love you."

He glanced back at her, his gaze softening. His nose was swollen and his lip was puffy, but he attempted to smile. "I love you too. Shorty."

She smiled, his regular name for her when they were kids warming her heart. She slipped into the bedroom and found Micah passed out on the bed. It had seemed huge when she'd arrived, but now that he was stretched across it, it seemed so tiny. His hair was still wet and she knew without a doubt he was naked beneath the covers. Her body yearned for his. She had discovered she didn't like sleeping without Micah by her side.

Tears welled up again in her eyes. Dammit, she hated that. She couldn't help it. He'd come for her. He had searched for her, found her and walked into what he thought was danger to save her. Her heart warmed at the thought.

She had known she cared for him, more than any man in her life. When she thought of her reasoning, that it was because he was her first, that she'd grown attached, she smiled. She knew now she was hip-deep in love with the man. He didn't like attachments and he definitely had never said anything about loving her. *Tough*, she thought as she pulled her T-shirt over her head. She shimmied out of her shorts and went to join him in bed. The guy was just going to have to get used to having her around. When this was all cleared up, she would just refuse to give him up.

She snuggled against him, her body sighing with relief at his body heat surrounding her. She settled her head against his shoulder and closed her eyes.

It was only a few moments before she felt his hand slip down her body, his fingers dancing over her flesh.

"I thought you were asleep."

"Kind of hard to do that with you thrashing about like a hoard of elephants." His voice was gravelly, tired. She knew it wouldn't take much for him to fall asleep so she tried to stay as still as possible. "Besides, not sure I could sleep knowing you would be beside me tonight."

"I'm sorry I worried you."

He kissed her forehead. "We'll talk about it later. And we will, but I don't think either of us is up to handling your punishment tonight."

Even as tired as she was, her body tingled at the promise in his voice. He tugged her on top of him. She sighed when she felt his erection nestled against her sex. He slipped his hands up to cup her face. Brushing his thumbs over her cheeks, he pulled her down and kissed her. Here was the passion, the need she was used to. His tongue thrust into her mouth.

He pulled away, and rested his forehead against hers.

"Don't ever run again." Every word seemed to be pulled from some dark place inside of him. His voice vibrated with anger...and fear.

She could feel the last few days well up, spill over as tears. "I'm sorry. I heard Conner's voice and I panicked. I didn't really think."

"I'm not asking you to think. Just to trust me."

"I do."

He shook his head. "In bed you do, I know that. But if you don't trust me outside, then it cheapens what we do here."

Her vision blurred.

"Oh, baby, don't cry. Please. I didn't mean to make you sad."

"No. No, you didn't. I am so sorry. It is just, I couldn't help reacting. Before I could even think straight, Devon was there."

She felt him swallow. "I don't think I will ever get over walking into your house and finding it that way."

She heard the pain there, the anger, but there was something else, something that touched her heart. Fear. He had been afraid for her. It was odd to be warmed by his fear. But to have a person care enough that they would worry about your safety, damn, it had been a long time. Besides her brother, she'd never had that from the opposite sex.

"I'm sorry." She kissed his chin and then brushed her mouth over his. "I'm so sorry," she repeated against his lips.

He rolled them in bed, his body hard with desire, with need for her, to join with her. She understood, knew exactly what he was feeling.

"Let me love you," he said.

fourteen

Micah kissed his way down her body, her smooth skin sweet beneath his lips. Now that he knew she was safe, he needed this. It was worse after hearing her tell her brother what had happened. He had a feeling that she hadn't told another person outside of the FBI. The heart break in her voice had been easy to hear, and he had felt it as if he'd been knifed in the chest.

He had wanted to gather her up there, but he had known that brother and sister had needed their time together. His plan was to wait until morning. But she had been here, undressing, her body against his...he couldn't resist.

He slipped between her legs and breathed in her scent. It was the most wonderful fragrance in the world. Unique. Seductive. *Dee*.

He spread her legs and cursed the fact the light was off. He wanted to see her, see that gorgeous pussy glistening with her need for him. She was beyond aroused. He could tell even before setting the flat of his tongue against her pussy lips. Lord almighty. He didn't think there would ever be a time that he would be able not to have her.

He laved her cunt, groaning as her essence drifted over his taste buds.

"Micah." She breathed his name, her need threading through her whispered plea.

She slipped her hands through his hair, molding her fingers to the back of his head. Always ready to please her, to do anything to make her happy, he pressed his tongue over her clit, nudging the hardened nub with the tip. He did it again and again, knowing that it wasn't enough to make her come. As he continued his assault, he slid his thumb to her pussy, gathered her juices and then pressed it against her anus.

She moaned his name. Long. Loud. It was enough to make a man come just from the sound. He continued, and eased his finger into her anus, knowing how much she loved it, how hot she got when he did it.

He didn't think he could wait, knew he couldn't. He stopped long enough to don a condom and then joined her back on the bed. Needing the connection, to be inside of her, he rose to his knees, pulled her hips up and entered her with one hard thrust. She gasped then moaned as he started to move. He knew his control was slipping, and for once he didn't care. He needed to feel her come, feel her go over the edge. He thrust into her, over and over, pushing both of them closer.

He felt his release coming upon him at the moment she fell over the edge. Her muscles contracted around his cock, tugging him deeper, pulling his own orgasm from him. He shouted her name as his orgasm burst through him and then let himself fall into oblivion.

Micah closed the bedroom door behind him as softly as possible. He didn't want to wake Dee. The moment he'd pulled her against him, she had passed out. He could have stayed there, snuggled deep beneath the covers, if he would've been able to keep his hands off Dee. He knew she would never deny him. But she needed sleep. He required it too, but at the moment, too much stuff was still running around in his head. And he wanted to be sure that he talked to Devon without Dee around.

Micah hadn't paid attention to the suite before, but now it hit him just how huge it was. Damn, it was probably bigger than the apartment he kept in Honolulu. The living area was sunken, with a bar to the right and a bank of windows that allowed for a wonderful view of the Vegas strip. He found her brother sitting there. Devon was looking out the windows. Micah took a second to study him. There was a lot of resemblance in his face. Although their coloring was different, they had the same stubborn chin.

"Are you going to stand there in the dark or join me for a drink?"

He smiled. "Most people can't hear me."

"I'm not most people." Again, he didn't turn around.

Micah took the chair opposite of him. "Who trained you?'

He glanced out of the corner of his eye, a look that he had seen from Dee. "What do you mean?"

"Please, don't bullshit me. You're trained. FBI. Military. Someone. Like I said, most people don't hear me, unless they're trained."

He looked back out the window and took a long pull off his water bottle. "I was at a special training school for the CIA. I wasn't at school in England when all this went down. They had me in training twelve hours a day. That's why I didn't hear about any of it."

"With your family background, it's amazing that you got in."

He nodded. "They didn't really care. I was considered a sort of wunderkind, and the CIA knew my father wanted nothing to do with me. Plus, they caught me hacking into their computer systems so they figured they should bring me to their side. I'm the best hacker they ever trained, or so they said."

"So you were training, your sister almost gets killed, then what?"

"I came back for a visit...pretend school break." He laughed, but there was no humor in it. "The family told me she was away. Just away. I knew better. And so did my superiors. They knew exactly what was going on."

"And they didn't tell you."

He shook his head. "After I discovered what they had kept from me, I left school. I went in search of my sister. But by then she had been reported dead."

"But you didn't believe it."

"No."

"So you used the skills they had taught you to find her."

"And create my identity."

"Devon Striker. Creator of Strike Force One."

He nodded, his lips curling. "Bastards let me hang out at school, shut off from the world for months, not telling me what had happened to Dee. I used what they taught me to create the game."

Micah whistled. "They can't be happy about that."

"They can't link me to Devon Striker. Never have. Never will. One of my jobs was helping our operatives disappear and then set up new identities. They were the ones who made sure that I could do it. When I faked my death, I'm sure there were some who thought I might not be dead, but they knew better than to look."

"What? State secrets?"

When he looked at Micah, Devon looked much older than his twenty-seven years. "You have no idea."

Micah decided to change the subject. "So do you think this is safe? I have my reservations about it since I found you so fast."

Devon shrugged again. "Doesn't matter. She's about to disappear again."

Anger and fear curled in Micah's stomach. "Think again."

"It's the only option." Her brother's flat tone let Micah know he was serious. Knowing his background, the bastard would be able to make her disappear.

"Your father will be going to prison. One of the guys who participated in the killing is testifying."

Devon shook his head. "No. He's dead."

Shock washed over Micah and then soured his stomach. Fucking FBI. "They still have a mole."

"Yep. Our FBI isn't doing their job. Whoever they have has been there for a while. Seems to know all the players, must have their hand in everything. I can't figure it out. Everyone comes up squeaky clean, and that is even with my computer skills."

"Either way, she's not disappearing now. And we need to move. As early as possible. This can't be safe."

"She's safe."

Micah shook his head. "You can't guarantee me that."

"You think I would put my own sister at risk?"

"Why not? You left her with that family of yours. You had a chance to escape and you took it."

He leaned his head back and sighed. It was odd, but the lonely sound reminded him of Dee's sighs. "We didn't know."

"Tell that story to someone else. Your IQ is too high not to have picked up on something. You were recruited as a teenager by the CIA, but you had no idea that your father was in the mafia? You knew and you left her."

Even in the dark, Micah could see the flash of anger in his eyes. "I didn't know."

"Bullshit."

Devon sighed. "I meant I never knew he did those things. I knew he was laundering money. That was obvious. But I didn't know he did things like he did to Sam."

"You knew him?"

"Yeah. He had worked as an accountant for my father for years. We grew up with him." He swallowed. "I knew Dad had a temper, but that had nothing to do with this. It was cold blooded, evil. I am sure my brother played the biggest part of it."

"And you left her alone with them."

"Fuck, I didn't know my father would go after her, okay? I knew he was ruthless, knew he would do things to get ahead. But I didn't think he would torture a man for hours, or that he would put a hit out on my sister."

The anguish he heard in her brother's voice told him that he had felt guilt for that all these years.

"What about this Dillon guy?" Micah asked.

"Clean. I thought he was stalking her because he wanted to finish the job, but after I got into some of his files—"

"His files?"

Devon smiled. "I'm a top-rate hacker."

"My tax dollars at work again?"

"Yep. Thanks for that by the way. But he was pulled off the case. That struck me as odd. It had been his case for years. He had a real hard-on for getting Dad behind bars. So I had to dig deeper. Apparently, the pervert had a thing for my sister."

Everything inside Micah went cold. "She was seventeen."

"And other than the hair and the leaner muscles, she looked like she does now."

Micah sighed. "So you don't think we should worry about him."

"My worry is that he'll lead our father's people to her. He's good, but he isn't that good. And he is former FBI. If he needed help, he might go to them."

"And that could tip off whoever's been selling her out."

Devon nodded. "Right. Why are you worried about him?"

"He'll find us here."

"No he won't. I told you—" A knock at the door interrupted Devon. He pulled out his gun and rose slowly from the chair. Micah followed him.

"You didn't order room service I take it?"

Devon shook his head.

They got to the door. "Who is it?" Devon asked through the door.

"Open up. It's Conner Dillon."

"Fuck off." Devon apparently wasn't going to be friendly.

"I know Micah Ross is in there."

Micah pushed Devon aside and looked out the peep hole. Dillon was with the black Irishman from the other night. Micah felt another person there, but he didn't see him.

"Who's with you?" he asked.

"My partner and my sister."

He put his hand on the door and felt the cold metal of Devon's gun against his neck. "You might want to think about that again."

"You said yourself that he's clean. He's here. Not like we can go anywhere. And you can shoot him if he does anything you don't like."

Devon hesitated, then nodded and moved away, but he kept his gun out.

He opened the door and found Dillon frowning at him, the man with dreads looking down the hall, and the Amazon with long inky hair and big green eyes.

"Come in." He stepped away and the entourage walked through the door.

Dillon picked up on Devon's gun right away. "Want to put that away?"

"No."

The Amazon laughed. "Oh, I like him already. Mr. Ross, I had the pleasure of experiencing your club a few nights ago."

He remembered her and the hulking man behind her from his club. He shifted his attention to Dillon. "So that's how you found her?"

"An ad."

"I found her," the woman said. "I have a facial-recognition program and I found her in your ad. Most people wouldn't since I'm the only person who has it."

The ad. He had forgotten about that. If she had told him the truth from the beginning, he would have made sure that she didn't show up in any ad.

"Conner?" the woman in question's voice filtered out over

the crowd, and even before he knew he what he was doing, Micah was moving toward her.

"Marjorie." Dillon said.

"Dee."

He opened his mouth and then snapped it shut.

"So what the hell is going on here, and just why do you all think you can discuss me as if I am a child."

Fifteen minutes later, Dee couldn't believe the crap the men in her life tried to pull on her. "Listen, I understand you all want to walk around dragging your knuckles on the ground. But someone needs to explain to me why being under this protection in Vegas is any good to me."

Micah said nothing as he sat stoically by her. And that pissed her off. Okay, that was stupid because she could take care of herself. Had for a long time. But there was a tiny part of her that wanted someone to take over. Take her away.

"You'll be safer here. Under our protection."

She thought she heard Micah call her brother a dumbass under his breath, but she ignored him.

"Really? Gee, in ten years, no one has found me. They all thought I was dead. And now, in the span of forty-eight hours, a former FBI agent, my brother and my lover all make enough of a mess of things that any idiot could find me."

"You have to know if I found you, your father could."

Dillon's simple words sent a shaft of ice to her heart. The coldness seeped into her blood. "Of course, as your sister said, no one else had that recognition program. So how would they have found me without you leading them to me?"

She thought she heard a snicker and decided it was from Conner's sister.

Devon wasn't in the mood to play nice. "I've been keeping tabs on you for years. First your sister and her boyfriend—"

"Boyfriend?" both parties said.

"Uh, I thought..."

Dee ignored them. "Finish your comment, Devon."

He pulled his attention away from the pair. "What I was trying to say was that first they went to Hawaii, then you followed less than a week later. Anyone who has any kind of tracking will know. And thanks to you, we will be on the move again."

"No," she said.

Everyone turned to her.

"You have to, honey. It will be safer that way," Devon said.

She crossed her arms over her chest. "I'm sick of running."

Conner shook his head. "Guerro is going to testify this week—"

"He's dead." Devon's announcement caused silence to fill the room.

"Fuck. How did you find out?" Conner asked.

"I have my connections."

"Or maybe you still have connections to Daddy." Conner fairly spit out the words.

Devon started for the former agent with rage burning in his gaze. Dee stepped in front of him to try and stop him. He made a mistake by pushing her aside. Before she knew what was happening, Micah was there, his large hand taking a handful of Devon's shirt and raising him off the ground.

"You want to rethink what you are doing here. And you *will* want to apologize to your sister."

Devon looked ready to fight, but Dee stepped up and put her hand on Micah's. "Put him down."

"Your brother needs to learn respect for women."

"Yeah, I agree. But he's my brother. I would really hate it if the man I love were to beat him up again."

Micah's head whipped around. He watched her, those gray eyes studying her to make sure she wasn't lying. Then he released her brother, allowing him to collapse on the floor. He pulled her into his arms and kissed her.

"While this is all nice, we need to be on the move again if Devon's information is correct. Her father is severing all ties," said Conner, always the FBI agent.

She shook her head as she snuggled closer to Micah and laid her head upon his chest. She'd made her decision. "No. What am I supposed to do, run my entire life? I can testify."

"No." That came from the two most important men in her life.

She looked up at Micah, who was grinding his teeth, then at her brother. "It's what has to be done. The only problem is getting a hold of the prosecutor. Can we trust him?"

Devon shrugged. "I guess as much as anyone. He wasn't involved in this when you disappeared, so the chances he is on the take are really slim. Even saying that, there's someone involved. Someone in the know around the FBI has been feeding your father info. Still."

"Could you find out who has been on the case? There has to be someone that is connected. We just have to find out who has been there all these years."

Devon nodded. "I can try. I worry because I left so fast, I didn't bring any of my security gear for the computer."

Maura stepped up with a smile. "That's where I come in. I have mine, and some of it is like my facial-recognition program. It's not on the market."

Devon smiled at the tall woman. Dee thought she heard a growl from Zeke, but when she looked at him, he appeared bored.

"Get to work on that. Conner, you have your connections still, right? You can contact this prosecutor?"

He nodded.

"Make sure he doesn't know where you are when you contact him. Tell him you have another witness." She sighed. "I need a shower. Come on, Micah."

He followed her into the bedroom with a smile on his lips. When he shut the door, he leaned back against it. "You liked being in control out there."

She nodded. "I did a little bit. It was more about not letting my father ruin my life. I have allowed that for too many years, dammit. I want my life back."

"It was sexy." The way he was staring at her made her heart turn over. He looked like he wanted to devour her.

Her stomach fluttered. "Yeah?"

He nodded. He just kept watching her with those gray eyes.

"What?" she asked.

"Did you mean what you said out there?"

She worked back through the conversation, trying to pick up on what he was talking about. But she couldn't remember anything that would put that look on his face.

"You said you loved me."

Well, crap. "I did not."

"You did. When I was threatening your brother."

Did she? Oh, God, she did.

"And you can't take it back."

She closed her eyes. "It's your fault, all of you. I haven't had a good night's sleep in two days. I'm stressed... God, I can't believe I said that."

He walked to her then. Even though his feet were silent on the plush carpeting, she could sense him just in front of her.

"Can't take it back."

She glared up at him when she saw his smile. "Why not?"

He grinned. "You said it in front of witnesses."

She sighed. "They can be bribed. I have a feeling my brother would never be happy with any man I was involved with."

"Well, I'm the only one you are, have been, or will be involved with."

She cut him a look as he pulled her into his arms. "Is that some kind of ultimatum?"

"Reality."

She huffed out an irritated sigh. "You're not going to order me around."

"Yeah?"

She settled her head on his shoulder. "What the hell have I got myself into?"

He chuckled but said nothing as he slipped his hands beneath her legs and lifted her off the floor. She would never get used the way he carried her around as if she weighed nothing. He walked into the bathroom and then set her down. He pulled off his T-shirt and then shucked off his pants.

God, he was beautiful. Tall, golden, he was the picture of masculine beauty. She allowed her gaze to travel down his body and settle on his cock. He was hard. She licked her lips. He groaned, but before he could tell her no, she dropped to her knees in front of him and slipped her tongue over the head. The salty precome danced over tongue, skittered over her taste buds. She cradled his sac in her hands as she leaned forward and pulled his cock into her mouth.

He groaned, the sound echoing in the bathroom. It spurred her arousal. Delicious heat spiraled through her blood, warming her body from within. Inch by inch she took him in, adding her other hand to the base of it. Then she started to suck so hard it hollowed out her cheeks. His fingers slid through her hair, then gripped it as she started on him in earnest. Each thrust into her mouth drew him closer to his orgasm. She could feel it there. He grew harder as he started to flex his hips in rhythm, the head of his penis bumping the back of her throat. But she didn't care. She wanted this. She wanted to feel him come in her mouth, taste him.

Soon he groaned her name, his hot seed shooting into her mouth and sliding down her throat as he held her still. She licked and sucked it up. He sighed, leaning against the tiled bathroom wall, and looked down at her. The hands that had been gripping her hair gentled, then slid down to cup her face.

She rose up to her feet, brushed a kiss over his lips, then led him to the bed. He collapsed, then rose to his elbows as she climbed in beside him.

"I need to give you pleasure."

She smiled and rose up to kiss him. "You will. Now go to sleep."

He sank down on the mattress, pulling her with him. "Just so you know, I'm not going to let you boss me around."

She smiled as she snuggled up against him, not caring just

who was in charge at the moment. All that mattered was that he was there with her.

Micah walked out of the bathroom and looked over at Dee. She was snuggled in the bed, her face relaxed in sleep. The woman was tying him up in knots and she had no idea. He knew, or at least was beginning to understand.

From the moment he had become sexually active, his need for control, to dominate his partner, had always been a compulsion he rarely ignored. Dominating her added to the satisfaction, but the fact that he didn't seem to need it to feel complete scared him more than anything he'd dealt with before.

He sighed. This wasn't the time to worry about it. They had to figure out just what the hell they were going to do about her father. Then they could get on with their lives. He bent down, brushed his lips over her cheek and then walked out the door into the hallway.

"We have to have some kind of plan."

Micah heard the irritation in her brother's voice the moment he stepped out of the bedroom. He rounded the corner and found Devon facing off with Dillon over the bar. It was still unbelievable to him that he was in this situation. His life had never been easy. The hard road to his success had been filled with pitfalls. No one would choose to become an ultimate fighter, or a bounty hunter. But it had suited him and the money had been worth it. He'd had worse jobs before he found those. Now he was in love with a woman who was on the run from her father who wanted to kill her. Her older brother wasn't only a pain in the ass, but a multimillionaire...if not billionaire. And he was having to deal with a former FBI agent who'd had a hard-on for Dee when she was seventeen.

"I agree, but going after your father head-on is never the answer."

Devon made a sound of disgust and whirled away to pace. Nervous energy vibrated off him in waves.

"Sorry to interrupt the little pow wow here, but I think I can add my two cents."

Both of them tossed him an irritated look. He smiled.

"Now I agree that going after your father face to face is stupid."

"Fuck you," her brother snarled.

His smile turned evil. "No, thanks."

Devon snarled again and then collapsed into a chair.

"What do you think you can add to this discussion, Ross? Hell, you led Dillon right to her."

The irritation in her brother's voice didn't surprise Micah. He could understand it himself. He was still pissed off he was so worried about getting to Dee that he hadn't taken precautions. But the past was past, and they needed to move on.

"I know how to take care of her better than either of you," said Dillon.

Micah rolled his eyes. He knew they didn't have time for the macho crap, as Dee often called it.

"I think all of you need to settle down. A girl could faint with all the testosterone in the room," the Amazon said. She walked into the room with a swagger that made him smile. "We have to bring all you idiots together to help Marjorie."

"Dee. Her name is Dee now," Devon said.

She smiled at him. "Of course, sorry. Dee wants to testify."

"Not going to happen."

Micah settled against the bar. "I think it is."

Devon glared in his direction. "Don't you have any control over her?"

Micah shrugged. "Sure, I could talk her out of it, for a time. But it's what she needs to do. It's what she wants to do. If that's what Dee wants, that's what Dee gets."

Dillon decided to add to the conversation. "I have to side here with Devon. It would be best if she didn't testify."

He glanced at the former agent. "Oh, you do? Was it best that you couldn't be on her protection team, so you allowed them to remove you from the team and left her open to attack?"

Dillon clenched his jaw. "Be that as it may, I understand her father better than anyone. It took me a long time to be able to bring the bastard down."

"You didn't. He's still out there," Devon pointed out. A flush of anger filled Dillon's cheeks.

"Yeah, just a little reminder here, if you had brought him down, it wouldn't have been because of you. It would've been because a scared girl put her life on the line. She allowed you to protect her and you fucked it up. So don't tell me you know her father well. No one knows him better than Devon and Dee. Dee probably better than Devon since he ran away to play spy."

"Oh, that's how Striker Force is so realistic, right?" Maura asked, admiration in her voice.

"Stay on track, Maura," Zeke spoke for the first time.

She shot the dangerous-looking man a dirty look but said nothing else.

"So, we need to figure out a way to get to Rizzoli," Zeke said.

"How? I admit to knowing more than the FBI knows, but even then, it would be hard to get to him," Devon commented.

Micah glanced at him. "How would you know? When was the last time you even talked to your father?"

"The day he told me my sister was dead."

A beat of silence filled the room.

Dillon sighed. "Well, I think the best thing, the one thing that your father would listen to is—"

"A threat," Dee said. They had been so intense in their discussion, they hadn't noticed that she'd joined them. "He would only listen to some kind of threat."

She looked tired. There were smudges beneath her eyes, and she looked so tiny wrapped up in the big, white, fluffy robe. Micah went to her, took her hand and led her to a couch for both of them to sit on.

"She's right," Devon said. "Dad doesn't believe in negotiations. If we wanted something from him, it took threats."

"So how do we threaten him?" Dillon asked.

Micah studied Dee for a moment and read what she had decided. With a sigh, he said, "We tell him Dee is still alive."

fifteen

All hell broke loose.

Dee would have laughed if all the noise hadn't added to her already fragile nerves. She had listened to all of them fighting over her, over what to do, and she had gotten sick of it. For ten fucking years she had given up her life for her bastard of a father. She was tired of living with an axe hanging over her head.

"Shut the hell up," Dee yelled. When everyone had, and was looking at her, she said, "It wouldn't be done in person. Devon is a computer genius. You can email Dad some way, right? I mean, make sure you hide who and where you are, right?"

He nodded. "Yeah, that's kid's play. Dad probably has some top-notch computer folks though, so we need to be careful."

"I can help," Maura said. "We have some accounts that we use for work that are completely untraceable. That is if my brother and Zeke agree."

Both men nodded.

"Well, we need to email him, let him know I'm alive, and then set up something." She was scared, that was true. She didn't care. She wanted this over one way or another. Her life wasn't worth anything if she couldn't live it freely. No more hiding. Micah stroked his thumb over the back of her hand.

"Be honest. Mention Dee is still alive. Say that she is ready to talk for some money and he'll come running."

Dee looked at Micah with surprise. She had expected him to throw a fit when she announced her plan. In fact, she'd thought he would be the one fighting her the hardest. The fact that he trusted her judgment made her heart happy. Men in her life had not always been that trusting of her opinion.

As if on cue, her brother shook his head. "So you want to use yourself as bait? I don't think so. No way."

Her brother was being the pain in the ass, which was a little surprising. He'd always been the one who'd backed her up, and now he was refusing her. She had thought he might be a little easier than anyone else.

She held up her hands as if she could ward off his objections. "Listen. It'll work. Dillon can set it up with the US Attorney's office. They can watch the whole thing. We can accuse him of killing someone. Hell, you could be the one to do it. It's not like you don't know how to protect yourself."

He gave her an odd look and it made her want to roll her eyes. Did they all think she was stupid? Some of what she was feeling must have shown on her face because she caught Micah's smile.

"You were up to something, Devon. You gained twenty pounds of muscle when you went away to your fake college. Correct me if I'm wrong, but most people gain fat when they go to college. Then there was that one time you had a call, had to leave right away."

He grimaced. "I thought I hid it."

"You did, from everyone but your twin. I knew better than to pry. Are you going to tell me what you were doing?"

Devon glanced around at everyone, then shrugged. "In school for the CIA."

She nodded. "Figured it was something. Anyway, we can have you be the person to confront him. Conner'll make sure there is some muscle around."

She glanced at Micah, waiting for him to say something but he kept watching her with a strange expression. Then she remembered what he said about watching her order people around. A blush burned her face and she cleared her throat and tried to pull her attention away from him.

"I have my secure computer here with me," Devon said, heading to his bedroom.

"No. Use Maura's. Hers has some stuff on it you could only dream about," Dillon said. "Some of our computer security programs are kept in-house, not released to anyone."

He nodded as he followed Maura, who grabbed some bags and they headed into the kitchenette area of the room.

Zeke followed, apparently not happy to have Maura around her brother. Then, when the room was cleared, it was just Micah, Dillon and her.

"I wanted to talk to you about what happened before." Dillon looked uncomfortable, more than uncomfortable. He looked positively ill.

"Go ahead."

He sighed. "I was pulled off the case. It wasn't my choosing."

"I understand."

"No, you don't. I had lost my focus. I was too worried

about you. I had gotten emotionally involved, and my bosses didn't like it."

She swallowed. "And so you were forced to leave."

He looked at her with bleak eyes. "Both John and I fought it, but they refused. We had to actually break up our partnership because of it. Neither of us wanted to leave, so John insisted that he would stay."

Pain swirled in her chest then slammed into her heart. He'd died, and he could have left.

"Don't." His voice was as gentle as it had been years earlier. It made her want to lean on him, take comfort in the fact that there was someone there who would take care of everything.

She could feel the tears burning the backs of her eyes.

"I never wanted anyone to get hurt. And if he had left, he would have watched that little girl grow up."

Dillon walked to her then, took her in his arms. "I know. But it was his job. And even if I had wanted to talk him out of it, I couldn't have done it. We both knew just what your father would do to you if he found you. And we knew he had someone on the payroll when you got attacked."

She sniffed and pulled out of his arms, away from him. He had been the man she had leaned on all those years ago. And yes, he'd had to leave because of the job, but...she was sick of people leaving her.

"The last thing he told me was to run. To not trust anyone. It was what kept me alive."

Conner shook his head. "I wish you would have come to me."

"How was I supposed to do that? I didn't know where you were, what you were doing. Besides, John said whoever attacked us was someone in the FBI and he was the only one I trusted at the moment."

She regretted the words the moment she said them. Pain etched across his features in sharp lines.

"Yeah, well, I don't blame you."

She nodded.

"We'll get him this time."

She nodded again. "I need to get dressed."

As she walked back to her room, she knew better than to expect anything good to come out of this. She wanted to get this crap done and over with. Getting on with her life had become so damned important. When she shut the door behind her, she closed her eyes and sighed with relief. She couldn't handle any more surprises.

"I think I deserve points for not ripping his arms off his body and beating him senseless with them."

She laughed as she opened her eyes and found Micah watching her. God, it seemed like a lifetime ago that she had been lusting after him, not really knowing what to do about him. She hadn't known if she could trust him. Strange, because now she trusted him more than any other person in her life. Even her brother.

"You want to beat Conner? Why?"

"He touched you." He shrugged. "It happens again, I'll remind him who you belong to."

She rolled her eyes. "There are times you sound like some kind of knuckle dragger."

He smiled, but not the tender smile he'd shared with her earlier. This was something else, seductive and a bit...wicked. It sent a rush of tingles racing over her skin, through her blood.

"What?"

"I think I remember saying you would be punished for not coming to me."

A lick of fear and arousal slipped down her spine and she drew in a deep breath.

"I was going to."

One eyebrow rose.

"I was. I can't help that instinct. I heard Conner talking and I panicked. It had been ten years since I'd heard his voice, and seriously, I had no idea if he was involved or not."

He cocked his head. "But you don't think so now."

"No. Devon has done a background check on him."

"Let's get back to the punishment."

"I said I would have called you. But Devon drugged me."

Oh, shit. She shouldn't have said that. A deathly calm washed over Micah as his face turned from the seducer she knew to lethal man.

"Well, not really."

"Did he or didn't he drug you?" Every word was measured, and while part of her was upset with him, another part of her sighed over the fact he was ready to protect her against anything.

She sighed. "He did."

"I'll deal with your brother later. You will be dealt with now."

"But I said that I would have called you."

He nodded and started walking toward her. No, he was stalking her. His slow, long strides reminded her of a jungle cat stalking its prey.

"Yes. But once you landed here, you didn't. You're a smart woman, Dee. You could have figured out how to get a hold of me."

He stopped within a few inches of her.

"I didn't want to put you in jeopardy."

He shook his head, his hair sliding over his shoulders. "You knew your brother had devices to hide your connection from anyone watching me."

She opened her mouth, but the look he gave her made her snap it shut.

"Strip."

Heat rolled through her, her body reacting immediately to the soft command. She'd known this was coming, known that he would have to exert some kind of punishment for doing what she'd done.

"I need room." She took two steps back as her hands went to the belt of her robe. Once she undid the knot, she allowed the robe to fall off her shoulders onto the floor. His gaze moved over her, his nostrils flaring.

"I should have known you were naked underneath."

She opened her mouth to explain, but he shook his head.

"No talking unless you're answering a question or using your safe word."

She said nothing as he approached her. Her nerves were shot, really, and she didn't know just how to handle this, what was to come. Micah needed this, and there was a part of her that needed it, yearned for it. He walked around her, and she stood trying to keep her wits about her. She knew tonight would be about a complete submission, her complete indoctrination into the life. And she knew part of her should be scared, but she wasn't. In fact, she wasn't sure that anything had ever felt so right before.

He slipped his hand down her spine to her ass, then skimmed the crevice between her cheeks. She shuddered, her need rising. From the first time he'd mentioned it, she had been dreaming of him taking her ass.

He must have read her mind. "Not tonight. I want to... damn I want to. But just not tonight."

She wanted to ask him why, but she didn't, knowing the rules.

He stepped closer, moving his hand around to her waist and pulling her back against him. Damn, he was hot. His body heat warmed her back, his jean-encased cock pressed against her rear end. He slipped his hand up her torso to her breast and plucked at her nipple. Pleasure with a shot of pain spurted through her. He took her other breast in his free hand and gave it the same treatment.

"Tonight you will not come until I give you permission. I will control everything. Your pleasure is mine to give and if you can't understand that, you will be punished."

His breath feathered out over her sensitive flesh, his heated words causing her to shiver. Before this, she would have never guessed just talking about it, about how he would control her, would get her wet. But she was. Her body pulsed with arousal, with an overwhelming need that shot straight to her sex. It made her want to rub against anything to release the pressure building between her legs.

He stepped away, his hands falling away.

"On the bed, on your knees, that ass up in the air."

For a moment she couldn't react, couldn't get her body to move. It had nothing to do with fear, but the arousal now pounding in her blood. He had her ready to come just from ordering her onto the bed.

"Dee, do it now."

She forced herself to act, crawling onto the bed, moving to

her hands and knees. He said nothing else, but she could hear clothing being removed. She wanted to look, needed to watch him strip, but she knew better than to turn around.

The dip in the mattress told her that he had joined her on the bed. He kneeled beside her, and she did chance a glance over at him. He was nude, his cock thick and hard bobbing against his stomach. She licked her lips.

Smack.

Without warning, his hand came down hard on her ass. Vibrations spread out over her body.

"You should have known to wait in the bedroom. I would have kept you safe in Hawaii."

Smack.

The sting intensified as did the throbbing in her pussy.

"Don't ever run again."

Smack.

She moaned this time. She couldn't help it. The last one had sent a heated wave of desire rolling through her body, causing cream to fill her sex, her clit to pulse, and her nipples to tingle.

She thought he would spank her again, but instead he smoothed the palm of his hand over her ass. His cool skin against her heated flesh was arousing. His mouth followed, his tongue moving over her.

He shifted, moving behind her.

"I was right. Your ass does look sexy red." His voice had deepened, the arousal in it easy to hear, to feel moving over her nerve endings.

His hands smoothed over her cheeks and then he smacked her once again. She moaned again.

"Feel good, baby? I bet it makes that pretty little pussy hot and wet."

She couldn't answer him even if he'd wanted an answer. Her heart was smacking against her chest, her body shivering with the anticipation he was slowly building. Her cunt was weeping with need.

He skimmed one hand between her legs, dragging a finger against her slit, then back up to her anus. Slowly, he eased a finger into her anus.

Before she was ready for it to end, he pulled away.

"On your back, Dee."

Arousal left his voice rough, her body shimmering. She did as he ordered as he slipped from the bed. He bent down and picked something up off the floor. Her robe. He took hold of the belt and pulled it from the loops.

"I think you understand now to trust me."

His gray gaze watched her, moved down her body. Licks of heat followed the path, leaving her flesh hot, burning. She wanted his hands there, needed them touching her, teasing her, driving her crazy.

He dropped the robe on the floor and walked back to the bed, the belt hanging loosely from his fingers.

"Hands up, over your head."

She did as ordered and he slipped the belt beneath her wrists, then around to tie them together.

"I'd like to tie your ankles down, but I don't have anything to anchor them to."

The image that brought to mind had her head spinning and her body yearning. He leaned over, his hands skimming over her aching nipples.

"I love you in this position. Like an offered treat for me."

She glanced up at him, the small smile on his face curling into her heart. She had wanted him for so long, but being wanted, desired by this man who could have just about any woman he wanted, was a thrill.

"Arch your back a little, offer me up those pretty breasts."

She did as he ordered and he dipped his head. His mouth closed over her nipple and the sensation of his tongue moving over the tip, then the graze of his teeth, shot straight to her pussy. Another layer of her cream coated her inner lips. She pressed her legs together, trying to ease the ache. Micah didn't like that. He slid a hand down and insinuated it between her legs, keeping her from doing anything. He raised his head, a wicked smile curving those full lips.

"Naughty Dee. I told you that your pleasure is for me to give, not for you to take." He slipped one finger into her pussy, then up and over her throbbing clit. "And if you're bad, I'll make you wait longer."

He continued his lazy movements as he moved to her other breast and pulled her nipple between his teeth, teasing it. Every nerve in her body felt electrified, in tune with what he was doing, anticipating what he would do next. Soon he was kissing his way down her body, his teeth grazing her stomach before he settled in between her legs. His silky strands slipped over her skin. He pushed her thighs apart and set his mouth against her. His breath heated her core, brushed over her clit. She couldn't stop the shiver that moved over her. She really had lost complete control of her reactions. She could not contain her need, keep it hidden. She didn't want to. What she wanted, what she needed, was to feel Micah push into her, feel his long, hard cock, have him push her up over the edge.

He slipped his tongue into her pussy, licking first, then nipping with his teeth. Her orgasm shimmered there, just on the edge, but she couldn't seem to make herself go over, could not allow herself the free fall into pleasure.

Micah's finger moved into her anus as he continued to tease her pussy. The dual sensations pushed her even closer, near the bliss but not quite.

Again, before she was ready for him to pull away, he did and moved to the nightstand.

"I told you, not until I'm ready to have you come, and I want to be deep inside that tight little pussy when you come."

She opened her eyes as he ripped open a condom and pulled it out. She couldn't look away as he rolled it on, his large hands moving over his penis.

"Ahh, you like that. I might have to have you watch me masturbate some time while I have you tied up."

Just the idea sent shivers of delight moving through her as her gaze shot up to his. His face was flush, his eyes dilated and his nostrils flared with each breath he took. The fact that the scenario aroused him too just made her want to see it more.

"I knew you were naughty. I'm just glad I'm the one who brings it out in you. And while I'd like to do that, I don't think it would be a good idea tonight."

He leaned over, set his hand against her pussy and gave her clit one last press before joining her on the bed. He moved between her legs again, his cock in his hand. He moved it over her slit and then entered her in one hard thrust.

Her muscles flexed against him as he started to move. His thrusts were slow, even, shallow, and she could do nothing to change his pace. When she settled her feet on the bed and tried to push against him, he rose to his knees and took her hips in his hands, lifting her feet off the mattress. She was now completely under his control and he knew it from the smile he gave her.

Soon though, his thrusts sped up, deepened. Flesh slapped against flesh, her body hurdling toward her orgasm.

"Baby, come now, do it."

She couldn't do anything else but obey his command. Her release crashed through her, sending a wave of heated pleasure over her nerve endings as her body convulsed with it. He shouted her name and thrust into her one last time, the tendons in his neck strained, his whole body rigid as he came. She watched even as her body was still recovering from her orgasm, entranced by the sight.

He was stunning.

Long moments later, he lowered her hips and pulled out of her. He bent down, his eyes filled with tenderness, and she realized then that something big had happened. She knew it the moment she couldn't come without an order from him. But it was then she realized he knew it too, that he had expected it.

Dee waited for the fear, for the panic to set in, but as he undid the belt from around her wrists, a strong sense of rightness settled within her. This is what she wanted, what she needed. He slipped from the bed, set the belt on the dresser, threw away the condom and then joined her back in the bed. He pulled the sheet over them and then tugged her into his arms. As the warmth of his body surrounded her, his lips brushed her temple.

"Thank you."

She sighed and let the sleep dragging on her take her, knowing that the man she loved had given her a gift that no one else could.

sixteen

"It's set up," Dillon announced the moment he got off the phone. "I made sure that no one at the FBI knows anything about it, and I threatened a certain US Attorney with some bad press if he didn't make sure that all of this was taken care of discreetly."

"So are Dad and Petey going to be here?" Devon asked.

"Yeah, both of them. They were already planning a trip here."

Devon's face showed his surprise and a little guilt.

"No. Not your fault. He was planning this trip for a while. He was apparently genuinely surprised to find out that you two are alive."

Knowing that Devon wanted to know more, and that it would slow them down, Micah took over. "What are we doing? Where do we all need to be?"

"They are going to meet downstairs in the casino."

"Isn't that a little risky?" Dee asked.

"It's safety. Your father might not think twice about kidnapping you, but he wouldn't do it with witnesses. If we can get the bastard on tape admitting to the killings, there will be no problem with the trial. In fact, it might keep you from having to testify, and it will offer some protection. Killing you will not stop a trial."

She sighed and leaned against Micah, and he could feel her muscles relax a bit. She would testify if she had to, that much he knew. But she would be happy not to have to go through it.

"We need to wire you."

Conner stepped forward and Micah almost growled. The former agent must have seen his expression. "I have to wire her to be able to have the recording."

"Her brother can do it."

Devon stood and grinned at Micah. "Yeah, I know how to do a wire. Come on, Dee. Where's the stuff?" he asked Conner.

Conner led him to another area of the expansive suite.

"You can stop trying to come up with ways to kill my brother."

He looked up at Maura, who had been pretty quiet up until then. It was only the two of them in the living area as she sat down on the oversized chair Devon had just vacated.

"How do you know I was?"

She laughed. "You have the whole predatory male thing down. But he has no interest in Dee that way."

"That's not what her brother said."

She shook her head. "How did he find out?"

"Said something about the case file."

She shut her eyes and shivered. "Oh, he hacked the FBI. Be still my heart."

He was smiling when she opened her eyes.

"My brother didn't have a thing for her. What you have to

understand is after my folks died it was just Conner and I. He practically raised me."

"And?"

"Okay, move your male stupidity out of the way and think. Dee and I are about the same age."

His mind turned over what she said and then it hit him.

"Yeah. His judgment wasn't clouded because of his interest in her sexually. It still disgusts him people thought that. His problem was every time he saw her, he saw me. It was hard to separate from that. I had just left for school. Then Dee falls into his lap. He blames himself."

"And his superiors think he had the hots for her."

"Yeah." She made a face. "He lost all interest in keeping his career after that. Especially after John died. He resigned after they couldn't find her."

"Why did they think he had an interest in her?"

She shrugged. "He doesn't know. John would have never said something like that. He had talked to Conner about it. Why?"

"There's a good chance whoever accused him of misconduct is the mole in the FBI. Or someone close to him was in the position to do it. You find out who did the report and you can find the person who got John killed."

"I don't know why I didn't think about that," Dillon said from the edge of the room. "But you're right. If whoever got me out of there, got me off the case, is still around, there's a good chance that is whoever sold Dee out to her father. Why the hell didn't I think of it?"

The disgust he heard in the other man's voice should have made Micah happy, but it didn't. "You had just lost your partner, and I'm guessing at the time, your best friend. A young woman who reminded you of your sister had just been attacked and was possibly dead, and you had been pulled off the case. Most people wouldn't think of it."

He said nothing but walked away, the anger and guilt vibrating off him.

"Well, shit," Maura said. "I should have thought of it too. It might have given us some kind of insight into what was going on at the time."

He shook his head. "I think it might have been a good thing."

"You think Conner being pulled from the case was a good thing?"

"No, but him being smart enough to suggest they leave her on her own is probably what saved her. At the time, she wasn't strong enough to testify. You know the FBI wouldn't have protected her without any information. After the attack, I am pretty sure she would have had a breakdown if she had been forced to testify."

She nodded. "Still, you can't understand the guilt he feels."

"No? I led you to her. How do you think that makes me feel?"

She offered him a smile. "I knew after seeing you together at the club that no matter what happened, you would follow her. Zeke and my brother weren't too sure."

"You need to talk to your brother."

She nodded and headed off in the direction her brother had gone in.

"Oh, and Maura."

She turned around, her inquisitive eyes sparkling behind the lenses of her glasses.

"Consider yourself a lifetime member of Rough 'n Ready."

Her lips curved into a smile that normally would have tempted him. She was just the type of sub he liked, but it seemed the position had been filled. Permanently.

"Thanks."

As she strode away, he tried to wrap his mind around everything that had happened. It was hard to fathom that just weeks ago all he wanted was Dee in his bed. He should have known there was something under the surface, something that was drawing her to him. He walked to the bedroom, his mind on the future. He hadn't thought of it for years. Micah planned business, not life. It was one of his mottos. His main one in fact.

When did things get so turned around?

That was easy. It was the day that Dee had walked into his club. At first, he'd kept his distance, but that hadn't worked. Granted, she had very adamantly said she wasn't into the life, and if that was expected of her she didn't want the job. His lips curved as he thought of the memory, the righteous indignation pouring off her.

She had been a thorn in his side from the moment he'd hired her. One of the best bartenders, but hard for him to resist.

He shook his head and decided to call Evan. He had to let him know everything was okay and check in on the business. He poked his head inside where Devon was wiring Dee.

"Hey, do you have a secure phone?"

Dee twisted around and smiled at him. Just that small curving of the lips and his entire body came alert...but scarier was the way his heart tripped at the sight. Jesus, if the woman knew just how much power she had over him, he was fucked.

Devon looked at him. "Sure." He handed him a cell phone.

Micah took it and dialed Evan's number as he walked back to the living area, realizing that life as he knew it was gone. For some reason, what he'd lost didn't bother him that much. He looked at the door to the bedroom. Probably because of what he had gained.

"God, what a sad sight."

Dee looked back over her shoulder at her brother. "What do you mean?"

"Micah."

"Do you think there's something wrong?" She couldn't keep the worry out of her voice. The fact that the man hadn't run like she'd expected, like she'd expected of everyone, still had her heart dancing the Lambada.

"Other than the fact that he's whipped?" He shook his head. "No."

She snorted. "Sure, he's whipped."

"Turn." She did as he ordered and he studied her. "Are you that stupid? I always thought you were smarter than that."

"I don't have time to worry about my relationship with him. I have to get through the next few days without getting killed. That's the priority."

He said nothing for a few minutes as he concentrated on his task. The only sounds in the room were his movements.

"You think..." She let her words trail off as he glanced up at her with an amused look.

"Yeah. Jesus, he followed you. He tracked you down. Men don't usually do that unless they're whipped."

She shook her head, trying to dismiss her brother's words

even as hope speared through her. "Micah just doesn't like being lied to. And he always thinks he's right."

Her brother laughed. "Believe me, I would have tracked down a woman who had lied to me, but I definitely wouldn't go about trying to save her unless I was whipped."

She stared down at him, still unable to believe that Micah would feel that way about her. Life just didn't happen for her like that. Men left. Men weren't dependable. But there was something there, something deep in her heart that needed this to be true. She yearned to have a man to be there, to lean on, to trust.

Stupid girls trust. Smart girls depended only on themselves.

Oh, how she wanted to be a stupid girl. For once.

Devon finished his task and she pulled her shirt back on over her head.

"Why don't you think you deserve him?"

She glanced at her brother and then away. "What're you talking about?"

He sighed. "Don't bullshit me. Tell me."

"I really don't know what you're talking about."

When he said nothing, she looked over at him. He'd crossed his arms over his chest and was staring her down. Damn, she forgot just how irritating he could be. As twins, they often knew each other better than anyone.

"Everyone leaves." Her voice cracked on the second word and she closed her eyes. It was a waste of time because tears started to slip from her eyes. "Oh, shit."

"Everyone doesn't leave."

She knuckled the tear away and tossed him a nasty look. "Really? Tell me where in my life that you think that hasn't happened to me. Every important man in my life has let me down."

The moment she said the words, she regretted them. Devon's face lost some of its coloring and his jaw flexed.

"Devon—"

"No. You're right. I knew what those bastards were like and I left. You had no idea, but I did. But I escaped, reasoning what you didn't know couldn't hurt you."

She could hear the condemnation in his voice. "Devon...I don't blame you."

"No? Well, I would."

She shook her head as she walked over to hug him. "At seventeen, I probably would have done the same thing. Seriously. If I had known what they were like, I would have run a long time before I did."

"But I should have—"

"What? Told me that our brother and father were sadistic fucks?"

He snorted.

"Not sure I would have listened to you then."

"Probably not. You were pretty hard-headed."

She sniffed. "Yeah, well, at least I didn't do illegal things."

He pulled back and smiled down at her. "Only faked an identity."

"Hey. I paid my taxes and was a good citizen for ten years."

"Go see your man."

She turned to leave but then paused. "You really think he's whipped?"

He nodded. "You might have had every man walk away from you, but there was one who didn't. In fact, the man raced across an ocean to come get you."

She smiled as she slipped out the door and walked toward Micah.

"I don't give a fuck. You tell Franklin that we aren't paying more for the liquor."

She laughed. He might play the carefree Dom, but the truth was he was a businessman. She should have known he would be talking business with Evan. She must have made some kind of noise because he turned to look over his shoulder. Heat flared in his eyes as his gaze locked in on her. She stopped, unable to walk. Her whole body sizzled, her nerve endings sparking. Jesus, all the man had to do was look at her and she was lost.

"I gotta go."

Evan said something because Micah smiled. "Tell May I owe her a drink."

He clicked off the phone and without a word walked toward her. He stopped inches from her, cupped her face with his hands and leaned down for a kiss. He didn't close his eyes. Heat, delicious and familiar wound through her veins and wrapped around her heart.

He pulled away. "Did Devon get you all wired?"

Her heart was smacking against her chest and there was a lump the size of a boulder in her throat. She swallowed past it and nodded.

"Hey, are you okay with this? If not, we can go."

Tears prickled the back of her eyes and she shook her head. "No. I outed myself. I need to go through with it. Who knows what else my brother and father will do if I don't get them behind bars."

He nodded and pulled her into his arms. "I'll do whatever you want. You want to stay and fight or run, just let me know."

Again, another rush of tears filled her eyes. Damn, she was crying again.

She wanted to run far away from Micah. If her father found out how much he meant to her, he would hurt Micah to hurt her. At the same time, she wanted him here by her side. She was making about as much sense as this situation.

"Dee?" Dillon's soft voice drifted through the room and brought her back to the present.

She leaned back and looked at Micah, a man she thought never to have, the one she had thought out of reach, too dangerous. He hadn't been the kind of man she had dreamed of years ago. But beyond everything else, he had given her back her dreams...her tomorrows. No one had thought enough of her to do that, had loved her enough to put their life on the line to ensure her happiness.

She rose to her tiptoes and brushed her mouth over his. With her lips still against his, she said, "I love you."

Anyone watching wouldn't have seen his reaction, but she did. His eyes widened and his hands flexed on her waist. He opened his mouth, but she pulled away and shook her head.

"I just had to say it. For me, I had to say it."

Micah studied her for a second and then nodded. "Don't think we won't talk about this."

"Dee?" Dillon said. "Time to go."

She nodded and turned, but Micah followed.

"You can't go," she said.

Micah frowned and crossed his arms over his chest.

"No, you can't. Conner can go, because well, he has the connections. If my father knows anything, and I am sure after that email he sent out feelers, he knows how important you are to me. You'll become a target."

"You shouldn't be going alone. I can go. I can take care of myself."

"I have to agree with him," Devon said. She glanced at her brother. "If Dad knows about him, he will think it's odd he isn't there."

She looked at Conner who nodded.

With a sigh, she rolled her eyes. "Freaking men. Okay, come on, but let me handle it."

He gave her a smile that told her he could care less about her warnings. With a huff, she followed Conner out of the room, with Micah close behind.

As they stepped on the elevator, she realized this was the first day of the rest of her life. She just hoped that life didn't end today.

Something cold slithered down Micah's spine the moment he spotted Peter Rizzoli. Just like the last time Micah had faced him, Rizzoli didn't look like the bastard he was. In better shape than most men his age, his dark hair was now threaded with gray and his face almost unlined. More than likely Rizzoli had been botoxed. The man was vain enough for it.

He was dressed in a conservative tailored suit, the only splash of color the red tie. The young man standing next to him had to be Petey, the oldest and the one Conner had said was completely out of control. Rizzoli was a bastard, a murdering bastard, one who put a hit out on his daughter. It was business. While Micah couldn't understand feeling that way about another person, he knew the type. His mother had been that way. Dee was in Rizzoli's way, so he put out a hit.

The brother though, he had been getting some notice. As Micah studied him, Petey offered him a cynical smile. He could see his resemblance to the twins, but he was more his father's child. Cold eyes, hatred seeping from his every pore. He wasn't cool-headed like his father. Instead, he had a temper that often got him in trouble. His father had been cleaning up his messes since high school, when he'd nearly beaten a fellow student to death. He enjoyed violence. As Dee said, he got off on it. He could only imagine how someone like that reacted to torturing someone. And Dee had heard it.

He glanced down at his woman and smiled. Anyone looking would see a cool competent woman. But he knew. He felt all those little nerves that were simmering beneath the surface. He wanted nothing more than to pull her into his arms and take her back upstairs. That would have to wait though.

They walked up the stairs to the restaurant. The moment her father realized it was her, Micah thought he might have seen a flash of recognition along with regret. Well, there was at least that. The brother sneered though.

Dee stopped by the table. "I see you got the message."

Her father studied her for a moment. The look in his eyes, the cold calculation Micah saw there, made his blood ice over. He looked at her as if she were a specimen.

"I didn't think you would be clever enough to send an untraceable email."

Micah grunted his annoyance and she shot him a smile that calmed him. She was really something.

"I'm a lot smarter than you ever gave me credit for."

"How do you figure that, sis?"

The sneering voice of her brother had Micah curling his fingers into his palms, but Dee laughed.

"I've always been smarter than both of you."

She was antagonizing them. Not a good idea in Micah's book.

"Really?"

"I've held down jobs for the last ten years. Jobs my daddy

didn't get me." She shrugged. "Not to mention that you guys couldn't find me for ten years."

Her brother growled, but a look from their father had him quieting down. It was then that Micah realized the warped relationship here. From the look of it, her father treated Petey like he was an unruly pet. One he would kick out of the house if he ever crossed a line. Killing wasn't the line, and that is just how strange the family was.

"Won't you sit down? Both you and Mr. Ross?" her father asked, but there was no doubt it wasn't a request.

She nodded and took a seat.

"What do you want?"

"Five million, in an offshore account."

For a moment, there was a deathly silence around the table. The only sound was the milling crowd, the slot machines...the music. Her father studied her for a long moment. Of course, neither of them said anything. Petey was the one who couldn't handle it.

"What the fuck, Marjorie? You turn us in, ruin your life, and now you want money?"

She shrugged and looked bored. Micah wanted to shout with laughter. Her move looked so natural.

"I realized a long time ago that there was no beating you. That's why I left the FBI and ran. Losers. Of course, I would have been safe if you hadn't had a man on the inside."

Her father's lips curved slightly. "So you want money. Do you have the account?"

She nodded. "If you hadn't killed him, this would have never happened you know."

Her brother shook his head. "Bastard was stealing money. We had to kill him."

A sigh of irritation slipped from Rizzoli, telling Micah he had realized what his son had said. Of course, he assumed they both knew. But it wasn't smart...proving Dee's point.

She offered a slip of paper to her father who looked it over and then handed it to his son. "Take care of it."

"Now," Dee said.

Her brother rose from his chair and pulled out his cell phone. "You were always a pain in the ass, Marjorie."

When they were alone, her father switched his focus from Dee to him. *This* Micah could handle. He hoped the bastard took a swing at him, tried something, although he knew her father was too cool for that.

"What is your roll in this, Mr. Ross?"

"I'm here for Dee."

Her father swirled his drink in his glass before taking a small sip. "I think it might be a little bit of payback on your part. After what I did to your business, I thought it might be the only reason you were around my daughter."

Micah offered him a smile, knowing there was nothing but animosity behind it. "If you think that, then you don't know your daughter. She wouldn't put up with an asshole bent on revenge. In fact, looking back, it was the best thing that could have happened to me. I ended up in Hawaii. And I ended up with your daughter in my bed."

The older man's jaw clenched again, but Micah could tell he was pissed. No matter what, he was still Dee's father and hearing about a man sleeping with her wasn't something any father wanted to hear. Especially the owner of a BDSM club.

"It's done." Her brother broke up the staring contest.

"For my silence about your roles in the killing," she smiled. "Not too much to pay, I'm sure."

Her father's smile left Micah's soul cold. "I didn't say we had anything to do with it."

"Sure, *Dad*. You can fool yourself. Of course, the truth is both of you are too cowardly to admit to doing it, let alone doing it. What I remember from my childhood was that neither of you did a thing. You ordered people about, but you didn't actually do any work." She tossed a sneering look at her brother. Micah looked at him, realizing that his face had flushed and his lip snarled.

"And you. Hell, until he dies, you will always be his *little boy*. The one who couldn't think without an order. I'm amazed you can even go to the bathroom without his help."

Petey bounded over the table at her, but Micah stopped him by grabbing his collar.

"You little bitch. Of course we did it. It was easy enough and you know what's the best thing? I enjoyed every fucking minute of it. Nothing like hearing Sam beg for his life while we questioned him. Dad might allow you this, but the truth is that someday, I'll do the same damn thing to you."

Micah's already frayed temper ripped away as the inner monster he kept at bay came screaming to take control. He took hold of the bastard by the neck and forced him down on the table as he pummeled him with the other hand. He enjoyed the sick sound of flesh meeting flesh, the way it felt to use his hands on the man. He hit the bastard for threatening Dee, but there was more to it. For everything he took away from her, for all the injustices done to her over the years, he couldn't seem to control himself.

A second later, LVPD swarmed the area, but Micah barely noticed.

"Micah."

It was then that the red haze dissolved and he realized that Dee was tugging on his arm. Again. He looked up and noticed the police and FBI agents with their guns drawn.

"Let him go." Her voice was gentle, and he could barely hear it about the noise of the casino. But he could see her lips move, see the tears in her eyes.

It took every bit of his power to pull back, to gain control of the monster that still clawed at his belly to escape. He dropped the little bastard on the table with a thud and moved away. One of the FBI agents smiled as Petey groaned.

"Micah."

He finally really looked at Dee and realized she was as white as a sheet. He must have scared her.

"I-I'm sorry, Dee."

Tears poured over and down her cheeks. "I was just so worried about you. You never know what Petey is going to do."

"You think I couldn't take him in a fight?"

She laughed. "Of course you could, but then Petey fights dirty."

"Ms. Rizzoli—"

"Sumner. Her last name is Sumner."

The FBI agent in charge nodded. "I need to talk with you."

She nodded and pulled away from him. Panic clutched his stomach.

"Go clean up. I'll talk to them and then meet you back in the room."

She leaned up and kissed him. "My hero."

She walked away.

Conner watched Micah Ross and sighed. There were things that needed to be said, things that needed to be done, and he didn't want to do it. Granted, Devon was her biological brother, but he had never been much of one.

"You did a good job down there."

Micah pulled on a fresh shirt and tossed his hair over his shoulder. "I know."

He snorted. "I know we could have done it without you, but it was definitely easier with you there. I trusted you with Dee."

Micah faced him then. "Your sister said you didn't have feelings for Dee."

Conner shook his head as he dropped into a chair by the massive floor-to-ceiling windows. "No. She reminded me a bit of Maura. It was hard to keep my perspective, but Marjorie... Dee was so lost. I just kept thinking of Maura, what we went through right after our folks died. I couldn't imagine either of us getting through that on our own. Here was this girl without any connections of her own. What she thought of her life was now a lie. It would have been terrifying at any age, but she was young and had no one. Then that report happened."

"We were talking about that. Who wrote the report?"

"Michelson. That bitch was after advancement, and she got it with that. I would have suspected her of being the mole, but she was too much into her career. Her whole family is in the FBI."

"Too bad she died while on assignment."

Conner frowned. "She didn't die. She was wounded, but she survived."

Micah stilled in his action and looked at him. "She's alive?"

Conner nodded. "Yeah. In fact, I just saw her a few minutes ago."

"Fuck," Micah said as he headed toward his door. "Where is the FBI? Who's protecting her?"

He rose and followed Micah. "What the hell is going on?"

Micah picked up a massive knife and slipped it into a holder on his hip.

"Whoa, Micah."

"Tell me."

"Not until you tell me what the fuck is going on."

"Dee said Michelson was dead. That your partner said she was useless to them."

For a moment, his head didn't work, then everything seemed to lock into place. "That fucking bitch." He started for the door.

"Let's get her. They're a floor beneath us."

eighteen

It took about thirty minutes to finish up the recitation of what had happened. She was offered protection once she returned to Hawaii, and while she would accept that, she wasn't going to change her name. She refused.

Her brother was shaking his head. "Dee, you need to go into hiding."

"I can do that. But I'm not running again. Ever. I want my identity cleared up. I want to be Dee Sumner for the rest of my life."

Agent Talon stared at her and then nodded. "Considering the FUBAR of your last protection, it is the least we can do. I'm going to call my boss, get this all cleared. You'll be all right?"

"Devon's here, I'm fine."

As he left them alone, Devon pulled her up out of her chair and hugged her. "I almost lost you again."

She scoffed at that and leaned back. "Not with Micah there."

"You really have that much faith in him?"

She nodded. "I love him. What's more, I trust him."

He sighed. "I guess I can't forbid you to see him."

She laughed. "Honey, there isn't a person who can keep me from him now."

"I think you might be wrong about that," a female voice said from the doorway.

Dee looked at the woman she thought dead and cold seeped into her veins. She couldn't move, couldn't even think. Apparently, her brother had no problem. He pushed her down behind a chair and started toward Michelson.

"No Devon—"

It was too late. Michelson shot him before he could do anything. He crumpled into a heap on the floor.

"Jesus, you've been one pain in the ass," Michelson spat out. "Come out or I hit him with another shot. This one will be in his head."

The calm tone told her that Michelson would do it. She wasn't some hothead like her brother. No, this woman was like Dee's father.

She rose from behind the couch.

"I can't believe after all these years..." She motioned with her gun and Dee followed her directions.

"I thought you were dead."

Michelson chuckled at that. The sound of it sent another icy shaft of fear slithering down her spine.

"And that saved me. Hell, I had to have Petey shoot me in the leg to make it look good."

"So when John said you were of no use..."

She nodded. "John had figured it out." She shrugged. "I'd already decided he would have to die. There would be no way to get to him. He was a straight arrow."

"Of course he was. He couldn't be bought like some dime-store whore."

Michelson walked up to her and hit her across the face with the butt of the gun. Pain exploded, stars forming before her eyes as she fell to the floor.

"Shut the fuck up, *princess*. I might be bought, but I wasn't cheap. I went for big dollars, and I've got enough saved up to disappear now. Of course, I have to tie up some strings...you being one. You thankfully took care of your stupid father and brother."

She stepped up and Dee rolled to her side to look up at her. The years hadn't been kind to the agent. Lines had deepened around her mouth and her eyes were cold, almost desolate.

This woman would kill her.

Dee knew she had little chance, so she kicked her foot out, connecting with Michelson's shin. She screamed out in pain and bent down. Dee rose to her feet. The years of training kicked in and Dee fisted her hands and gave the agent a swift right hook to the jaw. The force of the blow caused her to drop the gun. Dee punched her again, but Michelson had grasped the situation. She gained her wits and returned with a punch of her own. The power behind it threw Dee back and she tripped over her own feet. She hit the floor hard, the back of her head connecting with the tile. Stars formed in front of her eyes and she shook her head, trying to make them fade. By the time her vision cleared, the only thing she could see was the barrel of the gun. In the next instant it was gone.

"Argh," Michelson yelled out as Dillon grabbed her. Before she comprehended what was happening, Micah was there, pulling her off the floor and into his arms. His whole body shook as he enveloped her in a hug and then squeezed her so tight she almost lost the ability to breath.

"Micah, Devon's been shot."

He let go of her and looked around. It was as if he hadn't noticed her brother lying on the floor in a heap bleeding.

She ran to the phone, her head still woozy from the hit to the jaw. She dialed 911 as Micah checked out her brother. He grabbed an FBI shirt sitting on one of the chairs and pressed it against Devon's arm.

"He's all right. He did hit his head on the way down, which is why he is unconscious."

She pulled in a long, shaky breath. Her head was still spinning and for a moment, she worried she would pass out.

Agents and police now started to pour into the room, and at some point the EMTs showed up. Her brother woke up as they put him on the gurney. She breathed a sigh of relief as her vision wavered.

She glanced over at Dillon, who now had Michelson in cuffs, and from the looks of the agents, they knew she had sold out one of their own.

"Dee, are you all right?"

She looked at Micah and was alarmed as the light started to dim around him.

"I think I need to sit down." And with that, her world faded to black.

"She just had a blackout, Micah. Sit down," Dillon muttered. She could tell he was annoyed, but did he have to be so damn loud about it?

"Yeah, with your brilliant plan she was really safe."

"Listen, it wasn't my plan, it was her brother's, and none of us knew that Michelson was dirty."

At the mention of her brother, she said, "How is Devon?"

She couldn't open her eyes. Didn't want to.

Micah slipped his hand into hers, startling her a little. As usual, she hadn't heard him. "He's okay. Lost some blood, but going to be okay. Doctor said the bullet passed right through."

She sighed, relief coursing through her. She felt her whole body relax.

"Can you open your eyes?"

"I think it might hurt."

"Being a wimp, Sumner? Should have figured that you would be."

She frowned, drew in a deep breath and opened her eyes. The first sting of light wasn't so bad. Micah apparently had made sure the lights had been turned down. The white walls told her she was at a hospital.

"Why are we here?"

"The doctors thought it best," Conner said gently.

"And since you've been out cold for about an hour, I would say it's the smart thing. Not stupid, like trying to confront Michelson," Micah said.

Conner's voice was gentle as if he was worried he might upset her. Forever the big brother. It was in direct contrast to Micah's tone which was sharp. It should upset her. The man she loved should be trying to calm her worries. But instead it soothed her. If he was comfortable enough to be mad, everything must be okay. Plus, Micah was stroking his thumb over the back of her hand. The gentle caress reminded her that his bark was worse than his bite.

She glanced at the former agent. "Thanks."

"What are you thanking him for? He almost got you killed twice."

She smiled. "It wasn't his fault."

Micah snorted.

"Could you give us a minute?" she asked.

Conner tossed Micah an amused look. "Sure. The FBI wants to talk to you."

"I'm sure they do."

He slipped out the door. Silence filled the room as Micah glared at her.

"What?" she asked.

"You almost got yourself killed."

"I did not almost get myself killed. I didn't know that bitch was still around."

He let go of her hand, twisted away from her and started to pace the small room. "Well, yeah, if the FBI wasn't such a fucked-up organization they would have known."

"I agree. Of course, she was pretty good. If I remember correctly, her father was FBI too, so she was raised in it."

He snarled at her over his shoulder. "Don't make excuses for them, dammit. They fucked up and you almost got killed."

He yelled the last few words and she winced as they bounced off the walls.

"Actually, they have a track record of that. It's the reason I ran."

He stopped and turned to her, his frown blacker than the worst storm cloud. She couldn't fight the jubilant feeling shifting through her. She knew men, and she now knew Micah better than most. He was pissed, but he was pissed because she had almost been killed. Because he cared for her.

"This isn't something to make a joke of."

She pursed her lips. "After so many years, I would think that it would be imperative to find some humor in it."

He snarled again and she couldn't help the rush of giggles. For the first time in years, she was free. She didn't have to hide, didn't have to pretend to be someone else. She could live her life for herself.

Before he could yell at her again, the door cracked open.

"Are you up for being debriefed?"

She snorted at Conner's question.

"Sure, come debrief me."

An older gentleman came in, his hair military-short, brown and threaded with gray. The kind blue eyes sparked a memory. "Agent Davis."

He smiled, one of those fatherly smiles he had given her the first night she'd been taken in. "I wasn't sure if you would remember me, Ms. Rizzoli."

"It's Ms. Sumner," Micah growled. A look passed between Conner and Davis.

Conner stepped forward. "Hey, Micah, why don't you come with me?"

He crossed his arms and said nothing. She wanted him here, more than anything, but she realized she needed to do this on her own. This one last thing she needed to do on her own, stand on her own two feet.

"Micah, babe, could you give us a few minutes."

He said nothing.

"You need to trust me to handle it."

He glanced down at her, a look of irritation and possibly hurt passed through his gaze before he hardened it. "Okay."

Without another word, he stomped out of the room. The moment the door shut, another few agents came in, one carrying a small camera to film her discussion. Panic rushed up front, and she had to fight the need to call Micah back. She worried she had done something wrong, something that would not be able to get fixed.

"I'll keep an eye on him," Conner said, a smile curving his lips.

"Thanks." He left her as Davis pulled the only chair in the room closer.

"Are you ready?"

"You have no idea."

nineteen

Micah stomped down the hallway, irritation, fear and pain twining through his blood. Damn woman. He'd died a thousand deaths as they rushed to save her and she orders him out of the room...like a lackey. Like someone beneath her. He should have expected it from a Rizzoli. People like them always thought they were better than everyone else, like they were some kind of fucking royalty who had the right to do what they wanted.

"Micah," Conner said, jogging up behind him.

"What do you want? Shouldn't you be back there?"

He shrugged. "Not FBI anymore. I have a feeling if I hadn't offered to chase you down, I would have been kicked out."

Micah stopped and looked at him. "Chase me down? Did she order you to do it?"

Conner's face went blank, then a slow smile curved his lips and his eyes lit with amusement. "Holy shit. You love her."

Micah started walking again, refusing to look at him. Conner didn't take the hint.

"I wasn't sure, not the way you react most of the time. I

238

mean, I understand wanting to save her, to protect her. She's kind of tiny and delicate."

Micah snorted. "Delicate as a bull. Jesus, do you even know the woman?"

"I knew her. Then. I'll say that she was a bit of a hot-house flower then. Needed to be looked after."

Micah stopped again and faced the former agent. "You *really* don't know her. She heard her father and brother torture a man, and what does she do? She goes to the FBI and says I'll testify."

"Well, yeah—"

"Then, because of an FBI fuck up, she is left on her own. Nothing but a few thousand bucks and a fake id. And what does she do?"

"She runs."

Micah shook his head. "No. She survives. She lived on her wits alone, with no one, not one fucking person to help her. It wasn't something the FBI did for her."

"We gave her that first identity."

"Well, woo hoo for that. So your fuck up doesn't count? Of course, she used that identity what, a whole month? Then she had to change it to protect herself because there was no one there to protect her."

"I didn't want to leave."

"But you did. You left because you were ordered. You knew there was something wrong with it, but I guess your career was too damned important to you. So you let it go."

A flush of anger reddened Conner's cheek. "It happened in a matter of three days. I was trying."

"Three days?"

"Yeah, I was off the case and less than seventy-two hours

later my partner was dead, the case blown to shit and Marjorie had disappeared."

"Her name is Dee. Get it right." Micah bit out every word.

Conner rolled his eyes. "Either way, you can't blame this one on me. And on top of it, you have to let her do this on her own."

"I don't have a choice."

"She asked you to leave, but you could have stayed."

Yeah, he could have, but she had told him to leave. He had hurt, deep down where he had promised himself he would never go again. It was the kind of wound that ripped your heart to shreds and left you lying in the dirt bleeding. His mother had done that to him. Micah never wanted to be that vulnerable to a woman again. Now, though, he wanted something else, wanted to have her in his bed and in his life. He wanted more than that, more than just today.

Fuck. He wanted forever.

He had known it the moment he'd fallen for her, the moment she let him take her, that she was his forever. It was the reason he'd avoided her for so long. He had known the power she held over him. And now he was whipped. Damn, he didn't want to face Evan or Chris once they got back to Hawaii.

Without a word, he started off for the exit.

"Micah," Conner yelled. "Where ya going?"

"Shopping. Tell Dee I had something to take care of."

Dee smiled at her brother as he frowned at her.

"They aren't keeping you overnight?"

She shook her head. "They want me to stay in the area and gave me some warnings, but I don't think I need to worry."

"I want out."

She laughed. "Well, there is a difference between being pistol whipped and being shot. One allows you to leave the hospital earlier."

"I tried to force them to let me out."

She snorted. "Bribing doesn't always work with doctors."

"Yeah. I was told that today by two of them." He glanced at her. "Where's Micah?"

She shrugged, her nerves coiling her stomach. She had thought he would be waiting in the hall, but Conner had told her Micah had run out for a few things. What he needed, she had no idea, and she worried about asking him to leave earlier. What if she'd screwed things up?

"He's gone."

"Not for long I'm sure."

She glanced at her brother. "Yeah, how would you know?"

"He's gaga over you."

Restlessness seized her and she rose from her chair to the window. She saw nothing outside as she remembered the look on his face when he'd left. He'd been pissed, but he had been wounded too.

"I really upset him."

"I'm sure you did. Ordering a guy from the room in front of other men, not a good idea."

She glanced at him. "I haven't had much experience in the last ten years with men."

"Male egos are fragile, but that guy ain't going anywhere."

"How can you be sure?"

"He won't leave. And he loves you."

She sighed. "Yeah, but I might have really screwed up. It's been three hours."

"I can imagine what he's going through. That guy is dealing with some shit. You have to give him some room to deal with it."

"Oh, and I'm not? Jesus, my brother just tried to kill me, and a woman I thought dead rose from the grave and tried to kill me. Instead, she hits me and shoots you." Her voice caught on the last two words. She would never be able to get over the fact that she'd almost gotten her brother killed.

"It was my fault, Dee."

"No, it wasn't."

"I should have known, should have picked up on that. I investigated the whole thing."

She looked at him then. His swarthy skin was finally gaining some more color, and part of it was anger. But getting upset, especially for something that wasn't his fault, was stupid in his condition.

"It isn't your fault. I thought she was dead, yes, but how would we have known? And she was the only person to survive. The FBI debriefed her. They never picked up on anything."

"That's because the FBI has their heads up their asses."

She smiled. "Some spook rivalry?"

He returned the smile. "In a way. Don't get me started on MI-6. Those bastards drive me crazy."

"So do you have any secret spy gadgets I can play with?"

His smile faded. "I can't believe you aren't more upset with it. Most women would be pissed."

"First of all, you say that like we are some kind of weak sex. We are not. We're stronger than you whiney babies."

"That's—"

"Or are you assuming that it is just me that is weak?" She crossed her arms and waited for him to answer.

"Run away from that answer, Striker. Women will get you every time."

The sound of Micah's voice had the usual effect on her. Her pulse raced, her body tingled, but there was something else there. Something she knew was because of her fear that she had lost him. She had been so intent on reading her brother the riot act, she hadn't heard the door open, but that was nothing new. The man was a cat.

She turned to face him and swallowed. The need to run to him, to jump into his arms, almost overwhelmed her, but she held on to her control...and her pride. He was giving her the meanest look.

"Where have you been?"

He shrugged. "Out."

She tried to hold on to her temper. "You felt the need to run away?" She didn't miss the dangerous glint in his eyes as she turned toward her brother. "I told you. Men are the cry-baby weaker sex."

"I did not run away."

Pain and fear twisted in her heart as his cold words whipped out.

"Whatever. I have some papers to sign."

She said nothing more as she held on to what little bit of temper she could as she stepped out into the hallway. It wasn't much, but she had pride. If he was going to be some kind of baby, she wasn't in the mood.

And if he was willing to be a bastard because she'd asked to do something on her own, she didn't want anything to do with him.

If she kept repeating it, she might start to believe it was true.

"You might as well go after her."

Micah glanced over at the man who would soon be his brother-in-law and frowned. "The woman never lets me do anything. You would think by now she would be more submissive."

Devon rolled his eyes. "Please, I don't want to hear about that. I mean, she's a grown woman, and I know you would eat glass rather than hurt her, but please, leave any kind of sexual comments out of it."

Micah sighed. "She's a pain in the ass. I swear, you try and do something nice and what does she do? She walks out."

"Well, go get her."

"I will, but she needs to learn that I'm not going to chase her every time she runs. Damn sick of it."

A loud of bark of laughter rent the air. "What a liar. You would run her to ground no matter what the situation."

Micah didn't deny it because it was the truth. He knew it even before he admitted it to himself. He might have put feelers out for Dee if she had been any other sub. But she wasn't. She was his sub.

"What are you waiting for? Go. And turn the lights off when you leave. It's fucking bright in here."

"We're going to go to one of those little chapels."

Devon smiled as he closed his eyes. "She's going to be hard to handle."

"If I legally bind the woman to me, she's sort of stuck."

"Good luck with that. If you think she's going to settle down because you put a ring on her finger, think again. You should know Dee better than that."

Micah glanced at the younger man with a sinking feeling churning in his gut. He knew Devon was right, but he didn't have to admit it. Lord knew Dee was going to drive him crazy.

"So I take it you have no objections?"

"Like that would matter to Dee, but no. Now go get her, otherwise she'll come back in here and mope."

"See ya later."

Micah hit the lights as he slipped out of the room. Once outside he glanced at the signs and followed them to the accounts payable department. She was coming out of the door as he strode down the corridor. She was tired. He could see the weariness weighing on her shoulders. Her long hair was tangled and her clothes were still covered with Devon's blood. She was one big mess and the most beautiful woman in the world.

The pain of the last few hours slammed into him. He'd held it at bay for as long as he could, and with it came a healthy dose of anger. Anger at her for being so hard-headed. Anger at himself for not protecting her.

He understood her need to stand on her own, to tell her story. He had come to grips with that. Truthfully, that hadn't bothered him as much as the fear. In his life he'd been in situations that had scared him, but nothing had prepared him for the terror that had twisted in his gut. It held him by the short hairs, much like the woman. He had almost lost her, not once but twice in less than seventy-two hours. And that was something he was not equipped to handle.

He didn't say anything as he grabbed her hand.

"Micah."

He ignored her. He didn't have the capacity to deal with her questions or to sweet talk her. Now was the time for action. He dragged her down the hall and out of the hospital. He saw Maura and Zeke walking from the parking lot.

"Hey, Micah, how's Devon?" Maura asked.

"Fine." Micah bit out the word.

"I think I want to spend time with my brother," Dee said.

He all but tossed her into the car and then walked around the hood and slipped into the driver's seat. Ignoring the amused looks of Maura and Zeke, he threw the car in reverse, then into drive, then sped out of the parking lot. He kept quiet, trying to keep his temper in control as they headed to the strip. After a few minutes she sighed.

"Are we going to Devon's? He gave me the keys."

"No."

She didn't say anything for a few minutes and he knew it was killing her. She shifted in her seat, fidgeting with the bottom of her shirt. That was one of her big tells. Dee never had a problem standing still, taking in what was around her. But when she was nervous or agitated she couldn't keep still.

"Where are we going?"

"The strip."

She crossed her arms beneath her breasts. "I don't want to go gambling."

He laughed, but with little humor. "Well, you are, and the biggest gamble of all."

"What the fuck are you talking about?"

"You. Me. Little chapel."

Another beat of silence filled the car. "And?"

"We'll get a honeymoon suite somewhere."

"That's not what I'm talking about." Frustration poured over every word.

He shrugged. "I don't think we have much else to talk about."

She grunted. "No, I thought you might want to propose."

"Not giving you the chance."

"Dammit, Micah, I deserve a proposal. And I am not agreeing to anything unless you ask me."

Anger and guilt had him pulling over to the side of the highway. He put the car in park and took a moment to compose himself. What was it about this woman? He loved her, he knew that, but from the moment he'd met her, she'd intrigued him. Everything about her fascinated him. He'd been patient with her, taken his time, and now she wanted something more from him.

"Fine. Will you marry me?"

"Why?"

Irritation whipped through him. "Because I asked."

He thought he heard her strangle on a laugh.

"That's not good enough. I thought it might be because you love me."

He said nothing but kept looking ahead, unseeingly at the traffic passing them by and racing into the Nevada night.

She sighed. "Fine, well, I'll marry you because I love you, but I am getting sick of your inability to express your feelings outside of the bedroom. Really, why did I get stuck with such a Neanderthal? I need a little nerdy accountant who tells me every day how much he loves me."

He looked at her then. The moment he saw the amusement in her expression, he felt his temper cool.

"You'd roll right over him."

She shrugged. "It might be nice to have a little romance in my life. I have had very little of it."

His heart melted at hearing the yearning beneath her tone. She might project the woman who doesn't need all the hearts and flowers, but she needed them, deserved them. He'd done a good job at it before now.

"What's more romantic than a man who chases down his idiot woman when she runs away?"

"First, I didn't run away. Second, calling her an idiot really ruins it."

He smiled. "But I did it. You have to admit that no one else has done that."

Her eyes softened. "You still called me an idiot."

"If you don't know how much I love you, you have to be an idiot."

Her eyes widened. "How am I supposed to know? How do I know?"

He raised his hand to her jaw and cupped it, then rubbed his thumb over her cheek. "Because when I thought I might've lost you, I didn't care about anything else. I could have died there on the spot and been happier than living without you. I might not be the most expressive man...and I'm sure I'll continue to piss you off by being the way I am. But know this, you are all that is good in my world. Until you were mine, I didn't know what I was looking for, had no idea what I needed. The moment I touched you, it was as if I had come home. You are the first person I want to see in the morning, and the last touch I want at night. I love you."

Tears had welled in her eyes and were now pouring down her face. "Oh, Micah."

Without warning, she jumped toward him, clasping his face in her hands and planting her mouth on his. The kiss was sweet and hot. Need, pleasure and love entwined and sped through his blood. Her tongue slid in against his and he started to ease her back onto the seat of the pickup when there was a tap on the window. It took him a second to realize someone was there.

He pulled back and turned to find a Las Vegas policeman standing by the window.

"Is there a problem here, sir?"

Dee giggled as Micah felt his face turn red.

"No, sir. We just got engaged."

The older gentlemen smiled. "Congratulations. But it isn't safe to be out here."

Micah nodded. "I understand."

"Good luck and buckle up."

He walked away and Dee collapsed into giggles. "Oh. My. God. That was too funny. We got caught making out on the side of the highway."

He looked at her, trying to be mad, but at seeing her joy he couldn't drum up the frown. The woman had been so buttoned down for so long, it was good to see her happy.

He grabbed her and planted a kiss on her mouth and then let her go. Buckle up."

The lights flashed in the mirror.

"Sure thing."

He pulled back onto the highway. "We're going to make record time to the chapel. I plan on getting you into the honeymoon suite and not letting you out for a week."

She slipped to the middle seat, put on her seatbelt and then snuggled up to him. "I like the sound of that as long as we stop somewhere for clothes. I am not getting married in these clothes."

Micah punched the gas and laughed as they sped down the street and onto the rest of their lives.

twenty

ABOUT A MONTH LATER

Dee hummed as she looked around at all of their friends and family. They filled Rough 'n Ready to the rafters for their belated wedding reception.

After clearing it with the FBI, Micah had taken her on a whirlwind of a honeymoon, including three days in some insane suite in Vegas, a stop in New York, and then London. She would like to say they saw a lot of stuff, but most of it had been spent in the bedroom.

When they finally arrived back on the island, May had yelled at Dee and insisted on throwing them a reception. Since she and Micah saw many of the club's employees as family, they'd closed the club for the night and had the party here—sans any play. May's father and grandfather were there for Cripes' sake.

Dee laughed as she watched May's grandfather try to talk one of the floor managers into opening a room. May hustled him away, and even though Dee stood quite a ways from them, she knew May was blushing.

She sighed when she noticed Danny sipping an Old Fashioned and standing with Evan. Keisha had indeed broken his heart as Dee expected she would. By the time Dee and Micah had returned from her honeymoon, Keisha had moved to Maui with some guy she'd just met without even a text to say good-bye. It hurt her, but Danny seemed to have taken it the hardest. Also, Keisha better not ever cross paths with May. Dee was worried that her new friend might hurt the other woman. May protected what was hers.

As that thought popped into her head, a hand slipped around her waist. She knew without looking who it was. His earthy masculine scent hit her first, then the warmth of his body as he stepped closer.

"Having a good time, wife?"

She smiled. Micah loved referring to her as his wife or his bride. Her heart sang each and every time he called her his. The possessive tone never failed to send a rush of tingles through her entire body.

"I am," she said, turning around to face him. As she stared at him, she wondered how she had gotten so lucky. The heat in his dark eyes had her body throbbing with need and awareness. "Thank you for doing this."

He snorted. "Didn't have a choice. All the floor managers texted me while we were on our honeymoon that it was a done deal."

She was touched by everyone's acceptance of their relation-ship. They welcomed her even after she had essentially lied to all of them for two years.

"Hey, Dee," May said, stepping up beside them. "You had enough Micah time on your honeymoon. Time to hang out with the girls."

Micah smiled and leaned down to whisper in her ear. "Go. I know I get you all to myself as soon as we get home."

Even as my face heated, I kissed him. "Thank you."

Then, I let my friend drag me away to where a bunch of women are standing.

It's been over an hour since May dragged his woman off. Their two weeks alone was heaven, but it didn't feel like he had enough of her. He never would. Micah was counting the seconds until he had Dee all to himself again.

"Give it over, Ross. She's part of the family. You're going to have to allow her time with them," Evan said as he sipped his drink.

Micah spared his best friend a glance. "Oh, really? I seem to remember that you kidnapped May and took her to your house after our attack." Micah had been watching May when the woman who had been stalking her attacked her. The result was May in the hospital, and Micah had a broken leg. "You left me to care for myself while you convinced her to marry you. And how did you do that, by the way? Bribery?"

"Definitely bribery," Chris said, sauntering up. He'd closed his restaurant for the night to cater the party.

"Fuck off," Evan said with little heat. In the next instance, he sobered. "How's Jocelyn?"

Chris' sister had been through something back on the mainland and ended up in the hospital. Christ has been a little tightlipped about it.

"She's doing better, but I convinced her to come here soon. Cynthia told her she could stay at the cottage."

Micah noticed his new brother-in-law avoiding people, especially the women approaching him. He really didn't know what to think of Devon. He was a genius but also a smart ass who continued to look at Micah with a deadly glare. It was as if Micah made Dee cry, Devon would end him.

"Catch up with y'all in a bit," Micah said as he started off toward Dee's brother. "You're supposed to mingle, Stryker."

That earned Micah a side glance. "Don't care for it much."

"Surprising," he said, sarcasm lacing the word. "I'll say that you've ignored all the women who approached you."

He shrugged. "Not interested."

"And the men."

Another look. "Not my thing."

"So, who are you pining away for?"

"I'm not hung up on a woman. Haven't had a woman I could trust since my father killed my girlfriend."

There was something in his voice that told Micah that might have changed recently. "Yeah? What about the one?"

Devon frowned. "What the hell are you talking about?"

"I might be wrong, but it feels as if you are trying to convince yourself you like to be alone. And don't even try to lie to me, Stryker. I run a BDSM club and spend my nights observing behavior."

Irritation stamped the other man's features. "I can't find her."

"Wait, what? You lost her?"

He sighed. "I had to run off to get Dee. I couldn't take the chance of losing my sister again, so I left the woman in Vegas, thinking she would understand. By the time I got out of the hospital, she was gone."

"Well, it had been a few days."

"I can't find her. The woman is a ghost. Doesn't exist. Her image has even been scrubbed from security footage."

Micah frowned. "That's—"

"Odd. Yeah. I think I might have gotten played. Or worse, she was taken or something. I don't know. In the grand scheme of things, it doesn't matter. If I can't find her, no one can."

Micah wanted to argue with him. Devon had taken Dee, but Micah had tracked her down quickly enough.

"What are you two being so serious about?" Dee said, interrupting anything he wanted to say. Whenever she was near him, he couldn't think straight.

"Nothing. Micah's being pissy because I'm moving over here."

"Yay!" Dee hugged her brother, who shot a look at Micah. He would keep his brother-in-law's secrets. There was no need to tell Dee. If Dee knew her brother was smitten, she'd want to go back to Vegas to hunt for her.

When she stepped back, Micah slipped his arm over his shoulder. "You should talk to Evan, Devon. He's worried about the security of our club's computers. As we have gained some notoriety, we've had a few cyberattacks. They spend a lot of time trying to get our member list."

"Gotcha." He leaned forward to kiss Dee on the cheek before glaring at Micah. "Take care of her, Ross."

Then he slipped away before Micah could say anything.

"The nerve of him. '*Take care of her, Ross*,'" Dee said, mimicking her brother's voice.

Micah laughed. "He just loves you."

She snorts. "As if I can't take care of myself. I survived for years without him."

"You can take care of yourself. How about we get out of here?"

She blinked, more than likely trying to get her brain back in line. Dee liked holding onto her mad.

"May will get mad."

I glanced over at Evan, who had his arm around May. He signaled with a chin lift. "She'll understand."

"Then yes, let's get out of here."

It took them more than ten minutes, but once they stepped outside, Micah sighed with relief. They walked side by side, their hands entwined. As they stepped up to his vehicle, Micah opened the door. Before he helped her in, he raised their joined hands to brush his mouth over her fingers.

"I love you, Dee."

Her eyes softened as the cool Hawaiian air slipped over them. "And I love you."

Once they were on their way, he took her hand again. He knew that no matter what came their way, they would face it together.

epilogue

THE NEXT CHRISTMAS EVE

"Spread those legs and show me that pretty little pussy of yours," Micah said.

Even after more than a year of marriage, his commanding voice sent shivers of lust racing through Dee's blood. He didn't even have to say a word. Just seeing him completely nude was enough for that. He stood at the foot of their bed, his golden skin shimmering in the candlelight. Her gaze traveled down his body to his cock. He was fully erect, the head wet just a bit from pre-come. She licked her lips.

"Dee, you better do as I ordered. Now." He hadn't raised his voice. He didn't have to. There was enough dominant control in his voice to get her to do what he wanted.

She did as ordered, but she took her time about it. His nostrils flared as if he could smell her arousal. Maybe he could. She was so damned turned on she wouldn't doubt it. His eyes narrowed, then he reached out to her pussy. He slid his index finger along her slit. The simple touch had her body reacting. Just that simple little touch had her shivering.

"You're being especially bad tonight, Dee."

She smiled at him, and she could tell he was trying to keep from returning one. Micah loved being tested, and after a year together, she knew what he needed, what he wanted from her in bed. Although each time they did come together, it wasn't boring. Her love for him grew stronger, their passion higher.

She sucked in a quick breath when he spread her pussy lips and slipped the tip of his finger inside her. He had just shaved her, and she was extremely sensitive at the moment. He moved his digit back and forth, then over her clit. She moaned and closed her eyes. While he continued to tease her, he bent his head and took a sensitive nipple into his mouth. The feel of his tongue against her nipple shot straight to her pussy. Soon he moved on to her other breast, giving it the same treatment.

"I would really like to punish you tonight." The tone of his voice made her open her eyes. The intensity of his stare had her curling her toes into the covers. "And I will. But...being that it's my birthday, I think you need to start behaving."

She laughed. "What fun would that be?"

"I did not ask you a question. You aren't supposed to respond."

He slapped her pussy, and her eyes almost crossed. Whenever he did that to her, she wanted to come. It was such a wonderful combination of domination and sexiness that she couldn't resist opening her mouth again. She knew what would happen. He slapped her pussy again.

Then, without a word, he dipped his head and slid his tongue over her labia. *God.* She closed her eyes and felt her legs quiver. The man was a demon with that damned tongue of his. After he teased her for a few more moments, he slipped his tongue into her. Her stomach muscles tightened, her whole body readying for her orgasm as he shifted away. He grinned up at her.

She frowned and then he laughed. He leaned forward, and without breaking eye contact, he pulled her clit between his lips. Lordy, the man was going to be the death of her. He grazed his teeth over the tiny bundle of nerves, and she moaned as another gush of liquid filled her pussy. She was so damp. If she had been standing, she knew the tops of her thighs would have been wet with her arousal.

Over and over he licked her clit, and just when she thought she couldn't hold back her orgasm any more, he stopped. He moved away from her and grabbed the vibrator sitting on the bedside table. He turned it on and pressed it against her clit, then moved it away. Over and over he pushed, prodded, and teased her to the limit. By the time he pulled away, she was almost ready to beg for her release. Almost, but not quite.

"Up on your knees. Put that pretty ass of yours in the air."

It took her a few seconds to respond because she was so aroused. She was shaking with her need to come, but apparently he didn't care.

"Get up on your knees now, Dee."

His voice was a bit harsher, but she heard the arousal. He was just as turned on, and it was taking a lot of work for him to control himself. She finally got into position. He moved behind her. "Spread your legs wider."

She did, but again she took her time. It earned her a slap on her ass, his flat palm against her sensitive flesh. He took the vibrator and eased it into her, then turned it on a slow hum.

"You know the rules. I am in control of everything, so no coming until I give you permission."

She said nothing. She couldn't. To keep from coming, she was using every bit of her control.

"Naughty girls have to be punished."

It was all he said before he pulled back and smacked her. The sharp sting of the slap turned into more as it filtered over her skin. The pain combined with the low hum of the vibrator in her pussy had her barely holding her own. Over and over he smacked her. The pain twisted through her, turning into the same overwhelming arousal he could build in her each time. When he stopped, her ass was stinging, and she was sure she was red from the smacks. She didn't care. The combination of arousal and pain had her pussy dripping with need. She was just proud of the fact that she hadn't come. She was close, and it had taken all her effort to stay in position, but she had kept control of that.

He spread his hand over her ass, the light touch of his cool hand easing some of the sting and adding another level of arousal to her out-of-control libido.

When he moved off the bed, he reached for the lube. She closed her eyes, trying to fight the need to come. The vibrator was still humming in her pussy, and knowing he was going to fuck her ass had her barely holding on. She curled her fingers into the duvet of their bed.

He climbed behind her.

"I guess I could say this is punishment, of course, I know how much you like having my cock up your ass."

She shuddered at the dark words, the lust that deepened his voice. Over a year together and he could still get to her.

He reached between her legs and increased the speed of the vibrator. It rocketed through her system, pushing her that much closer to her release. Next, he settled between her legs, his fingers skimming over her flesh. She felt his cock at her back entrance. Even though she knew it was killing him, he eased his way in slowly. With the vibrator going and his cock up her ass, she almost lost her mind. Once he was deeply seated in her, he started to move. With each thrust she climbed closer and closer, her body barely holding back from the release it needed so badly.

His fingers bit into her skin as he held onto her hips, thrusting harder and harder.

"Come for me, Dee."

She was already coming, unable to hold back any longer. It only took two more thrusts and Micah joined her.

Long moments later, they collapsed. Micah removed the vibrator, switched it off, and set it on the table. Pulling her into his arms, he settled back against the pillows.

"That was a pretty fine gift, Mrs. Ross," he said as he kissed the top of her head.

She smiled and sighed with contentment. "And the best kind because I got to share in it."

He laughed, and the sound of it rumbled against her ear. The sound of rain pattered on the roof, and she sighed again. Life was just about as good as it could get in her opinion.

Micah woke a short time later and found himself alone in bed. For a moment, he laid there content to hear the rain. It wasn't one of the big thunderstorms he had hated in Georgia. It was soft and musical. It always relaxed him.

He stretched and moaned. His muscles were sore, and not just from their lovemaking. He was getting old. He would never admit it to anyone else, but working three days straight of twelve-hour shifts had done him in. He was glad that they were shut down for the holidays for the next few days.

He sat up and then stood. The smoky scent of the Kalua pork Dee had made for his birthday dinner filled the air. He knew she was in the kitchen, puttering around, getting things ready. He smiled. A man couldn't ask for much more than having someone to look out for him the way Dee did—or to be able to return the caregiving. It was one of the greatest joys of his life to have someone to take care of.

After cleaning up and pulling on a pair of shorts, he walked to the kitchen. He stood in the doorway and watched her. God, she was a beauty. All tough exterior and soft gooey center. He knew she could dropkick him without much effort, but he also knew she had a thing for puppies. His lips twitched when he heard her singing "Happy Birthday" in Hawaiian. The one thing she could not do well was sing.

"Smells good."

She jumped and turned around. "I told you to stop doing that 'sneaking up on me' thing."

He chuckled as he walked over to her. "Sorry, babe. Old habits of very old bounty hunters die hard."

She rolled her eyes. "You're not old."

He pulled her into his arms and sighed. "I feel like it. Rough 'n Ready was crazy this month."

She slipped her arms around his waist and settled her head against his chest. It was always odd to remember how tiny she actually was. Dee projected herself as someone so much bigger.

"We might need to hire a third key. You know someone past

you and Wesley? I can't function that way because we always want to be off together."

He nodded, knowing she was right. The club he and his best friend, Evan Chambers, had started several years ago now had two locations and a waiting list for membership. She gave him a squeeze, then stepped back.

"Everything is on the table. Why don't we go sit down?" she asked, smiling up at him as if she had a secret.

He followed her into the dining area. Next to the bay window sat their first Christmas tree. Dee had taken such delight in getting the house ready for Christmas. As they sat down, he noticed a small box on his plate. It had a bow but no wrapping paper.

"Ah, Dee, I told you not to worry about a gift."

She smiled. "But it's your birthday. We have Christmas tomorrow, but I wanted something special for tonight."

He looked up at her. How did a man get so lucky? He grew up on the streets and was a self-made man, but it still amazed him every day that he had the love of his life to cherish every day. Considering that he had almost lost her, he knew how lucky he was. He leaned over and gave her a kiss. When he pulled back, her eyes were misting.

He cupped her face. "Don't cry, baby."

She sniffed. "When you look at me like that, it's hard not to."

And he knew how much she hated showing that. Even now, even knowing she trusted him, Micah knew showing any kind of vulnerability was hard for her. That she allowed him to see it meant the world to him.

"Open your present."

She was still sniffing and grabbed a tissue as she watched him. He untied the bow slowly, and she sighed.

"You always take too long," she said with a smile. He knew she wasn't really complaining. Dee knew what his childhood was like and the fact that he rarely had birthday gifts. She made a big deal out of every holiday mainly for him.

When he opened the box, he found tissue paper. He frowned as he lifted it away and found a pair of little white baby socks. He lifted them out and studied them, then he looked at her. Tears were streaming down her face, but she was smiling. His heart clutched as he held them in his hands.

"Does this mean what I think it does?"

She nodded. "What do you think about that, Daddy?"

Micah tried to swallow the lump in his throat as he set the socks back down. Without a word, he grabbed her and pulled her onto his lap.

"How do I feel?" He cupped her face and wiped away the tears with his thumbs. "I can't say. No one has ever loved me the way you do. Thank you."

He kissed her, brushing his lips over hers softly before pressing his open mouth against hers. Dee hummed against his tongue, and he smiled as he pulled back. "No wonder you've been so tired. I couldn't figure out just what the hell was going on. I was kind of worried you might be coming down with something."

She snorted. "Coming down with something, that's for sure. And in about thirty-three more weeks, you'll get to help with that something."

He settled his hand against her stomach. "Thirty-three weeks? You've known how long?"

"Just a little over a week. We've been so busy that I didn't even notice I missed my period. But, I woke up about a week ago and thought I was going to die."

Then it hit him what they did earlier. "You should have told me before tonight. I could have hurt you."

She rolled her eyes and slipped her hands behind his neck. "I talked to my OB about that. She said we'll just have to be careful. And most play will have to be toned down. We'll talk about that later. Don't worry so much, Daddy."

He smiled at the name. "I like hearing you call me that. I like it a lot."

She sniffed, and he worried she was going to start crying again. Dee must have seen the look of panic in his eyes, and she sighed. "Better get used to the emotions, babe. We have a long haul in front of us."

He gave her a hug. "We need to call the family."

She smiled. "Let's do that, and first on the list needs to be my brother."

He grunted, but she ignored him. Her brother and Micah had finally come to an understanding, but neither of them really trusted the other. The only thing that kept them civil was their love for Dee.

"Then we'll call Evan and May."

She nodded, her eyes still brimming with tears as she pulled out her phone.

"Devon. Yes, I know what time it is, but I have no idea where you're at."

There was silence.

"Well, I was just calling to tell you that I'm pregnant." Silence again. "Of course Micah's the father. If you're not nice, I'm going to hang up on you."

Micah chuckled. Even though Devon was a pain in the ass,

putting up with him was worth it. He got Dee in the bargain. He sat back and listened to the love of his life yell at her brother.

Dee hung up the phone with a frown.

"What's up?" Micah asked as he slipped his arms around her waist. "What did Dillon have to say?"

"I didn't talk to him. I talked to his sister, Maura. Apparently, he was rushed to the hospital today."

And she couldn't forget the fear she heard in the younger woman's voice. Dee could understand it. Conner Dillon was Moira's only family.

When she turned to face Micah, he was frowning. "Something happen on the job?"

It was a logical question because former FBI agent Conner ran a security agency. "No. That's the odd thing. Moira said he had chest pains. It turned out to be nothing, but they kept him overnight."

"I'm sure he's getting good care. Remember, he is in Miami. They've got to have some good heart doctors there with all the retirees."

She smiled. "That's true. He apparently was stressed out."

Micah raised his eyebrows. "Interesting. Of course, he is kind of uptight."

"I'll call back in a couple of days." She stood on her tiptoes. "So, still feeling good?"

He smiled at her, and she felt as if she owned the world. She did, in her opinion. "Yeah. In fact, I think I need to show you how good I feel."

"Yeah?"

He bent down and lifted her into his arms. "Yeah. Let's go back to the bedroom and I'll demonstrate."

She sighed and settled her head against his shoulder. He took her to their bedroom and laid her on the bed. She smiled at him.

"You don't have to be so gentle."

"But I want to show you just how I feel," he said as he inched her shirt off.

As he joined her on the bed, she felt tears well up in her eyes again. He leaned down to kiss her.

"I love you." He slipped his hand down to her stomach. "Both of you."

She smiled as her heart burst full of love. As he kissed his way down her body, gently loving her, she realized that now everything in their world was perfect.

It was her last coherent thought for hours.

Thank you so much for reading A LITTLE HARMLESS LIE! If you enjoyed Micah and Dee, please think about leaving a review at your favorite book retailer or review site.

A LITTLE HARMLESS ADDICTION

Falling in love might not be the smart thing, but it might be the one thing they both need.

acknowledgments

No book is ever written without some of the most supportive people in the world. My big thanks to Kris Cook, Brandy Walker, Joy Harris, Ali Flores, Bonnie Hoffmaster, Tina Dowds and the rest of you crazy Harmless fans. You keep my heart light. Of course, a massive thank you to Heidi Moore, editor extraordinaire, for her mad editing skills and for being a calm presence in this crazy business we both love.

Of course, always to Les, Audrey, Eliza and Belle the dog. Your sacrifices are plenty, your contributions huge and my love for all of you knows no bounds. Thank you for everything.

}

about the author

From an early age, USA Today Best-selling author Melissa loved to read. When she discovered the romance genre, she started to listen to the voices in her head. After years of following her AF Major husband around, she is happy to be settled in Northern Virginia surrounded by horses, wineries, and many, many Wegmans.

Keep up with Mel, her releases, and her appearances by subscribing to her <u>NEWSLETTER</u>. If you want to keep up with cover reveals, new behind the scene info on her writing, and when new excerpts are posted, follow her MelissaSchroeder.net News News. Or you can do both! They are low traffic, so you will not get tons of emails.

Check out all her other books, family trees and other info at <u>her website!</u>
<u>If you would want contact Mel, email her at: melissa@ melissaschroeder.net</u>

instagram.com/melschro

amazon.com/author/melissa_schroeder

facebook.com/MelissaSchroederfanpage

bookbub.com/authors/melissa-schroeder

goodreads.com/Melissa_Schroeder

tiktok.com/@melissawritesromance